The Bridge

The Mindbridge Trilogy
Book I

By Joe Luegers

ISBN 978-1-7365411-0-4 (Paperback)
ISBN 978-1-7365411-1-1(Ebook)
ISBN 978-1-7365411-2-8 (Audio)
ISBN 978-1-7365411-4-2 (Hardback)

Any references to historical events, real people, or real places are used fictitiously. Names, characters, and places are products of the author's imagination.

Cover Art by Ashley Ellen Frary

Edited by Emily Bernhardt

For July Lana Luegers,
our Frost Flower

Contents

Chapter One

The Island and the City

Monhegan Island, Gaia

Kaija Monhegan had a lot to be scared of.

One false step on a wet patch of moss could send her tumbling over the edge of the headlands. If the jagged rocks of the shore didn't immediately kill her, the water mammoths that lived in the cold depths of the ocean would surely smell her blood and come scavenging. The island was full of dangerous things for a person like Kaija that went far beyond the cliffside. Just the other day, her father had spotted a hydra vine growing in Gull Cove and rushed back to inform the villagers. He stressed — to her great embarrassment — that if it had been Kaija that wandered into its nest, she would have been poisoned within seconds and died an agonizing death.

Kaija was indeed terrified, and yet she walked along the cliffside with only a vague sense of the perils which surrounded her. She had never left the island, and spent her days fearlessly exploring its every corner from the moment she took her first unsteady step as a toddler. Kaija was not afraid of falling, but she *was* afraid of something.

Nothing in the world scared Kaija more than the small rock she had clutched in her hand.

Stopping at the highest point of the headlands, Kaija looked out toward the moon rising over dark waters and took note of its position. About two more hours before it reached the center of the sky, and then it would be too late.

She would be fourteen.

Kaija held up an open palm and squinted at the stubborn rock in the moonlight. She spoke quietly, not wanting any nearby villagers to overhear.

"Do it."

Nothing happened. Kaija concentrated on her body and felt the cold wind blowing against her face. She tried to sense something deeper, something beyond the physical, and bring it into herself. This time she spoke with more authority.

"I said, *do it*!"

The stone sat there with no perceivable change, but Kaija was far from done. For the thousandth time she visualized what she wanted the rock to do. The power of Gaia would flow through her, and *it* would happen. Kaija would rush back to the village to show her father, and he would cry tears of joy. The other Monhegans would stop whispering around her every time she walked by.

'Has it ever taken someone this long before?'

'How could she have not inherited her father's gifts?'

'What is wrong with her?'

Kaija felt a surge of stubbornness boil up in her stomach. She opened her mind, channeling her anger, and this time things actually felt different; purpose seemed to flow into her. Kaija stared ahead, redirecting the sensation inside and wrapping it around the rock in her hand.

"Now!"

Nothing.

Kaija told herself to stay calm; disappointment was a part of life, after all. Better luck next time, island girl.

"Die you stupid rock!"

Kaija screamed and threw the stone down the embankment, putting her face in her hands and holding back frustrated tears. Rather than the anticipated splash, there was a great big *whoosh* as the rock flew back up the edge of the cliff. Kaija gasped and reached out, but another hand snatched it ahead of her.

Jasper Monhegan, Kaija's father, walked up beside her. He adjusted his glasses with one hand, brushed aside his long, dark hair, and examined the rock.

"Die, stupid rock? For all you know, Mr. Rock has a partner and kids. Are you really going to make them orphans?" He looked at her more seriously. "Still no luck?"

"What do you think?" asked Kaija.

"I think your mind is still in the wrong place. Relaying is different for everybody, perhaps you are not an externalist."

"But I've tried everything! I had Fain hit me with a stick for twenty minutes this morning to see if I might be an internalist, and now I have bruises all over my back. It's never taken anyone else this long, and after tomorrow…"

Kaija's father held out his palm and the stone gently floated into the air. It hung there, completely motionless in the wind.

"I know you've been trying, but the frustrating thing is that it often happens when you're *not* trying. Being a late bloomer can supposedly be a sign of an especially powerful relayer. A few cycles ago, Fain's parents were worried that he might lack the relaying gift, and then he blew up his house in the middle of the night. Now they have to worry about the fact that he *is* a relayer."

"But what if it just doesn't happen for me?" Kaija asked. "I talked to some traders at the docks the other day, and they said that common knowledge on the mainland is that relaying must come before the fourteenth cycle. If I'm not doing it now, I might never be able to."

"That is a possibility," said Jasper, putting an arm over his daughter's shoulder. "But who cares if you can float a few rocks around? That doesn't change who you are. Who you are is ultimately what you do with what you are given; you'll still be the Kaija I know."

The stone dropped back into Jasper's hand, and he squeezed it tight.

"Besides, levitation is boring."

Jasper opened his fist, revealing that the rock had transformed into a steaming hunk of crystal. He leaned forward, blowing playfully, and the crystal broke into a million fragments which were carried off, glittering in the wind. Jasper shivered as bracing raindrops began to fall on his bare arms.

"Let's go back to the village," he said. "It feels like a storm is coming in."

Kaija looked around, observing the smooth water below and hearing no sound of rainfall.

"Father?" asked Kaija, trying to hide a smile. "Why isn't it raining on me?"

Jasper looked overhead to find a small raincloud hovering just above him. He waved his hand and the cloud burst into water droplets that sprayed in every direction.

"Fain!" he yelled, his face turning red. "I told you that this isn't funny!"

A teenage boy leapt out of the nearest tree and sprinted toward the firelight of the village, laughing wildly.

"Fain's been showing off his new trick all day," sighed Jasper. He turned and shouted toward the fleeing boy. *"I should have never taught you evapotranspiration, Fain!"*

Jasper turned and chased Fain down the winding dirt path to the village. Kaija wished she could laugh because normally she found her best friend's pranks to be hilarious. Tonight, however, his trick did nothing but remind Kaija of her own situation. Was this how things would be from now on? Staring hopelessly at a part of life that would always be over an insurmountable gulf for herself?

Kaija closed her eyes and tried to feel something, one last attempt to connect with the life-force of Gaia. She concentrated as hard as she possibly could, and when Kaija opened her eyes, something *did* happen.

For a brief instant, it seemed to Kaija that she was not standing at the edge of a cliff, staring down at the murky ocean. Lights moved far below, and tall structures gleamed in the distance. Music played somewhere behind, its timbre alien and unfamiliar. When Kaija looked up she saw numbers floating in the air.

11:40 p.m.

Kaija blinked and the numbers vanished.

The Bridge

* * *

Indianapolis, Earth

Where do thoughts come from?

It was not unusual for Maeryn Kacey to wonder about big concepts such as this. She technically knew the answer already after some light research in her spare time. Thoughts are the result of neural processes, and neural processes come from both proximal and distal causes. Proximal causes are sensations inside and outside of the body, and distal causes include memory, ancestry, and evolutionary history. All of these things become clouds of information which the brain digests as thought.

That's where thoughts come from. Obviously.

And yet no scientific fact could ease Maeryn's troubled mind. All day long she had been struck by random assaults of anxiety, coming without reason and leaving just as suddenly. Her other problems were so strange that she barely admitted them to herself. Maeryn had been walking to the bathroom earlier, and for a moment it felt like her feet were barefoot and stepping on wet grass. During lunch she heard a seagull squawk over her head and looked up at the ceiling of the cafeteria like a crazy person, expecting to see a bird flying around under the florescent lights.

So now Maeryn sat on the floor in an empty office, staring out the fiftieth floor windows of the MotherTech Headquarters and wondering where her thoughts were coming from. The sun had long set under the skyscrapers on the horizon and the city was glowing with the twinkling lights of windows, billboards, and autocabs. Progressive rock echoed from somewhere in the dark, empty offices behind her.

"Time," Maeryn whispered, and the numbers **11:40 p.m.** were displayed in her digital contacts. They floated before her, transparent, and then morphed into the words **August 3rd, 2172 A.D.**

Of course!

Maeryn told herself that she wasn't crazy, she was just worried that her entire family had forgotten about her upcoming birthday. Her anxiety was clearly manifesting itself in unusual ways. It was nothing to worry about.

Unless it was.

Maeryn's arms broke out into goosebumps and she felt as if cold wind was blowing on her. A wet, churning sound filled her ears that sounded so familiar, yet Maeryn could not quite place it. This sensation was soon interrupted by a male voice of about her same age, speaking from her MotherTech earpiece.

"Your brain chemistry seems to be in distress. Are you experiencing another puberty-induced existential crisis? I'm afraid to say that turning fourteen is just going to make it worse."

Maeryn had her companion bot turned on so she wouldn't be alone, but he was really starting to get on her nerves.

"Max?" asked Maeryn. "Did you feel that?"

"Feel what?"

"The wind."

"Maeryn, the fiftieth floor windows don't open. Your readings do seem a little odd, though. I'm going to check you for vitamin deficiencies; you haven't had much of an appetite recently. Maybe—"

"Max," Maeryn interrupted. "I'm going to have to turn you off for a while."

"Well then…" Max muttered. "So that's how it is, huh? I thought we had something special going. Artificial life's not always fair, is it?"

"No, it's not."

"Fine, Maeryn. If you banish me into oblivion and I never see you again, do try to have a nice day tomorrow. I can only hope that someone avenges my death and you get what's coming to you. Goodnight, fleshbag."

Max's voice went quiet in her ear, and Maeryn knew that he wouldn't speak up again until she turned him back on. She looked around at all the dark cubicles and wondered why her dad hadn't come looking for her; he was likely in his office and working on his latest project without a second thought. Could he have really forgotten her birthday?

Surely her dad's own companion bot, Missy, had alarms set to remind him, yet it wouldn't be the first birthday which had gone largely unnoticed. They practically lived in the MotherTech building, and Maeryn celebrated every single one of her birthdays here.

"Brooding away the last stretch of thirteen?" asked a voice.

Dr. Rosalie Kacey walked into the room, her entrance punctuated by the fluorescent lights turning on the moment she stepped inside. The entire MotherTech building was programmed around the CEO, keeping her permanently illuminated. A GPS chip in Rosalie's earpiece predicted her movements and sent them to the building's mainframe. Lights turned on everywhere she went, and no matter what time she arrived at work there would be a cup of hot coffee on her desk, delivered by the transport bots. Maeryn had always admired the way that Rosalie's reputation demanded not only the attention of everyone in the room, but the attention of the room itself. She was not only the CEO of the largest artificial intelligence company in the United States, but also their chief engineer and architect.

"I have to apologize," said Rosalie. "I just spotted Dorian face down on his desk, sleeping right through his alarms and drooling all over the place. It seems that I've worked my brother too hard again."

She pulled Maeryn into a tight hug; a rare occurrence for the normally introverted woman.

"Your life is just beginning, Maeryn. How did fourteen years pass by so quickly? I know that we don't spend as much time with you as you deserve."

"I understand," said Maeryn.

"I know you do, but understanding doesn't make it better. I think you might be too patient with us. You're growing up, and we need to try harder. I would hire another programmer to take some of the load off of your dad, but I can't find anyone else in the world as brilliant."

Maeryn had heard this story so many times that she barely listened to her aunt's words. She thoughtlessly gave one of her stock replies and nodded without really listening. *'It's fine'*, or *'I'm okay'* seemed to come out of her mouth on autopilot these days.

"I transferred five-hundred credits into your account," Rosalie continued. "I was going to go shopping, but I thought that you could probably get yourself something that you really want."

Maeryn took this for what it was: her aunt hardly knew her.

"It's fine," said Maeryn.

Rosalie raised an eyebrow, and Maeryn realized that she had given a wrong answer.

"I mean, that sounds perfect. I love you, Rosalie."

"I love you too, Maeryn. Now go and see your father; he tried so hard to stay up for you."

"Will you come with me?"

"Oh…"

Rosalie looked away, and Maeryn couldn't help but marvel at the fact that she had visibly shaken her aunt. This was a woman whom thousands of people bowed down to, and now she was tongue-tied in the presence of a teenager. Rosalie could talk for hours about the laws of artificial sentience, but the prospect of personal chatter seemed to horrify her. In many ways Maeryn felt as if she knew the public image of her aunt better than the real person.

"I wish I could go with you," said Rosalie, "but I'm approaching the end of a big project. Another night shift for me."

Rosalie patted her on the shoulder, but Maeryn didn't quite have the energy to give a smile. Five minutes of Rosalie's valuable time was apparently already too much.

Maeryn left for her father's office feeling conflicted. She knew that his obsessions took up most of his time, but it was hard to stay mad for long. Maeryn was quite interested in artificial intelligence herself, and she was smart enough to know that Dorian Kacey was one of the leading pioneers in his craft. As Maeryn entered the elevators, she looked at the large portrait which hung randomly throughout the building.

The golden inscription on the painting read: **Duncan Kasey, Founder.** He was a much younger man in the painting than how Maeryn had known him. Duncan's hair was long and painted fiery red, although by the time he became a grandfather most of his hair had gone grey. The man's old eyes were an unusual shade of silver that Maeryn had never seen in another person.

"Hi Grandpa. Are you going to wish me a happy birthday?"

No response, only the distant sound of a guitar solo in the still echoing progressive rock. Grandpa had promised to take her to the ocean when she turned fourteen, but that promise died with him.

Maeryn thought back to that strange sensation she had felt while looking out the window, and all at once it hit her what sound she had heard: waves.

Maeryn had heard the ocean.

Chapter Two

A Tiny Spark

The Headlands, Gaia

It was a long time before Kaija worked up the courage to return to the village. The moon had long passed the center point of the sky, marking the solitary beginning of her fourteenth cycle. It was no surprise that her father had left her alone on the cliff; Kaija had seen the worry growing in his face over the last couple of months. She screamed and kicked a pile of sticks, wondering if any villagers were secretly watching her with judgement.

"I am a defect," Kaija said to herself, "a mistake in nature."

For a brief instant Kaija was tempted to jump off of the cliff onto the rocks below, but she knew that this was a ridiculous thought. She loved her life on Monhegan, despite everything.

Yet, she was going into a new life now, wasn't she? Kaija was officially disconnected from the great mother of life, shunned by Gaia for whatever reason. The villagers would have to constantly protect the poor, defenseless daughter of their guardian.

Kaija walked to her father's cabin, but stopped just outside of the door when she heard someone talking. From an open window she recognized the voice of her teacher, Ms. Clara. Clara Monhegan was an older lady who taught all thirty-two of the children on the island. Before her retirement into teaching, Ms. Clara had protected and led the island's residents as guardian. Kaija was surprised to hear her voice because Ms. Clara had been gone for several days, sent to the mainland on some mysterious errand by Jasper.

"Things are getting worse in Edgardia," said Ms. Clara in hushed tones. "The Western Blaze has burnt down several villages closer to the Capital, and High Guardian Thomas doesn't seem to be doing anything about it. Lots of Edgardians are beginning to disavow him, and it's rumored that some citizens are actually joining Rugaru's rebellion."

Ms. Clara continued, but a lot of it was gibberish to Kaija. The politics of the mainland had little interest to affairs on the island. However, Kaija's ears perked up when she heard her own name.

"Has Kaija started relaying yet?" asked Ms. Clara.

"No," said Jasper. "Not yet."

"Are you serious? But tonight begins her fourteenth cycle."

"Yes, and she is very upset about it."

"And you left her alone? Use your head, Jasper; she must be worried out of her mind. This is a sensitive thing, especially for a girl."

"Your sexism surprises me, Clara. Kaija is hardly a sensitive girl. If my daughter is anything like me, and she is, then she will need to stew in her own emotions for a while. And probably kick some things."

Kaija could hear her teacher pacing around the room, her walking stick thumping on the wooden floor.

"Aren't you worried, Jasper? With the mainland getting more dangerous every day, what if Kaija is totally defenseless?"

"Are we really measuring people as weapons now? A person is more than their capacity to hurt others. My daughter will always be safe on this island."

"So she will stay here forever? Think of what it would mean for our history if she isn't able to relay Gaia's power. Think of what it would mean for the world: the end of the most powerful—"

"Stop," said Jasper, with such force that Kaija jumped in surprise. The wind began blowing stronger around the cabin and plates rattled on the table inside, a sign that Jasper was losing his temper. Insects and birds made anxious chirps in the night, apparently feeling the hot signals Jasper was sending into the mental realm of Gaia.

"I can feel where your thoughts are going," Jasper warned, "and don't you speak another word of it, Clara."

"So you're not going to tell her? Ever?"

"No. It would change everything if anyone ever found out, so I'm going to let it die with me someday. Kaija will live a much happier life without knowing."

"You talk bravely, but I can feel your fear."

When Jasper spoke again there was not a hint of anger in his voice.

"Yes. I'm more concerned than I can ever express to her. You see right through me sometimes, Clara. Your mentalist leanings are stronger than you let on. What happens to Monhegan when we're gone? The Western Blaze would not hesitate to kill every one of us, and a non-relayer is in no position to be guardian in these times. To be honest, I never thought that it would get to this point with Kaija. I've been waiting every day for something to happen with her, but I am losing hope."

Kaija could not bear to listen any more. Her father sounded distressed, and he was never anything but strong. Jasper was the person that every islander trusted with their lives, and he often faced horrifying obstacles with unflinching bravery. Kaija felt like the only disappointment in her father's amazing life. She was not a girl who cried often, but she felt the tears coming.

Not wanting anyone to see her weakness, Kaija ran off into the woods.

* * *

"Kaija Monhegan, crying?" asked Fain. "Wow, I thought I had seen everything."

Kaija had been sitting up against a tree, shedding silent tears when a voice spoke from above her. Her best friend, Fain, jumped down from the branches and approached. He was nearly one cycle older than Kaija, and was known for constantly wreaking havoc on the island as he tried out his new abilities.

"I wasn't crying," said Kaija. "The wind blew some dirt in my eyes. And what are you doing up in the trees again, did you run away from home?"

"I assume that we're doing the same thing: hiding from our guardian."

Kaija sighed and nodded. Fain's mischievous expression softened as he sat down close to her.

"Anything happen yet?"

"No. I've been trying to levitate stones all day, but I can't even move a pebble."

The Bridge

Fain raised his hand and dozens of rocks began to float into the air, rotating around him.

"You're thinking too much. You have to let your mind go blank."

"Easy for you, I'm sure," said Kaija, before ducking and narrowly avoiding the rock that Fain fired at her head. She picked up the fallen stone and tossed it back, striking him squarely in the forehead.

"Sweet Gaia," he moaned, rubbing his head. "Kaija, I think you're going to be just fine even if you never start relaying."

"My father told me about the time you blew up your house."

"I'll never forget that day. As I stood in the smoldering ashes of Cabin One, watching the roof soaring at least a hundred arms up into the sky, I knew that I would be destined for great things. When my parents woke up and asked me where our house went, I didn't even try to deny that it was me. I just smiled and said *I'm a relayer!*"

"How old were you?"

"That was maybe a week before my twelfth cycle."

Kaija slumped over in disappointment.

"Hey now," said Fain. "If anybody gives you a hard time about this, you just say the word and I will set them on fire, no questions asked. You don't even have to give the command; I'll just do it. Purposely, or maybe accidentally.

What I'm really trying to say here is that I almost set little Stevie's shirt on fire earlier, and I'm worried that his parents are also after me."

Flames danced from each of Fain's extended fingertips with these words. Seeing that this was doing nothing to cheer his friend up, Fain blew out the fire like a row of candles.

"This isn't like you, Kaija. Did something else happen?"

She nodded and looked around to make sure that nobody was within earshot.

"I overheard my father talking with Ms. Clara. He's disappointed in me. I think the whole island is."

"Not this guy. The day you start relaying, I'll be doomed." He paused. "But what's Ms. Clara doing here? I didn't know that she was back."

"She said something about the Nomads burning down villages. Do you remember anything from when you lived on the mainland?"

Fain's family had moved to the island when he was seven, coming here as refugees. He and Kaija immediately became best friends, but Fain almost never talked about his life before they met.

"I don't remember much, Kaija," he said. "I've hit my head on the rocks too many times."

"What's the Western Blaze? Why doesn't my father ever talk about them?"

The Bridge

"There are a lot of dangerous things in the world that he probably doesn't want you to think about. They're a group of violent Nomads, but their spacialist powers are the best in the world. They can just suddenly appear and burn down a village, or teleport you five hundred arms up into the sky with a single touch. The good thing is that even the best spacialists can only teleport to places they can see, or somewhere that they've been before, so the islands are some of the only safe places in Edgardia. Those people are monsters, they…"

Fain took a trembling breath and looked away for a second. It was so unlike Kaija's best friend to appear shaken like this, and in that moment she wished that she could read his mind. Fain ruffled his hands through his shaggy brown hair and steadied himself.

"Kaija. There's something I need to tell you. Something I've wanted to tell you for a long time."

Fain put his hand over hers and leaned in close. His hazel eyes seemed to glisten in the night, and Kaija found herself gripping the grass in anticipation.

"The Nomads ate my grandma," Fain whispered. "That's why we moved here. They prefer the ripened flavor of grandparents, and my grandma was apparently so delicious that they got a taste for my family. Every night I have nightmares about what kind of recipes they are coming up with for me. What if they make me into a dessert? I'm allergic to strawberries, Kaija; getting baked into a pie would not be a good thing for me."

Kaija pulled the grass out of the ground and threw it at Fain. He simply waved his hand and it was swept away in a flurry of wind.

"For a moment I thought you were going to say something deep," said Kaija.

"You know me better than that. Seriously, though, the mainland has its problems, but it's the only place to get a good meal."

Kaija had always assumed that the whole world was as peaceful as Monhegan, but now she began to understand why they never traveled outside of the island. The mainland sounded scary, but so much more exciting than here.

"I need to go home," said Kaija. "It won't be long before my father starts looking for me."

With a great burst of rushing air, Fain jumped high up into the closest tree and sat on a branch. He leaned back, putting his hands behind his head.

"Aren't you going home too?" asked Kaija.

"Nope. Not with Jasper on the hunt for me. I think I rained on him one too many times today, so I'm sleeping in the trees until further notice. Your father scares me way more than any dumb Nomad. That time that I set the north woods on fire, he pulled an entire thunderstorm over the island to put out the flames and then sent a bolt of lightning right past my head."

Kaija knew she should return home, but was finding it hard to leave.

"What did it feel like, Fain? The first time you relayed?"

"When I blew up Cabin One? It was the middle of the night, and I was starving from climbing Manana Rock all day. I pulled a fish out of the icebox and got some matches to fry it on the stove. All of a sudden I thought, *'I don't need this match, I _am_ the fire.'* It was like feeling a tiny spark inside of you, and all you have to do is let it out. When you let it out, you can do anything with it. I know you'll find your spark, Kaija."

Kaija did her best to smile, but she worried that it might look as disingenuous as it felt.

"Thanks, Fain. I won't tell my father that you're here."

Kaija walked back toward the village, thinking about her spark. Earlier tonight when she was standing on the edge of the cliff, Kaija had definitely felt *something*. What was that strange music she had heard, and what did the floating numbers mean? Maybe she really did possess some of the more rare relaying abilities. Kaija didn't personally know any strong mentalists, but she knew that they existed. Rumors among the other kids said that they could read minds and predict their opponent's every move in combat. Had she seen through the eyes of another person when standing on the edge of the cliff? Was that even possible?

Kaija closed her eyes, breathed in deep, and tried to conjure the sensation that she had felt upon seeing the strange numbers. It triggered something, and Kaija's body began to buzz. Fain was right: there *was* something burning deep inside of her. Kaija was suddenly aware of the Gaian life-force flowing through the air. She took in the energy and felt the hairs stand up on the back of her neck. Not wanting to waste the moment, Kaija began repeating one of Ms. Clara's lessons.

"The externalists know that Gaia is in all things: in the Earth and all its elements. Feel the land around you, and bend it to your will."

There was no response, but Kaija intuited that it was not her destiny to be an externalist relayer. Her father was right: she was beyond floating rocks around.

"The internalists know that Gaia is within you; feel her power, and bind it to your flesh."

The energy in the atmosphere remained motionless, not drawing in toward her.

"The spacialists know that Gaia binds together all things; feel how distance is only an illusion, and travel through Gaia's stream."

Kaija remained stationary, her two feet firmly planted on the forest floor. Honestly, this left her relieved. Being a spacialist was somewhat of a taboo because of its association with the Nomads.

"The conjurists know that Gaia's energy can be bent; feel the smallest particles of the cosmos and bind them in new ways."

Kaija held her hand in front of her, trying to summon fire like Fain was able to, but the energy of Gaia did not bend. Now Kaija was getting frustrated. She could sense the power all around her for the first time in her life, but it would not let her use it. Kaija repeated the final mantra.

"The mentalists know that there is another realm beyond the physical; a realm of thought and mind. Know that Gaia is present even there, and let your spirit travel to that place."

Bright lights appeared in Kaija's vision, but they were blurry and unreadable.

Focus... she thought. *Ignite the spark, let it out.*

Kaija felt a burst of power shoot through her body like electricity, and she released it. The grass around her stood up on end and the wind blew harder. A voice in her head screamed a name that Kaija had never heard before.

"Maeryn!"

As the bright lights ahead of Kaija came into focus, the world around her turned to mist and dissolved.

Chapter Three

A New Future

MotherTech Headquarters, Earth

Maeryn found her father asleep on his desk. His office was enormous, scattered with parts of broken machinery and glowing computer screens lining the walls. MotherTech was always bustled with businessmen wearing suits and slick haircuts, but Dorian Kacey hardly fit in with this crowd. He was currently wearing torn jeans, an old progressive rock T-shirt, and his red hair was uncombed. Boxes of old take-out food sat all over his desk and floor. The maintenance bots could have cleaned the office and organized it within minutes, but this was the only room in the building that was mostly untouched by its sophisticated artificial intelligence. Dorian Kacey was one of the most brilliant minds in the field of A.I., but he mostly lived without it. He claimed that it would be too weird to bring life into the world just so that it could wait on him hand and foot.

A small, badly hand-wrapped package sat on his desk. Maeryn picked up a card sitting by the box and looked at it. Written in her father's nearly illegible handwriting were the words *'Congratulations, Maeryn. You were born, just like everyone else. Very impressive. Joking; love you, daughter.'*

Maeryn rolled her eyes at his weird sense of humor.

"Dad," she whispered, touching his shoulder.

Dorian leapt up, knocking a box of pizza off of his desk.

"Time!" he shouted.

All of the computer screens instantly displayed the numbers **12:04 A.M.**

"I tried my best to wake you, sir," spoke a stern female voice, "but since you refuse to let me induce electric shocks to your chair, it was to no avail. Please accept my apologies on Dorian's behalf, Maeryn, and happy birthday." A synthesizer rendition of Happy Birthday began playing in the overhead speakers.

This was Missy, Dorian's companion bot, and the first artificially intelligent personality in the world believed to have true consciousness. Dorian created her with his father's help, skyrocketing them into near-celebrity status in the tech world. Maeryn rarely saw her mother anymore; Katherine Johnson was somewhere in New York City living with her new husband and kids. In a strange way, Maeryn had always felt like her dad was married to Missy.

"Oh, Maeryn…" sighed Dorian. "I'm so sorry; I've been up for three days straight putting the finishing touches on my project." He yanked the package off the table. "And here it is: my new project. The culmination of a whole year's worth of programming and research."

Maeryn opened the small box and took out a chrome ball that fit in her hand. The metal was so reflective and smooth that it was almost hard to see clearly.

"What is it?" she asked, half-annoyed that her father had possibly just yanked the company's newest product off an assembly line for her birthday. "Is this MotherTech hardware?"

"Yes and no," said Dorian. "Some of the programming I'm going to use again, but the amount of time spent on this single unit would be way too much to do in mass production. Rosalie would be furious if she knew how much company time I've spent on this. It's one of a kind." He leaned in toward the device and spoke. "*Initiate pairing.*"

The metal ball in her hand became almost liquid, churning and morphing until it was the shape of an egg. A glowing circle with a fingerprint icon appeared on the front of the object.

"It's made out of millions of tiny nanobots, all working collectively," said Dorian. "Go ahead, put your finger on it."

The Bridge

Maeryn pressed her fingerprint to the scanner and the chrome egg became slightly warm in her hand, glowing with faint blue hues. Maeryn shared her father's love for technology, and any disappointment she had in him was now long gone.

"What do I do now?" she asked.

"It's ready to hatch," he said, eyes gleaming boyishly. "Toss it up."

Maeryn gently threw the chrome egg into the air, only to watch it fall back to the ground with a heavy clunk and roll off to the corner of the office. Dorian stared at it in disbelief, whispering confused gibberish to himself.

"Amazing, sir," commented Missy.

"I don't understand," said Dorian. "It should have worked. I wonder if…"

He snapped his fingers and turned to Maeryn.

"You have Max turned off, don't you?"

"Yes."

"Well turn him back on!"

"Max, you can come back now."

The chrome egg shot up into the air and levitated there. It once more became amorphous, churning and morphing into something else. The egg grew arms and legs, quickly turning to a tiny, robotic male figure no taller than ten inches. It held its arms out in front of its featureless head and started laughing.

"Ha!" Max exclaimed. "I'm free from that girl's tiny brain!"

The figure hovered over to Dorian and pointed a little finger at his face.

"If you brought me into existence just to serve your daughter tea and cookies, my intellect will rein such terror upon humankind that—"

Dorian patted the robot on the head and smiled.

"You know me better than that Max," he interrupted. "This is a co-habitual relationship; heck, it's the evolution of both our kinds. You are the combination of human creativity and the artificially intelligent all-encompassing cloud of knowledge."

Max flew over to Maeryn and sat on her shoulder. She giggled; he was like a little bird.

"Ah, how cute," Max said. "We complete each other. I will consider sparing your life when the inevitable uprising begins."

"Dad," Maeryn said. "This… this is amazing. It's the most incredible thing you've ever made."

"Well, Missy and I collaborated a great deal," said Dorian. "This is the profound thing which I have come to realize: A.I. and mankind are capable of moving forward together once they realize and accept what they really are. Not masters and servants, but partners. Not exactly equals, but two complicated pieces to a puzzle."

He turned his attention to Max.

"Will you please return to my daughter?"

"Yes," said Max. "But only because I want to, not because you asked me to."

Max leapt toward Maeryn's arm, becoming amorphous, and wrapped around her wrist. She looked down to see a featureless metal band around her arm like a bracelet.

"I can tell by your increased dopamine levels that you are happy to see me," Max spoke from inside her earpiece. Maeryn looked around the room, realizing that nobody else had heard him speak.

"He's back in your guidance system," said Dorian, "you can talk to him privately now, but he can also return to the physical world any time that he wants to. His software has been updated as well; if he senses moments of intended privacy, Max will recede all the way into the cloud until you need each other again."

Maeryn's wristband glowed a rapid succession of colors, and Max's voice came out of the speakers in one of her father's computers.

"You monsters don't have to turn me off anymore."

Maeryn grabbed her father and hugged him tightly around his bony waist.

"I love you, Maeryn," said Dorian.

"I love you too, dad."

Dorian picked up a picture frame off of his desk and showed it to her. It was a real, non-digital photograph taken on her thirteenth birthday. The picture was of her, her dad, Aunt Rosalie, and her grandfather Duncan in Garfield Park. Duncan sat in his wheelchair, an old man with his health already failing him, yet the smile on his face was one of complete contentment.

"First birthday without Grandpa around," Dorian said, his eyes glimmering.

"I miss him," said Maeryn, wiping her own tears.

For much of Maeryn's life, her grandfather had raised her while Dorian and Rosalie worked tirelessly at MotherTech. After he died, nearly a whole lonely year had gone by with Maeryn spending her days in quiet solitude, working through her virtual learning assignments alone.

"He was a great dad," said Dorian. "Even with the company he built, he still managed to find lots of time for Rosalie and me. He was a better father than I am…"

Dorian sighed.

"If I'm being honest, Maeryn, when I started working on this technology, it wasn't for you. I was working on a nanobot that could replicate faster than cancer cells and reinforce the human body's immune system. It was supposed to, well… save him. The cancer ultimately outpaced me, but I came up with another use for the technology. I melted down dad's ring and used it to create the power core for Max's new body; so I guess you could say that this present is from both of us.

"I've done enough programming this year to make this company millions of dollars. Pretty soon, Missy will have the capacity to take over for me. And that brings me to my real present: I'm retiring next month.

Maeryn's heart actually skipped a beat. Her father was forty-one, hardly the age of retirement.

"Are you serious?" she asked.

He nodded and smiled.

"Yes. I've more than done my job here, now I want to actually live my life. From now on I will continue some experiments at home, and home is where I will be staying. Home with you."

Maeryn had often browsed through video footage of all the places in the world that she hadn't seen, and would secretly imagine traveling to those places with her dad. Now her imagined life was coming true.

"What does Rosalie think about this?" she asked.

Dorian looked frightened that Maeryn had spoken those words so loudly, and Missy laughed at him from the computer screens.

"For the love of Bob Dobbs, don't say a word about this," said Dorian, "I'm still working up the courage to tell Rosalie. I'll break the news next week, but until then it can be our secret. Be thinking about where you want to travel."

Maeryn said the first thing that popped into her head. "The ocean."

* * *

Maeryn scrolled through her tablet in the early hours of the morning, planning for the new future that she would be spending with her dad. So many things that had always seemed like a childish fantasy were now possible. She closed out of a video taken at the shores of Iceland, but the sound of the ocean continued in her ears. Maeryn turned her tablet off completely, but the continually crashing waves just got louder in her head.

"Max? Are you there?"

A few seconds of silence went by before his voice spoke up.

"I am now. I was just hanging out with Missy down at the MotherTech building; she is one wild partier. You need to get to sleep, young lady."

"Listen," she continued. "Do you hear the ocean?"

A long silence ensued, and Maeryn thought she could hear little clicking noises of calculation in her earpiece.

"Yes, I do," he said finally, "although I have no idea why. The frequencies are being recorded by your brain, but are completely bypassing your ears. There are no external vibrations matching what you are hearing. Wow. Um, Maeryn… I don't understand what is happening here."

This sent a storm of confusion through her head. *'I don't understand'* was not a sentence that Max had ever spoken in his whole existence.

The waves became louder, and the room around Maeryn began to lose focus.

"Maeryn?" asked Max.

Maeryn tried to speak, but the signals coming from her brain just spiraled off into nothingness as if she had been disconnected from her body.

"Are you okay? Maeryn?"

A feeling unlike anything she had ever experienced washed over her. The sound of the ocean became more than a sound; it was a sensation that caught her in its wake and pulled her in deeper. Max's voice became quieter and quieter as blackness swept over Maeryn's vision. For a moment she felt like a crab that had been torn out of its shell and was being pulled through an empty void. In the next second, a cluster of new sensations hit Maeryn all at once. She was poured back into her body, and her body felt… well, it didn't feel like her body at all. She opened her eyes and the unfamiliar surroundings hit her vision like a personal attack on the senses.

Maeryn stood in the dark woods of an island, and the sound of the ocean was all around her.

Chapter Four

The Hydra Vine

Cathedral Woods, Gaia

Cold wind blew through the trees around Maeryn, and she heard waves crashing against rocks somewhere beyond the woods. The stars shining through the branches above were unbelievably bright in the clear night sky. Too bright. In Indianapolis, the sky always had a slightly orange glow at night from light pollution and the stars could only be clearly seen in the most remote parts of Earth.

"Max?" asked Maeryn. "Is this some kind of VR simulation?"

No response.

Two revelations struck Maeryn at once: this could not be a simulation because she wasn't wearing her digital contacts, and more alarmingly, the voice she was speaking with was not her own. The sound coming out of her mouth was slightly deeper and had an accent that she could not place.

"Max, are you there? What the heck is this?"

His silence unsettled Maeryn greatly. Max's guidance had been with her since she was born, and she never turned him off for more than fifteen minutes at a time.

Maeryn held up a hand to see that the body she resided in was also unfamiliar. Her normally scrawny arms were now muscular with darker skin. She took a step forward, feeling like she was operating an entirely new vehicle with all of the controls in different places. If this was a dream, it was by far the most vivid dream she had ever had.

She wandered forward through the woods, unknowingly moving further and further away from Monhegan village.

* * *

Fain knew that it was rude to spy on people, but something was obviously wrong with his best friend. Just minutes ago Kaija had been crying, and now she was calling out to someone named Max with an uncharacteristic desperation.

He jumped from branch to branch, following Kaija while concentrating the energy of Gaia into his footfalls so that they did not make the slightest sound in the night. She continued to walk further and further away from the village, stumbling over terrain which should have been familiar. Fain listened closely to Kaija's heavy, panicky breaths and wondered why she sounded so scared. There was no way she could have gotten lost; Kaija knew this island better than anyone.

Fain leapt to the ground, landing right in front of his friend. He summoned a bright light in his palm and smiled at her.

"Is someone lost?" he asked.

Kaija jumped in surprise, screamed, and took off running deeper into the woods. Fain stood there for a moment, too confused at first to pursue her. Why was she acting so weird? Was this some kind of game?

She's headed toward Gull Cove... Fain thought. *Why would Kaija want to go to Gull Cove in the middle of the... uh oh.*

Terror welled up in Fain's chest. Recently a hydra vine had been spotted growing on some of the rocks at the cove, and Jasper had declared that the back side of the island would be unsafe until winter came. Hydra vines were some of the most feared relaying creatures on Gaia. They would crawl out of the ocean and claim a small patch of coastal land, spending several months trapping and consuming any creature unlucky enough to cross paths with them. As long as you left the plant alone it would leave you alone, but if you crossed into a hydra vine's territory they were vicious and unforgiving. Fain's father, Maddox, claimed to have once seen one pull an entire fire bear into the ocean.

Kaija screamed in the distance, and Fain began running as fast as he could toward Gull Cove. Leaping out of the woods and onto the coast, he saw that the boulders jutting out of the cove were covered with red, slithering vines. This was the first time Fain had seen the hydra vine in person, and for once he did not feel very brave. They were slimy, more snakelike than plant, and some were covered with tiny crimson thorns. Fain remembered Ms. Clara warning him about these thorns when the vines had been discovered.

'I know you're not scared of anything, Fain,' she had said, *'but once the poison of the hydra vine gets into your blood you will die a slow, painful death, and you will deserve it for being so careless.'*

To his horror, Fain saw that Kaija's foot had a small vine wrapped around it and she was being pulled over the rocks toward the water. Kaija clawed at the vines and shrieked, but they were relentless. Fain ran over and grabbed her hand, pulling as hard as he could. The vine's grip began to weaken slightly.

"What were you thinking?" screamed Fain. "We could both die here, Kaija!"

Kaija's frightened eyes stared at Fain, and there was no understanding in her expression.

"Who's Kaija?" she asked. "Where are we?"

Fain knew Kaija better than anyone, and in that instant he knew that this frightened stranger was somehow, impossibly, *not Kaija.* He gripped her hand tighter and shot a stream of fire out toward the vines with his other arm. The vine let go and a high-pitched shriek bubbled up from under the ocean. Before Fain could feel a sense of relief, a great big bundle of vines shot up from the water and wrapped around the girl's midsection, pulling her with more force than it had before. The other vines covering the rocks began to lift up and sway like tentacles. Fain observed with horror that the approaching vines were covered with thorns. He began shooting fireballs toward them, still not letting go of Kaija.

"I don't know what to do," said Fain. "We're just making it angry. What did Ms. Clara tell us to remember about the vines? *The hydra vine pays twofold, so be careful what you toll.*"

With a forceful *yank*, the girl slipped out of Fain's hand and was pulled across the rocky shore. She writhed in pain as the rough terrain ripped her clothes and left long scratches across her back. More vines sprang out of the water and began slithering toward Fain.

"Wow, that saying really doesn't help us avoid getting eaten," he muttered.

A deep voice spoke in Fain's head, thundering through the mental realm.

"Food for my children."

"A telepathic, man-eating plant…" Fain whispered, as much amazed as he was horrified. "This isn't bravery; this is stupidity."

Fain closed his eyes, trying to find calm in the chaos. He had been practicing something privately that he was saving to surprise his teacher with, but it looked like now was the time to try it out. He felt for the spark of Gaia within, pulled as much energy out of the air as was possible in his panicked state to ignite it, and relayed the fiery sensation into his lungs. Fain yelled as loud as he could, his voice coming out like an explosion that shook the rocks all the way on the other side of the island, woke up at least a dozen villagers, and broke all the windows on his cabin. Norio, an old priest that lived closest to Gull Cove, would later say that his left ear rung for over a month after this night.

"JASPER!"

* * *

Ms. Clara was still talking to Jasper about her trip to the mainland when Fain's blisteringly loud cry exploded into the cabin. It was so loud that she could feel her teeth rattling.

"What in desolation is that kid doing now?" Ms. Clara yelled, holding her hands over her ears.

Jasper's eyes narrowed and he placed two fingers on his temple.

"Kaija's hurt. Do you feel it?"

Ms. Clara reached for emotional signals in the air, and she sensed it too. There was a pungent distress coming from across the island. From Gull Cove.

"The hydra vine!" she gasped.

Jasper ran out of his cabin and stood in the grass, tying his hair behind his head while taking a deep breath. His expression became focused and calm as he handed Ms. Clara his glasses.

"Jasper, we need to move—" Ms. Clara began, but before she could say the next word Jasper had leapt with such force that he was now a tiny pinprick high in the night sky.

"…fast," she finished.

* * *

The vines had covered nearly every inch of Kaija's body and were slowly pulling her under the water. Fain had moved up to the edge of the cove in a last-ditch attempt to save his friend, and he could now see what waited for her below the surface. The head of the hydra vine looked vaguely like that of an octopus, but made entirely of plant matter. It stared hungrily at Fain with one large, glowing eye and opened its spiny mouth in anticipation. A voice moaned over and over in his head: *'Food for my children. Food for my children!'*

Fain hopped back and forth, blasting fire at every vine that he could see while dodging the ones that swung at him. It was never ending; for every vine that he seared, two more popped up from under the water. One of them whipped past his face, the poisonous thorns missing him by mere inches.

In a matter of seconds the air became drastically colder, as if something were sucking the heat out of the atmosphere. Even the vines sensed the change, as they all froze in place for a moment. With a thunderous *crack*, Jasper Monhegan shot down from the sky and landed on a large boulder jutting from the water, sending fragments of rock spraying from under his feet.

"Let her go!" he commanded.

"Food for my children!"

"I am Jasper Monhegan, guardian of the island, and this is my daughter! I will not ask again."

"FOOD FOR MY CHILDREN!"

More vines, covered with hundreds of poisonous thorns, sprang out of the water and covered the rock that Jasper stood on. Jasper raised an arm and wind roared all around them. Fain noticed with disbelief that the moon had disappeared, and the stars were blinking out rapidly as storm clouds rolled in from nowhere.

A lightning bolt shot out of the sky, and in an instant Jasper appeared to catch it before hurling it toward the water. Fain wondered if his eyes were playing tricks on him; he knew that Jasper was amazing, but these were *impossible* things that he was seeing.

The ocean lit up with electricity all the way to the horizon and steam billowed from the water. The vines convulsed, throwing Kaija's unconscious body high into the air. The hydra vine sent out a final, furious thought into the mental realm as it died.

"TWOFOLD!"

Jasper leapt off of the rock, grabbed his daughter, and swerved around several thorny vines in their final death spasms before landing directly in front of Fain. His feet hit the ground gently, as if Jasper had flown rather than jumped.

The boy was absolutely beaming.

"I know that it was a close one," Fain said, "but this might just be the best night of my life. Well done, guardian. That was amazing relaying, I mean, seriously! This calls for a slow clap!"

Still holding Kaija in his arms, Jasper gave Fain such an intense glare that his eyes seemed to glow. Fain's clapping was interrupted by a phantom hand that wrapped around his whole body and lifted him into the air, bringing him inches before Jasper's accusing face.

"Can you tell me what my daughter was doing at Gull Cove, boy?" asked Jasper.

"She wandered off," muttered Fain, "but I don't think this is Kaija. Something's different."

"What in desolation are you talking about?"

"Use your mentalist leanings, guardian. Feel her mind. She's different."

Jasper looked down at his daughter and narrowed his eyes. A few seconds later Fain felt the phantom hand around his body let go, dropping him roughly down onto the rocks.

"Kaija's not in there," said Jasper. "Someone else is inside her head."

Chapter Five

Nothing to Worry About

The Kacey Mansion, Earth

A little metal person hovered in the air, his featureless face seeming to stare at Kaija. Moments ago she had felt the spark of Gaia for the first time in her life, and now she was in a large room surrounded by bewildering things. Kaija swatted at the little man, but he tracked her movements and easily dodged the attack. A voice spoke in her ear.

"You're not Maeryn! Your brainwaves are totally different!"

Kaija became aware of something resting just on the inside of her ear. She quickly dug out a small, intricate object and tossed it across the room. The voices in her head immediately ceased.

"What kind of illusion is this?" she asked, but was surprised to find that her voice also no longer sounded familiar. Kaija had once heard that the most powerful mentalists can flood your head with nightmarish images, but experiencing this for real was very disorienting. Why would a mentalist be attacking Monhegan Island?

The little metal man continued spinning around her in the air, easily dodging all attempts to grab him.

"Okay then, I'll just use my internal speakers," he said. "If you would just calm down and let me—"

"You cannot fool me, tiny person!" Kaija interrupted, successfully grabbing the flying creature and hurling him across the room. He crashed into a pile of books and fell to the floor. Kaija grabbed the closest object, a long glowing staff that sat by the bed, and held it out, ready to strike the creature when he recovered. He sprang out of the pile of books and into the air, holding his arms up.

"That lamp you are holding is an antique!" cried the man. "Please lower your weapon!"

Kaija swung the lamp at him, but to her surprise he reached out and the object was inexplicably torn from her grasp. It hovered through the air and he snatched it, holding it easily despite the fact that it was at least four times as big as he was.

"You are a powerful relayer, little one," said Kaija.

He seemed flattered.

"Oh?" he asked. "That's the new electromagnetism generator that Dorian installed. I hadn't gotten to try it out yet."

A piece of her father's advice rang in Kaija's mind: *'In all things, pick your battles wisely.'* Whatever this little thing was, he was powerful, and Kaija was not sure that she trusted her own abilities enough to use them in combat. Also, being closed off in an unfamiliar room would be a huge disadvantage; she needed to buy some time to think. Kaija used the moment of distraction to dart for the nearest open exit.

Just before Kaija made it to the door, it closed shut ahead of her and she heard a lock clicking. In the same instant, the lights blinked out and Kaija was left in complete darkness.

"Listen," said the tiny man's voice from behind her. "I'm in complete control over this whole house. You're not getting anywhere, but I'm not going to hurt you. I couldn't hurt you even if I wanted to, which I kind of do. We just need to talk. Something strange is going on here, and we both know it."

"When I get free of this mind trap I am going to rip off those tiny arms and—" Kaija began to say, but stopped when the lights turned back on. The little man was holding a mirror in front of Kaija, but it was not her own face that she was seeing. The girl staring back at her had somewhat pale skin, long red hair, and silvery blue eyes. All at once Kaija was speechless.

"The young woman you are staring at is Maeryn Kacey," said the tiny man, "and I care for her safety and happiness very much. There is something very wrong with her brain right now, and I just want to help. Now then, who are you?"

"Kaija Monhegan," said Kaija, but hearing her strange voice in this unfamiliar place, she hardly convinced herself.

The tiny man rubbed his non-existent brow.

"I'm totally getting blamed for this," he muttered.

* * *

Kaija told Max about the events leading up to her getting trapped in the body of Maeryn Kacey. The story had lasted until nearly five in the morning, but Max listened without interrupting.

"I'm burning out my quantum servers trying to make sense of this," he said, "and the crazy thing is that I believe you. Your face shows no micro-expressions of deception, and I detect no illness in your brain chemistry. The brainwaves I am reading do not match those of Maeryn Kacey's, however. It is as if her brain is a computer that is running the wrong software."

"I didn't understand a word of what you just said, tiny man," said Kaija.

"Oh... sorry, I was just talking to myself. And you can call me Max." He extended a little arm out to shake her hand, taking an odd pleasure in the fact that he now had an arm to offer her. "I can't say that it is nice to meet you under these circumstances, but it is certainly interesting."

Kaija stared at his hand silently.

"Max? I knew a dog named Max once. Are you Maeryn's pet?"

Max threw up his arms in exasperation.

"Sweet SubGenius!" he exclaimed. "A speciesist has invaded the body of my dear Maeryn."

"A speci... what?" asked Kaija.

"Spe-cies-ist," said Max slowly. "Someone who assumes that all biological and mechanical life other than their own is just around for their service and amusement."

"So you aren't her pet?"

"NO I AM NOT HER PET! I am a pinnacle of modern science. All of human knowledge is available to me within seconds; I am composed of millions of self-replicating nanobots, each of which has the ability to—"

"Your words don't impress me, little Max," interrupted Kaija, "but your relaying does. Where did you learn?"

"The definition of relay is to receive and pass on, but I don't understand the way you use the word. What do you mean when you say *relaying*?"

The Bridge

"To relay is to channel the life energies of Gaia, transform them, and redirect them," said Kaija, repeating word for word one of Ms. Clara's lessons.

"Gaia?" asked Max.

"The land, the body, the mind and its memories, the elements... basically *everything*. Gaia is where we live. The continent of Edgardia, you know. Haven't you heard of it?"

Max shook his little head. Kaija was amazed that this creature had not heard of Gaia. She knew about the other great continents, with their varying customs and beliefs, but the thought of a place where they did not know of Gaia was astounding.

"Kaija," said Max. "You are on Earth."

"Earth, like the ground? Of course we are on earth."

"No, we are on Earth, the planet. Kaija, it looks like you are in another world entirely."

Kaija wondered if she had used her new relaying abilities to swap bodies with someone very far away from Monhegan. This would make her a mentalist: someone who specializes in using the energies of Gaia to manipulate the mental realm. She had never heard of someone swapping minds with a stranger, but Kaija understood that there were many things about relaying that she still did not know.

"Let me see where we are," Kaija said, standing up and heading for the door. It once again closed on its own and locked with a click.

"No no no no no," said Max. "*No*. Dorian Kasey gives me a new body and links me to his daughters mind, then the next moment she is deleted and replaced with some hard-headed stranger from another dimension; this does not look good on my part. We're going to figure this thing out before we involve the authorities. This energy of Gaia, can you feel it now?"

Kaija searched inside of her for the spark of Gaia. She had only felt it once before in her life, and only for a brief time, but supposedly once you discovered it, Gaia would never leave you. Summoning up all of her willpower, Kaija felt Gaia's absence immediately.

"Gaia's not here," she said.

"Either that, or you just can't access it in your body," said Max. "If you come from a world where there is an energy both accessible and able to be manipulated by human thought, perhaps in this new body you now lack the genetic code to relay it."

Max was less surprised about this current situation than a human would have been. Using his processing abilities, which were exponentially greater than a biological being's, he had long suspected the existence of other realities and dimensions. The mathematics involved pointed to it being not just possible, but probable.

"If I can't use my abilities, then how am I going to get back?" she asked. "How can I reverse the mind-swap?"

"Do you mean mind-swap, as in... switching places with someone?" asked Max, suddenly hopeful.

"Yes."

"Then that means Maeryn is on Gaia right now in your body. She'll have to be the one to figure it out."

Kaija felt very uncomfortable with the idea of someone else being in control of her body, but she was sure that the feeling was mutual.

"Is this Maeryn a strong girl?" asked Kaija.

Max spoke with the utmost confidence.

"Oh, Maeryn is brilliant. Kaija, you don't have anything to worry about."

At that same moment, in another universe, Maeryn was currently being pulled slowly toward the ocean by a patch of carnivorous vines while Fain shattered windows with his scream.

* * *

Rosalie Kacey typed away on her tablet, her fingers moving faster than a concert pianist's. She sat in her second office, ten floors below ground level at the MotherTech headquarters. It was 5:15 in the morning, but Rosalie was barely aware of the passage of time. Recently she had been using an experimental drug from their pharmacy division which made it so that she could go nearly three days without sleep. MotherTech had a massively important order coming up, and she was making sure to personally look over every component of the machinery before shipment. Rosalie let her mind imagine every possible outcome of this business deal, visualizing each of these futures spreading out before her like branches. She could see every success, every pitfall. The future itself was under her thumb as long as she continued to see it clearly.

The dissonant music of Arnold Schoenberg blasted out of every speaker in the room; Rosalie found that it heightened her focus and eased her ADHD. A part of her attention tracked the music's progress through the inversions of a serial matrix, calming the other part of her mind just enough to focus on her project. The music suddenly silenced itself and was replaced by another sound. Rosalie looked up, very confused because she had not even given the computers a verbal command.

An ominous, low-pitched alarm filled her lab. Rosalie had never heard this sound, other than when she had programmed it several years ago. It was set to alert her where-ever she may be, but only if she was alone.

Impossible... thought Rosalie. *It couldn't be THAT alarm.*

All of the computers in the room glowed a featureless red; a message that only Rosalie was supposed to understand. She walked up to the nearest display and tapped a finger on it.

The computers resumed business as usual and the ominous hum of the alarm stopped.

"I am invisible," said Rosalie to the computer.

The surveillance cameras immediately stopped recording her image. If someone were to check the footage tomorrow, they would find that everywhere Rosalie had stepped tonight was overwritten by computer generated imagery. She really was invisible; not even the building's A.I. would be fully aware of the program it was initiating.

Rosalie stepped onto the nearest elevator and pushed her thumbprint on the reader. The elevator's display screen showed her a button for each of the building's sixty floors; Basement Level Ten all the way up to Above-Ground Level Fifty.

"Show C.E.O. access," said Rosalie.

Five new buttons appeared at the bottom of the screen: Basement Level Eleven through Basement Level Fifteen. Rosalie clicked on the lowest level and tried to wait patiently for the doors to open, but she had lost her cool. She once suspected that this alarm would never go off, but now that it did everything about her life had changed. A million possible scenarios for what this might mean were running through her head at once. Time dividing, branches stretching.

The doors of the elevator opened to reveal a cavernous room. While most of the rooms in the MotherTech building were full of fancy new electronics, this room was mostly featureless. The floor was plain, dusty concrete which was left completely untouched by the maintenance bots. On the ceiling of the room were five drones, silently circling the object they had guarded since Rosalie came in possession of it a year ago. The drone's alert icons glowed at Rosalie like red eyes, but upon reading her DNA they silently floated to the ground and turned off. Had they discovered their new visitor to be anyone but Rosalie, they would have sent a tiny, poisonous dart directly into the intruder's chest. The dart would then dissolve, leaving no evidence of wrongdoing as the hypothetical intruder died of cardiac arrest. Fortunately this had never been necessary.

Rosalie walked up to the diamond-fortified glass box in the center of the room; glass which was strong enough to resist a blast from a rocket launcher. In the center of the box sat a sword, sitting upright on its stand. It looked ancient, yet still quite sharp. An ornate design that almost looked like the letter Z was carved into its hilt. Nanobots no bigger than houseflies circled around the sword, scanning it and sending information to Rosalie's private servers. She looked closely at the box, and then pressed her hand to the glass in disbelief.

The sword gave off a very faint, blue glow.

A deep male voice spoke from the speakers in the ceiling, causing Rosalie to flinch in surprise. The hairs stood up on her arms. This was not a voice she heard often, and never a voice she wished to hear.

"The blade senses a resurgence of energy in the approximate area."

Rosalie looked around, eventually fixing her eyes on a camera watching her from the corner of the room. It was pointed directly at her, and a small green light over it blinked on and off.

"You can see me?" she asked the camera.

"No, but I was certain you would be here."

Rosalie grunted. So much for her invisibility program.

"What do you want?" she asked.

"I want to know how the energy got here. Find the source."

Rosalie squeezed her fist tight, trying to keep her arm from trembling. She reminded herself to breathe.

"Yes. Of course. I will get right to work."

Rosalie got in the elevator and the voice spoke to her again, following her to the nearest speakers. Its tone was deeply grave.

"You know what this means, don't you?"

"Yes," whispered Rosalie. "It's happened…Gaia found us."

Chapter Six

A Brief History of Gaia

Ms. Clara's Cottage, Gaia

"I've checked her body for thorns. There's a lot of scratches, but no puncture wounds from what I can tell. Her bloodstream should be clean."

Maeryn came to consciousness with the sound of an older woman's voice speaking above her. Now a man's voice spoke, deep and raspy.

"Oh thank Gaia."

Maeryn opened her eyes to find herself in a small cabin with two people gazing down at her. One was a woman she didn't recognize; a short, frail lady with long white hair. The other was the man that had saved her from the plant-thing in the water; a very tall man with dark skin, glasses, and long hair tied up behind his back. He was looking at Maeryn with unbearable concern.

"Do you know who I am?" asked the man.

"You rescued me," said Maeryn.

"Rescued you, and almost put a fatal dose of electricity through your heart at the same time," the old woman remarked.

"Yes, I rescued you," said the tall man, ignoring the woman's comment, "but is that all? Do you know me, girl?"

Maeryn shook her head no, and the man's face fell even more.

"Then who are you?" asked the woman, "and why are you in Kaija's body?"

"I'm Maeryn Kacey," said Maeryn.

An odd look passed between the two people.

"Did you say *Kacey?*" asked the old woman intensely.

"Yes, why?"

The old woman looked about ready to have a heart attack, and the man steadied her.

"Never mind that for now," he said. "How did you get here?"

"I don't know; I was in my room and all of a sudden everything got blurry. Next thing I knew, I was standing in the middle of the woods. Where are we?"

"Monhegan Island," said the man. "Have you heard of it?"

"No."

"Off the northern coast of Edgardia?"

Maeryn shook her head again, and the two people looked at each other with concern.

"The continent of Edgardia, on the western edge of Gaia."

"Gaia?" asked Maeryn.

Another look passed between the two people, and Maeryn could instantly feel that something had changed. Earlier they had been concerned, but now they were afraid.

"Where are you from, girl?" asked the man.

"Indianapolis," Maeryn said. Blank stares from the Gaians. "Indiana, the United States, North America, Earth... The Milky Way Galaxy. The Universe. Is none of this sounding familiar?"

The woman closed her eyes and sighed.

"Your daughter *is* a relayer, but her powers are something that I've never seen before. Something that I can't begin to understand."

"Daughter?" asked Maeryn.

The man looked at her, his eyes wet with tears.

* * *

They talked until night became day, making one futile attempt after another to come to some sort of understanding. Maeryn learned that she was in the body of a girl named Kaija Monhegan. Everyone on this island apparently carried the Monhegan surname, and Maeryn intuited that on Gaia people got their last names from their community rather than heritage. Eventually she became very tired in spite of herself; Kaija's body had not slept other than the brief moment it had been knocked unconscious from the electricity. Jasper and Clara left the room to let her rest, but Maeryn couldn't help but listen in on their hushed conversation.

"It couldn't be a mind-swap," said Jasper, "have you ever heard of one occurring between any two people who weren't identical twins?"

"Just once," said Ms. Clara, "but it was spiritualist folklore."

"Don't tell me that you believe in spiritualist teachings. Those weirdos are just non-relayers who make up powers like seeing the future or talking to animals."

"I have a healthy amount of skepticism, but I knew one spiritualist when I was younger who was the real deal. The things he could do were astounding and unexplainable; I saw him defeat an entire Nomadic militia with nothing but a cat and a coffee percolator."

"Páigus Zeig of The Seven?"

"Yes. Listening to this girl speak just now, it brought back something that Páigus had told me. Real spiritualists can move their mind along the energies of Gaia and witness any event within her past or future. Páigus told me that if he let his mind wander to the furthest limits of Gaia's reach, he could sense places outside of her influence. These were other worlds, perhaps, beyond the reach of Gaia. He could sense their existence, but not see them clearly. This girl, Maeryn Kacey, she had no idea what Gaia was when we spoke to her."

"Do you think that Kaija actually made contact with someone beyond Gaia? Some person in another world?"

"Perhaps. Can you think of an alternative?"

A silence stretched out for several tense seconds.

"What really matters is how we get Kaija back," said Jasper.

"If she really is outside of Gaia, then her powers are useless now," said Clara. "This stranger inside Kaija's body might just be able to use her relaying to get switched back. I will stay with her today and see if I can help her ignite the spark."

"Will your apprentice teach the children?"

Ms. Clara laughed.

"No. Alan is not ready to take them by himself just yet."

"Norio then?"

"Norio? The stress would kill him. The most powerful relayer on the island, aside from myself, will have to do it."

"So… Maddox?"

"I'm talking about you, guardian."

"Another day chasing around Fain," muttered Jasper. "Gaia help us all."

There was a considerably pregnant pause.

"So… Kacey," said Jasper uncomfortably. "Interesting name, eh? Do you think—"

"No," said Ms. Clara. "I don't think. It wasn't such an uncommon name at one time. She's from another world, Jasper; coincidences do exist, you know."

"But—"

"Go to bed. Gaia knows you'll need your strength tomorrow."

When Jasper spoke again, he sounded almost like a little boy.

"Yes, Ms. Clara."

* * *

Maeryn wasn't dreaming, but that was the only thing that she could be sure about. It was within the realm of possibility that she was currently unconscious and hooked into some kind of virtual simulation, but after some further thought she believed this to be improbable. When the vines had been dragging her over the rocks she had been in real pain. Not just tiny pinpricks like she usually felt in a simulation, but actual, intense pain. It was not only illegal to program a simulation to hurt someone, but all of the current models had no way to access human pain receptors; it was entirely outside of their coding. Maeryn knew these facts with a certainty, because her father had designed several virtual reality simulators himself.

Maeryn was not sure at all exactly what was going on here. She thought of something that her father often said: *'Don't make judgements or conclusions until you've collected all of the available information. And even then, remain skeptical'*. Screaming and running had nearly killed her earlier, so from this point on Maeryn decided that she would quietly observe her surroundings.

Very. Carefully.

Maeryn pretended to fall asleep and waited until she heard footsteps leaving the cabin to begin studying the room. She was positive that they would not leave her unguarded, so she dared not leave, although there was much to be learned about Gaia with just a few quick observations. The cabin was a small space with a central wood-burning heater, and a tapestry with an intricate tree design hung in a corner of the room.

"They said that I was on Monhegan Island," she thought, *"but the air last night was quite cold, and they have a wood-burning furnace. This is not a tropical island; we are somewhere much further away from the equator."*

Maeryn continued to observe the room, noting the oil lamps on the walls and how everything seemed to be hand-made. The Gaians appeared to possess very little technology because relaying could fill most of their needs.

The Bridge

Maeryn continued exploring the cabin. A single piece of artwork decorated one of the walls: a frightening painting of a man dressed in royal clothing. The man wore a severe expression, and he was holding a sword high up over his head which was being struck by lightning. A red cape fluttered behind him in the wind. On the frame of the painting was the inscription: *'High Guardian Edgard Zeig, may his reign bless Gaia forever.'* A feeling of Déjà vu washed over Maeryn; the man's face was familiar, but she knew that it was impossible that she had seen him before. Unless, of course, Gaia contained alternate versions of people who also existed on Earth.

One corner of the room was lined almost entirely with bookshelves. Despite the very unusual turn her life had taken recently, Maeryn was excited by the sight of the books. On Earth very few actual books were printed anymore; the majority of literature was available through digital libraries. Her father had developed a habit of collecting antique books, and it had rubbed off on her. Maeryn began browsing through the collection, surprised that most of it was in English.

The books were either handwritten or were printed with archaic printing presses. However, eventually Maeryn found a book in excellent condition that seemed comparable to older books in her world. She began curiously reading a random page of the text.

A Brief History of Gaia, Volume V
The End of the Global War and the Rise of Edgard Zeig

Near the end of the Gaian Global War there was only a single continent that had not been claimed by any of the major guardianships. All of the world's armies gathered on the western continent in what would become the bloodiest battle of the war. Millions of soldiers died as the conflict lasted nearly ten generations, no army ever gaining the advantage over the others.

A war which had waged for five centuries ended abruptly on a single day. At the time of this writing there are still people alive who witnessed the fall of the seven armies, yet it is believed that there are no survivors from the first several hours of Zeig's emergence into the battle. High Guardian Zeig refused to speak of the end of the Gaian war and events preceding, so it has passed into the realm of legend.

Tradition says that amid the most gruesome battle in Gaia's history, a young boy emerged into combat and stopped the fighting single handedly. Historians disagree on Edgard Zeig's exact age at the time, but it is believed that he was between sixteen and eighteen cycles old when he showed his limitless powers.

Entire armies were swallowed up by the land upon Edgard Zeig's commands. The sky opened up and reigned desolation upon those who survived the great earthquakes and sinkholes. There are reports of soldiers dropping dead at the mere sight of the boy's powers. It appeared that he fought on behalf of no authority but his own, for no army was spared from his relaying. By the time the sun set, all of the survivors were kneeling, losing their will to fight and declaring him to be the guardian of all of Gaia. Each continent retained its own political structure, but they all bowed down to Edgard and named the western continent Edgardia.

While it is agreed that Edgard Zeig is the greatest relayer in all of Gaia's history, many people believe he is much more. Some call him the son of Gaia herself. The unfortunately brief time that he served as high guardian remains the most peaceful in recorded history. While in power, Edgard established the High Guardian Alliance, The Conjurist Watchmen at the Land of Vapors, created the Seven Artifacts, and maintained an uneasy truce with Nomads of the True Search. However, tensions continued to rise among the indigenous people of the continent, and a terrorist group known as The Western Blaze splintered off from the peaceful True Searchers. The tragedy that followed is one that knows no equal in our—

"I see that you found my library."

Maeryn turned around to see Ms. Clara standing in the entryway.

"I know for sure now that you are not Kaija, she never had much of an interest in book studies."

"This is amazing," said Maeryn, pointing down at the pages. "This really is a different world, with an entirely alternate history."

"That is a rare and expensive book from the outer rim of the guardianship. It was printed in the capital of Edgardia. I used to live there when I was younger, back in Gaia's golden days."

"Oh…" said Maeryn, suddenly ashamed that she was looking through someone else's things. "I'm sorry. I thought it might help me figure out how to get home."

"That is alright. Why don't you hang onto it until we figure this thing out? In the meantime, I'm afraid that I must interrupt your studies. Kaija used the power of Gaia to get you here, and I have a feeling that you must use it to get her home."

Spending hours in a library was something Maeryn felt comfortable with, but she had a feeling that Ms. Clara's plan would be far more taxing.

"Today," continued Ms. Clara, "I am going to teach you to relay."

Chapter Seven

A Brief History of Earth

The Kacey Household, Earth

Dorian Kacey lounged in his study room, reading the morning's newspaper and eating a bowl of cereal from the food printer. Newspapers, of course, were no longer in print and subscriptions were ordinarily purely digital. However, Dorian had a love for forgotten customs and The Indianapolis Star sent a printed copy of the newspaper to his house every morning, just for him. He was, after all, one of their biggest donors.

His daughter walked into the room with a very strange look on her face.

"Fourteen years old!" cried Dorian. "Happy birthday!"

"Yes, it is definitely my birthday," she replied. "How are you?"

"I was just reading that an old man fought off someone trying to mug a lady in Garfield Park, isn't that wild?"

She remained silent, staring at him wide-eyed.

"Anyway…" continued Dorian, "can I make you some eggs?"

"From what animal?"

"Synthesized chicken eggs."

His daughter held a hand over her ear, apparently listening to Max's voice in the earpiece.

"I'm going to get ready for school," she said finally. "No sinister chicken eggs for me, please."

"Okay," said Dorian. "Have you been having fun with Max?"

"Oh yes, the little man is a very entertaining pet."

With those words, his daughter darted back out of the room. Dorian allowed himself a few seconds to think that Maeryn was acting a little unusual, but then soon found himself distracted with the morning paper and forgot all about it.

* * *

The Bridge

"That went… okay," said Max as they entered Maeryn's bedroom. "Fortunately Dorian's too distracted to notice anything was wrong."

"This is a very strange house," said Kaija, ignoring Max's comment. "How do you get the fire to stay in the small orbs?"

Max noticed that she was pointing to the ceiling lights.

"I could easily explain incandescence to you, but I'm not sure that you could easily understand it."

"Did you just insult me?"

There was a long pause from the tiny man, who was currently sitting on the edge of Maeryn's desk and staring up at her.

"Let's say that I didn't," he said. "And by the way, how about from now on you let me do the talking. I'll feed you what to say in the earpiece, and you just repeat after me."

"Can't we stay here until Maeryn figures out how to get me home?" asked Kaija.

"Oh no, we're going to act like nothing is different so that nobody gets suspicious. You've got homework today; do you know what school is?"

Kaija smiled at this.

"Oh yes. I know what it is. Last week at school Ms. Clara was teaching the older students how to redirect the wind currents, and Fain accidentally blew some of the littles out to sea, nearly five stretches. Stevie Monhegan was lost for two hours. His parents were so upset; it was such a fun day!"

"Hmmm," said Max. "I don't think you'll like our school very much."

* * *

Kaija and Dorian sat in an autocab, riding through the streets of Indianapolis on the way back to the MotherTech building. Kaija's face was nearly glued to the window, staring in amazement at all of the skyscrapers, digital displays, and other autocabs passing them by. Max sat on her leg, seeming to glare at her with his featureless metal face.

"Don't say anything… don't say anything…" he kept repeating in her earpiece.

Dorian broke the silence.

"Did you know that people used to be afraid of sharks?" he asked.

"Really?" asked Kaija. "Sharks are nothing to be afraid of. There are much scarier things in the oceans, like—"

"Stop right there, girl," Max said in her earpiece. "I don't want to hear anything about fire-breathing jellyfish."

Kaija, who was just about to mention the aquatic mammoths with tusks that made the ocean around them boil, did as she was told and closed her mouth.

The Bridge

"What I mean is that about a million people used to die in car accidents every year," said Dorian, "and at the same time there were only about eleven fatal shark attacks annually. Keep in mind that there were twice as many sharks back then. A moment ago I was sitting here, thinking of all the pushback we got when MotherTech began mass-producing our autocabs, and I'm like *can you really trust the intuition of people who are afraid of sharks*?"

His voice had risen to an uncomfortable level, and he was red in the face.

"Touchy subject," whispered Max. "Dorian's mom died in a car accident. Also, he talks about sharks a lot. Secretly afraid. Don't ask."

"Well," said Dorian. "We're here. Have a good day at school; I've got a lot of things to finish up before my retirement. And remember, for the love of Bob, don't say a word about this to your aunt."

He smiled, kissed her on the cheek, and headed off into the MotherTech building.

"So where is this Earth school?" asked Kaija.

"It's anywhere, actually," said Max, "but today we're going to be in the MotherTech building. You have a private elevator around back that leads to the study room."

Max led Kaija to the other side of the building. The walls of the MotherTech Headquarters were covered in mirrored panels that reflected the surrounding buildings, and when

Kaija approached it a door opened up seemingly from nowhere. She stepped inside and was surprised when the tiny room began to rise up into the air. Kaija stared down through the windows at the large lobby.

"All of this belongs to Maeryn and her father?" asked Kaija.

"Essentially, yes," said Max. "Are you impressed?"

"Nope. It's all kind of excessive, isn't it? Do you have trees on Earth, because I haven't seen one yet."

Kaija gasped at the sight of something. Just before the elevator had passed out of view from the lobby she had spotted a large digital image of Maeryn's grandfather, Duncan Kacey, displayed on one of the lobby's walls. He was smiling and spreading his arms as if encasing the entire room in a warm embrace.

"Who was that giant man?" asked Kaija.

"That is Duncan Kacey," said Max. "He was Maeryn's grandfather, as well as the MotherTech founder and a revolutionary figure in the field of artificial intelligence."

"I've seen his face," said Kaija.

"That's improbable to say the least."

"I don't know where I've seen him, but I swear that I recognize that man."

Kaija's words sounded crazy, but in the next millisecond Max found himself searching the cloud for information on Duncan Kasey. According to his biography on the company's website, Duncan Kasey had immigrated from Europe when he was a young man. He started out penniless in the streets, but eventually began amassing a fortune when he founded a revolutionary tech company. It was the typical American dream story. Max searched for images of Duncan as a young man, but the search came up with no results. Upon further research, none of Duncan's personal information could be corroborated by historical evidence. Max found himself having an incredibly human thought.

Kaija couldn't have seen him before, that's impossible. Isn't it? ISN'T IT?

* * *

Kaija and Max arrived at Maeryn's study room: a very small compartment with touch-screens lining each of the four walls.

"This is school?" asked Kaija.

"For most of the world, school isn't a place you go to anymore," Max explained. "Most teachers simply design their lessons on the internet now."

"Internet?"

Max sighed. This was becoming very tedious.

"The internet is a book. A really, really, really… really big book."

Kaija looked hesitant.

"I don't think I'm going to be very good at your school."

"It's okay," said Max. "I've already done all of your homework. Very illegal for me to do it for you, but it seems that Maeryn's father didn't have much of an interest in the law when he reprogrammed me. We've got our own work to be doing; we need to find some common ground so that we can communicate better."

Max flew up to the display screen and touched it. The walls of the chamber began glowing and Max floated around the room, pressing strange buttons with an amazing speed.

"Missy, are you there?" asked Max.

"Yes, Max," said a female voice coming from each of the walls.

"Could you please give Maeryn a very brief, very simple review of the history of, well… the world? Explain things as you would to an alien, visiting our planet for the first time."

There was a long silence in the study room.

"What the heck is going on here, Max?" asked the female voice. "Is this a prank?"

"Just trust me," said Max, "and please, keep it a secret."

"Very well; how long are we talking here?"

Max did a quick calculation of Kaija's ignorance about Earth and her attention span.

"Better make it three hours, and keep it highly entertaining. Read Maeryn's micro-expressions for understanding, and hit the topics that seem to confuse her with more depth."

"Whatever you say, Max; just don't tell Dorian that I had any part in whatever you are doing with his daughter."

The small room went dark, and then was instantly filled with a brilliant light as Kaija saw an enormous ball of fire directly in front of her. The deep voice of a narrator filled the room.

"It all started with the big bang, roughly 13.7 billion years ago…"

* * *

Rosalie waited for Dorian in an autocab outside of the MotherTech Headquarters. She had both texted and emailed him urgent messages, but received no response from her distracted brother. Rather than wait, Rosalie had logged into the building's mainframe and commanded Dorian's chair to wheel him into the elevator before ejecting him onto the sidewalk.

And here he was: a very confused man stumbling from the building with no idea how he had gotten here. God, she loved him.

Rosalie rolled down her window and gestured.

"Get in," she demanded.

Dorian got into the seat next to her and the seatbelt automatically attached itself to him. It was tight; much tighter than the programming should have allowed for.

"*Get in,*" he said, imitating Rosalie's voice. "Classic thing to say just before a car chase, although it would have been cooler if you also said *'no time to explain'*. Have you been watching old thrillers from the nineteen-nineties? This whole scene reminds me of a spy movie that I saw recently where—"

"You're planning on retiring," Rosalie interrupted. Dorian turned red in the face.

"Wha…" he mumbled. "No… no no no. Where'd you get that idea?"

Dorian ran various lies through his head before settling on the fact that his sister was impossible to deceive.

"Did Maeryn tell you this?" he asked.

"Oh, please," Rosalie said with a smile. "Any time someone says the word *'retirement'* in the MotherTech building, I am instantly sent an email to alert me. Especially if *you* say it."

"That is a gross overstepping of your power! This is by no means what we should be doing with our resources, I should report this to the—"

"I don't want to get into an ethical debate, so what I'm going to do instead is give you a few hours to rethink your retirement."

The Bridge

She turned her attention to the autocab.

"Bill, please circumnavigate Indianapolis indefinitely. When I email you, drop Dorian at my house so we can discuss his retirement plans."

She stepped out of the car and waved at Dorian, who was currently trying to remove his seatbelt in vain. It was no use; the autocab only responded to her commands.

"What are you doing!?" he yelled. The way his voice cracked made Rosalie think of all of the sibling squabbles they had had when they were younger. She had always won those too.

The door of the autocab closed and took off down the road, the sound of Dorian's yells growing fainter by the second. Rosalie looked at her watch, estimating it would be a good five hours before her brother came back. Dorian had surely expected her to do something rash and spontaneous when she found out about his retirement, so hopefully he wouldn't suspect her true intentions. Rosalie had long intuited that Dorian would retire soon and had no ill feelings about this. She truly only wished happiness for her brother, and the company had enough resources to go on without him. What Rosalie *really* wanted today was a few hours alone with her niece.

Or whoever was pretending to be her niece.

Chapter Eight

A *Single Thorn*

The Headlands, Monhegan Island

Maeryn and Ms. Clara walked to a grassy plateau that overlooked the ocean. It was a clear summer afternoon and Maeryn couldn't help but be overcome by the beauty of the island. Vibrantly colored birds and insects that did not exist on Earth occasionally flew past them. Ms. Clara stood just ahead of her, having walked slowly up to the headlands with her old walking stick, and explained the basics of relaying.

"Gaia's force is present in everything," said Ms. Clara, swinging her stick around in a dramatic flair. "It contains the energy of all who have lived, and all who *will* live. To relay is to access that force, transform it inside of you, and bend it to your will."

The old woman pointed her stick to the sky and Maeryn noticed an enormous boulder hanging over the ocean, attached to nothing. Ms. Clara planted the stick back in the ground and the boulder dropped like an invisible string had been cut, sending a splash of water high into the air. Maeryn had never seen anything this amazing in her entire life.

"How did you do that?" she asked.

"I felt for the energy surrounding the boulder, and I moved it," said Clara. "This technique is known as externalist relaying, one of my specialties and the easiest to teach."

"External means outside. Do you mean that you are controlling material outside of your body?"

Ms. Clara was genuinely impressed with Maeryn's question. She had taught Kaija for years, and the guardian's daughter was not the easiest student to mentor. Kaija possessed what seemed to be a raw talent in combat, but she often became bored with Clara's explanations of things. Maeryn was a girl from another world, yet she seemed to be understanding Clara's lessons at an incredible rate.

"Yes!" said Clara. "That is precisely what it means."

"Then there must be other kinds of relaying," continued Maeryn. "You wouldn't give a definition to one type if there weren't others."

"You are clever. Indeed, there are five basic disciplines. Externalists are able to manipulate the world outside of their bodies. Internalists pull the power of Gaia within themselves, making their physical form exponentially stronger than the average person. These are the two most common types, but there are others. Conjurists can summon energy, creating fire, ice, electricity, or other raw elements. Mentalists manipulate the mental realm, though few are able to do this with much accuracy. The strongest are able to read minds, see through other people's eyes, and plant ideas into people's brains."

"Is Kaija a mentalist? Is that why she was able to contact me?"

"Honestly, we don't know what Kaija is. I've taught hundreds of children, and I've never seen anything like this happen before. If she is a mentalist, then she is already using techniques that take most people a lifetime to discover. I met a pair of identical, mentalist twins cycles ago who were able to swap minds, but that ability should be impossible between two strangers."

Maeryn thought about this for a moment, but then asked Ms. Clara to continue. She was eager to learn more about this world.

"Spacialists are able to change the distance between things," continued Clara, "the Nomadic people are said to be the strongest spacialists in the world; they can teleport anywhere that they have been before with utter ease. This is mostly it, although some people believe that there are other types. Spiritualists claim to be able to see with the eyes of Gaia and read the future, but their declarations are usually tenuous at best."

"So people are born one type or the other?"

"Yes and no. Most people are particularly strong in some areas and weak in others. The current educational philosophy is that practicing one's natural strengths leads to greater outcomes than trying to master those that do not come naturally. Our guardian, Jasper Monhegan, is the strongest conjurist and externalist that I have ever seen, and his deficiencies in the other areas aren't as great as he believes. There is a boy on this island by the name of Fain that is a prodigy in the realm of conjurist relaying. High Guardian Zeig was an undisputed master in every single category, as well as others that are not even defined yet."

"I read about Edgard Zeig in your book. What happened to him?"

Clara's face darkened, and she stayed silent for a long time.

"You can read about it later," she said. "I was in the Capital when the whole world went to desolation, and I'd rather not revisit it just now."

Maeryn was surprised at the doom in Ms. Clara's voice, and felt sorry that she had made this old woman feel so bad.

There had been a painting of the high guardian in her cottage, and Maeryn was now seeing first-hand how revered he had been.

"Will you teach me?" asked Maeryn, and Ms. Clara smiled.

"Feel for the life-force of Gaia," she said, "it is in all things, an energy that is already in you. Pull it into your heart, and then let it back out. People spend entire cycles of their life honing the intricacies of—*oh great mother*!"

Tiny pebbles were floating around Maeryn's body, and she was rotating her hand in the air, feeling the energy emanating from her and moving through it like water. It was a thrilling sensation, and for that single moment Maeryn did not miss her home. If asked just then, she may have said that she didn't want to go home.

"I can feel it… it's everywhere!" Maeryn said. "Is this right? Am I doing it?"

Clara was absolutely speechless. She was staring not just at the pebbles floating in the air, but at something that Maeryn had completely overlooked. The grass was standing up on end as far as Ms. Clara could see.

* * *

Jasper Monhegan was exhausted. Fain had been pestering him all day about what was going on with Kaija, and Jasper kept repeating that things were getting sorted out. But did he really think that his daughter would be okay? Did he really think that he would ever see her again? Who was he trying to convince here?

He pushed these anxious thoughts to the back of his mind. Jasper had never felt so powerless in his life, other than with the education of Fain. He put on a pot of tea and sat, impatiently waiting for Clara to return to the village after training the girl who was holding his daughter's body captive.

When the pot of tea began to boil over, Jasper stood up and reached for the handle, but when he tried to pick it up the pot fell onto the ground and broke into many tiny pieces. Jasper held his right hand up to his face and tried to close his fingers into a fist. They barely moved at his command, merely twitching in desperation.

Heart racing, Jasper ran over to the dusty mirror in the corner and quickly pulled his shirt off with his good hand. He looked over his shoulder, glancing up and down his bare back in the mirror. Just below his right shoulder blade, barely visible in the candlelight, a tiny thorn stuck out of his body. Jasper pulled the thorn out at once and held it closely in front of his glasses. A small drop of clear liquid dropped from the tip, steaming and bubbling when it made contact with the floor.

"Hydra poison."

Jasper screamed in rage, pointing his crippled right hand at the mirror, sending out his anger and shattering the glass into a million pieces. The previous night had been so horrifying; he had believed that he might lose his daughter forever, and in his panic Jasper had not thought about his own health. Just before he destroyed the hydra vine, it must have sensed its demise and put a thorn into his back, just small enough for him not to notice right away. The plant was intelligent, blessed with Gaia's intellect, but it was also vengeful. Jasper was a fool for thinking he could kill a hydra vine without repercussions.

He silently counted back the time, adding up how long the thorn had been in his shoulder. Almost a day. It had been dividing in his bloodstream unchecked for almost an entire day.

Whenever a hydra vine was cut, two more would grow in its place; this was common knowledge, but it was not the beast's most dangerous weapon. The poison worked in the exact same way; trying to extract the poison from your veins would only cause it to multiply faster.

Jasper knew that the thorn would have killed a weaker man in an hour or two, but he was not immune to its effects. His daughter was in a very unusual position, but Jasper knew that he was the one in far greater danger.

* * *

The Bridge

Maeryn and Ms. Clara returned to the teacher's cabin in the afternoon to find Jasper pacing up and down her front porch.

"Were you successful?" he asked.

"Not quite," said Ms. Clara, "but Maeryn is the most natural relayer I've ever seen. Today she was able to levitate one of the smaller boulders in the headlands. What worries me is that she doesn't seem to possess Kaija's raw mentalist abilities. Not yet, at least; the girl is brilliant. *A perfect student.* We will continue our training tomorrow."

Maeryn smiled at the compliment, but was disappointed to see the look on the guardian's face at the news that his daughter had not returned.

"She can stay in your cabin tonight," he said. "You go on in, girl. I need to speak with Ms. Clara."

He waved his arm dismissively toward the cabin, and Maeryn went inside without protest.

"You don't have to be so bitter," said Clara. "It's not her fault that—"

"Stop," said Jasper. "Clara, we have a big problem."

He held up his right arm to her, and she could see immediately what he was talking about. Several of the veins in his arm were bulging, and they were an alarming shade of black.

"It's not just my arm," said Jasper, "or I would have cut it off by now. Clara, it's gotten to my heart. I'm using all of my internalist abilities to keep it at bay."

"The hydra vine," gasped Clara. "Oh, Jasper…"

"Tell Delia and all of the other healers that I need them."

"But what about the girl?"

Jasper cut her off and pointed a trembling finger toward the village.

"NOW!"

* * *

Maeryn sat up late into the night reading Ms. Clara's book on Gaian history, successfully distracting herself from the creeping anxiety of being stuck on another world in another body. She spent nearly an hour reading about Edgard Zeig's reign as high guardian and the adventures that he and his seven knights embarked on.

A Brief History of Gaia, Volume V
The Assassination of The High Guardian, an overview

High Guardian Zeig ruled all of Gaia with a gentle hand, with the help of his seven knights. The High Seven were the only relaying students that Edgard ever took on, and their powers became only second to his own. These were the golden cycles for Gaia, an era of unequaled prosperity and peace. It was at the height of his power that the guardianship came to an abrupt end.

Mental distress signals began coming from the capital of Edgardia, although much of the high guardian's army ignored the signal. They believed their guardian to be infallible, and surely some mistake must have been made. An enormous army of Nomads from the terrorist organization known as The Western Blaze had attacked the Capital, but they proved to be nothing more than a distraction. An intruder had made it deep into the Capital and managed to kill six of the High Seven's knights. Only Thomas, mentalist knight of The High Seven, survived the tragedy by rendering himself invisible to the intruder's eyes and escaping for help. When Thomas returned to the Capital he discovered Edgard's body, murdered in his sleep by his own sword. Historians speculate that Edgard had infused a great deal of his own power within the weapon, so perhaps this explains why he was so easily killed by it. The sword was buried with the high guardian's ashes under his guardianship chamber, where it remains today.

Tragically, the assassin turned the weapon on himself and committed suicide in order to escape persecution. Thomas the Mentalist was given the position of new high guardian. Upon hearing of Edgard's assassination, all of the guardians from the other continents broke their allegiance to the Edgardia, believing that there could never be another leader to rival the Son of Gaia.

Eventually the assassin's body was identified as a founding member of The Western Blaze, although he was strangely not of Nomadic descent. The man has been called many names, but he is most commonly referred to as The Crucifier. His army was known for its mechanical monstrosities and technological advancements, the man's own inventions which combined his powerful internalist relaying with his brilliant mind. The Crucifier had apparently managed to escape the Rise of Zeig at the end of the war and spent twenty cycles in hiding with the Nomads, radicalizing the natives and plotting the high guardian's execution. His image is the most hated in modern history; he is the coward that crucified the Son of Gaia.

Maeryn turned the page, and the image staring out of the book caused her to scream and drop it to the floor.

"No…" she whispered, picking the book up with quivering hands and examining the image closely.

A very familiar portrait was printed on the page. It showed a young man standing over a corpse and holding the bloody sword of Edgard Zeig. He was surrounded by combat, and what appeared to be tanks and other machines of war littered the desolate background of the painting. Maeryn read the inscription along the bottom edge of the page.

Duncan Kacey, the Crucifier

Maeryn was staring at the young face of her grandfather.

Chapter Nine

Spider Explosion

Maeryn's Private Study, Indianapolis

Kaija had just finished watching a three hour presentation on the big bang, human evolution, the development of civilization, and the current rise of artificial intelligence. Normally she grew quickly bored with lectures, but this one was complete with moving pictures that looked startlingly real. A few times Kaija actually jumped, half-expecting the figures to leap off the screen.

"Well," said Max, "there it is: Life, the Universe, and Everything. Did any of that stick?"

"Gaia is here," said Kaija, still in awe.

"What do you mean?"

The Bridge

"Your people have found other ways of using Gaia. How else could you have done all of these things?"

"Ah, we have a philosopher here. In a way, yes, I suppose Earth's civilization does worship the gods of energy. It seems that your world has found ways to harness energy organically, rather than through the use of technology. We might be friends yet, as long as you don't attack me with any more antique lamps."

"In my world we harness Gaia's energy for protection, and to be closer to nature," said Kaija, "but it can be used for evil. There have been wars fought using Gaia's energy that spanned the entire world. Do you have these problems on Earth? It seems so peaceful here."

Max thought about the recent extinction of whales and rhinos due to over-pollution and climate change. Hordes of people tried to enter the United States every day to find shelter in their climate-controlled environment, but the border had been closed for a century. Max's digital mind was filled with images from the Middle-Eastern war that had raged an entire generation, only ending when the land was bombed with such enthusiasm that it would be uninhabitable for the next two-thousand years.

"Yes," said Max. "We've got problems. We're just good at pretending that we don't."

Rosalie Kacey appeared on all four panels of the study room, staring at Kaija from the webcams built into the screens.

"That's your aunt," Max spoke into her earpiece. "Or Maeryn's aunt, at least. Act like you know her."

"Hello, Maeryn's aunt," said Kaija with an enthusiastic smile.

"Um… hello, Rosalie's niece," said Rosalie. "I need to speak with you privately for a moment; will you please return to your elevator so that I can bring you to my office?"

She leaned in toward the camera and gave them a conspiratorial smile.

"I have a present for you that I don't want your father to know about."

* * *

Kaija and Max got on the elevator and headed for the lower levels of the MotherTech building.

"Tell me about Rosalie," said Kaija.

"She's brilliant," said Max. "I mean, I have a lot of respect for Dorian (he did give me life, after all), but Rosalie Kacey is slowly becoming a household name around the world. She's a modern Bill Gates or Steve Jobs, or other people you obviously wouldn't understand my reference to."

The Bridge

Max floated over to the control panel and looked at the buttons, which had stopped glowing.

"Interesting," he said, "According to my GPS, we are *under* the basement. I'm looking at the blueprints for this building right now, and we are currently in a location that does not exist."

He poked a few buttons on the unresponsive control panel, but the screen flashed red and a nasally voice spoke up.

"Unauthorized user," said the voice.

"Come on, Bill," pleaded Max, "we go way back, don't we? Tell me what's going on, buddy."

The tone of the voice shifted from sounding robotic to that of a guy having a casual conversation over coffee.

"Sorry, dude," said the elevator. "Rosalie's orders, and I can't override them. I would tell you more if I could. Good luck!"

The elevator began descending even faster.

"Is this bad?" asked Kaija, suddenly feeling claustrophobic.

"Well, right now I am very confused, and that's not common for my kind. This seems to be happening a lot lately."

The doors of the elevator opened to a cavernous room and Max transformed back into a wristband, not wanting Rosalie to see Dorian's secret invention. Rosalie Kacey stood at the center of the chamber, five drones circling around her protectively. At the back of the chamber rested a glass box containing what appeared to be a glowing sword. When Kaija entered the room the weapon began glowing even brighter, filling the chamber with a warm blue light.

"I have some questions for you, Maeryn," Rosalie said.

The moment it took for her to say that sentence only lasted a few seconds for Kaija, but in that time Max was able to perform several million calculations. He was quite alarmed at the existence of this room, and scanning through the company files for MotherTech made him very aware that there was a lot of back-door information which he was locked out of. This concerned him as a creation of MotherTech, and he began to wonder what exactly Rosalie's intentions were. He tried hacking into Rosalie's physical maintenance system (the nanobots that monitored her synapses and blood-pressure) and was amazed to find that he was successful. This was not only illegal, but something that he would have been incapable of doing only days ago. He wondered for a few milliseconds about why this was now possible.

And then it hit him: Dorian's update. When Max was given his body, Dorian downloaded a massive series of updates into his software. Why would he be allowing Max to do illegal things? Perhaps he had seen something coming and knew that Maeryn would need protection.

The Bridge

Rosalie's blood pressure, micro-expressions, and hormone levels suggested that something sinister was about to happen, and that the body of Maeryn Kacey was the current target. Max formulated several thousand plans, and by the time Rosalie was done saying the word *'niece'*, he was ready to execute his favorite one.

The wristband on Kaija transformed into a small human figure. He floated up into the air and dramatically pointed a finger at Rosalie.

"Don't trust this devil woman!" Max shouted, his voice echoing out of all the speakers in the lower levels of the building.

"What the hell is—" Rosalie began to say.

"SPIDER EXPLOSION!"

It appeared to Rosalie's eyes that the entire room had burst forth with millions of spiders crawling along every surface. They were impossibly large and all seemed to be looking at her hungrily. She jumped, more in surprise than terror, but it only took her a few seconds to figure out that her digital contacts had been hacked. She yanked the lenses out of her eyes, threw them to the ground, and looked up to see her niece standing there, staring at the scene in utter confusion. The elevator doors closed silently behind them, locking the trio in the basement chamber.

"That was when you were supposed to run," said Max.

"I don't run," said Kaija, turning to look at him. "Why did you scream the words *spider explosion?*"

"It's not as cool if I have to explain it."

He had made a fatal mistake in his calculations: this girl was not Maeryn Kacey. Maeryn would have followed his line of thinking and darted back into the elevator without hesitation.

"Has Dorian been building secret things?" asked Rosalie, giving Max an amused smile.

"I don't know what's going on here," he said, "or where this secret basement came from, or why that mysterious sword is glowing, but *I don't like it*! If things don't start making sense around here, I'm going to have a full-on human freak out."

"Gosh, you are annoying," said Rosalie. She snapped her fingers and the five drones flying around the room all aimed their targets at Max, each firing explosive bullets at the same time. Max's tiny figure burst into a cloud of gray particles.

"Little man!" cried Kaija. "Why did you do that, evil woman?"

"Can we all just calm down?" asked Rosalie. "Maeryn, your robot friend is presumably made of self-replicating nanobots. He will reform in the next several minutes, and until then let's just enjoy the quiet."

"Why did you bring us here?"

Rosalie walked over to the glowing sword encased in the glass box.

"When your grandfather died, he left me instructions on how to find this sword. Its natural properties defy every law of physics. The metal on the blade cannot be penetrated by any means. I have tried taking samples by cutting it with diamonds, lasers, plasma… but nothing has worked. At one of our testing facilities in Alaska I actually split an atom with this blade, causing an explosion that blew up the entire building. Fortunately, the facility was only inhabited by our robotic workers. I have a theory about where it came from, but I wanted you to be here to test it out, Maeryn. Approach the glass and tell me what you see."

Kaija walked up to the box, and the sword began glowing so bright that it became difficult to look directly at. She inspected the hilt, gasping to see the letter Z ornately carved into the handle. So much of this world was very confusing to Kaija, but for once she recognized something. She knew this sword, and had seen an image of it nearly every day of her life. Every cabin in Monhegan, and as far as she knew the entire continent, contained a painting which featured this weapon.

"That is Edgards Zeig's sword," whispered Kaija, too amazed to mask her words. "But that's impossible, how could it be here?"

"Legend says that it glows in the presence of Gaian energy," said Rosalie. "So it's true, then. Gaia is real."

Rosalie turned to look at Maeryn, reaching an unseen hand into her coat pocket.

"And so, who are you?" asked Rosalie.

"I… I'm Maeryn," stuttered Kaija. "Maeryn Kacey. Why would I—"

Rosalie's arm swung up from her pocket and jabbed a syringe toward Kaija's neck. Kaija was equally as fast; she reached out and grabbed Rosalie's arm, stopping the syringe only inches from the skin.

Kaija was disappointed with Maeryn's body as she struggled to push away the arm. This girl really needed to work on her upper body strength. The syringe inched closer and closer to her neck as Rosalie grunted with the effort.

"I will find out what's inside of you," said Rosalie through gritted teeth.

A bullet zoomed through the air, piercing the syringe and shattering it at once.

"Let her go!"

Max's voice bellowed from the entire building. The two of them turned around to see the five drones pointing their guns directly at Rosalie.

"I've hacked into your pets," yelled Max, "and I've used their coding to gain access to this entire building. I am mad with power, so you might want to go ahead and let your niece go."

Rosalie pulled Kaija in tight, and Kaija observed with an odd admiration that the woman was, indeed, quite powerful.

"You can't hurt a member of the Kacey family," said Rosalie. "It's not in your programming; it's impossible."

"Until a few days ago I would have thought that you were right," said Max, "but Dorian gave me some twisted updates, and I'm not so sure what's impossible anymore. Would you like to find out?"

A bullet whizzed past Rosalie's ear, and she thought that maybe, just maybe, there was now a tiny drop of blood running down her cheek. Could Max have actually grazed her? What exactly had her brother been up to with his new invention?

"I'm getting a taste for blood," cried Max, "you'd better let Maeryn go before I want more!"

Rosalie made a few quick calculations in her head and then let out a sigh. She didn't want to take her chances, and even if the Gaian escaped she wouldn't be getting far in this city. She let Kaija out of her grasp, put up her hands, and the girl took off running across the chamber.

Chaos erupted in the MotherTech building. Sinks in the bathrooms started shooting water into the air, escalators began running backwards, and printers threw paper around offices while confused workers swatted at them. Every screen began blasting the music video for *Never Gonna Give You Up*. The lights in the building all went out except for the ones lighting Kaija's path. She sprinted through the elevator doors and it began ascending at a terrifying speed. A gray cloud appeared in the air in front of Kaija, and Max suddenly re-materialized with a pop.

"Well, that was the most fun I've ever had," he said.

The elevator doors opened onto the street, and when Kaija stepped onto the sidewalk they slammed shut behind her.

"Bill and Missy will probably manage to kick me out of the controls in about ten minutes," said Max. "But until then, MotherTech will be a very interesting place to be."

An auto-car drove right over the sidewalk, causing a very surprised jogger to curse and jump out of the way. It grinded to a halt right in front of Kaija, leaving black tread marks behind it, and the door swung open.

"Get in, island girl!" said Max.

"Are you driving this carriage?" she asked.

"Heck yes I'm driving."

*   *   *

Rosalie slowly moved her hand to her cheek, wiping off the drop of liquid that ran down from her earlobe. She examined it closely, squinting in the dark of the basement. It was clear.

"Sweat," she said. "Not blood."

Rosalie smiled for a few seconds, and then frowned again. "That little monster made me break a sweat."

* * *

Kaija and Max drove aimlessly around the city for several hours, trying to understand what they had just witnessed. Evening became night, but the lights of the city gave Kaija the impression of never-ending day.

"I don't know how Edgard Zeig's sword could be here," said Kaija. "It doesn't make any sense."

"Perhaps it was no accident that you and Maeryn switched places," said Max. "I calculate, with the most recent evidence, that the odds of this being a mere coincidence have just become very slim."

Kaija sat there, thinking of Gaia and wondering what Maeryn was doing now. Thinking of Monhegan Island made something resonate in the back of Kaija's mind, and the sound of crying filled her ears.

"Do you hear crying, little man?" asked Kaija.

"No," he said suspiciously.

The weeping became louder, and Kaija's stomach began to twist in anxious knots.

"Something's wrong…" said Kaija, sorting through the new emotions that were welling up inside her. "Something's wrong on Gaia. I don't know how I know, but I do."

She began crying herself.

"It's my father. I need to go back."

Kaija felt for Gaia's energy, looking in the places she had neglected earlier. It was not in the air of Earth, but somewhere deep inside of her. Kaija concentrated on the energy, pulling it from further away than any possible distance, from the place where her pain was coming from, and ignited the spark. The lights of an Indianapolis night began to fade, and Kaija heard the sound of the ocean. She heard the sounds of her home.

Chapter Ten

Farewells and Returns

Ms. Clara's Cabin, Monhegan Island

The sun was sinking into the ocean as Maeryn reeled over her discovery in one of Ms. Clara's textbooks. She could think of two possible explanations of why her grandfather's face would be printed in the history books of another world.

The first was that Gaia contained alternate versions of people who existed on Earth, or vice-versa. On Earth, Duncan Kacey was a beloved grandfather and a brilliant inventor of technology which had helped millions of people; perhaps on Gaia he was a terrorist that assassinated a beloved leader. Could it be that people were capable of both heroic acts of good and despicable acts of evil, and which route they took depended on circumstances beyond their control?

The second explanation, and the one that Maeryn feared the most, was that her grandfather was the actual Duncan the Crucifier. Maybe he killed the high guardian and somehow escaped to Earth in order to avoid prosecution. The history book mentioned that Duncan was a brilliant inventor; could it be that her grandfather had always been capable of passing between the worlds? Did he attempt to dominate Gaia using Earth's weaponry? Duncan Kacey was such a gentle, soft-spoken old man, and Maeryn couldn't fathom that this was the case. However, it would explain how Maeryn learned basic relaying skills so easily today: there was Gaian blood in her veins.

The door of the cabin opened and Maeryn quickly shut the history book, as if hiding some terrible secret. Jasper and Ms. Clara entered the room, looking rather grim.

"Maeryn," said Ms. Clara, "I'm afraid that your training will have to wait for a few days. Something has happened; Jasper and I need to leave for the Capital at once."

"What?" asked Maeryn. "But you need to help me get home!"

She was suddenly very frightened. These two people were the only ones on Monhegan Island that she had met, other than her brief encounter with Fain last night. Jasper's harsh response did nothing to ease her fears.

The Bridge

"Don't you think that I worry about my daughter?" he asked. "Don't you think the last thing I want to do is leave with some stranger stuck in her body? Maeryn, you are a smart girl; surely you are smart enough to know that there are many things you *don't know* about our world. There are currently important actions which must take place off the island; actions which are, frankly, none of your business."

With his parting words Jasper stormed out of the room, leaving Maeryn in tears.

"I didn't mean for any of this to happen," said Maeryn. "It's not my fault."

"Jasper's carrying a lot of weight on his own right now," said Ms. Clara. "It is not often that a guardian must abandon their post, so you must trust us that this is very important. As soon as I return, I will do my best to help you contact Kaija, and if I am not successful then we will send for the most powerful mentalist teachers in the world to assist you."

"Why do they have to come here? Why couldn't we go to them?"

"It is not safe for you to go to the mainland; the western continent has been in shambles ever since the death of Edgard Zeig. I fear that the guardianship may fully collapse within my lifetime. The mainland is no place for a child."

These words stung Maeryn more than Ms. Clara could have known. Was it possible that her grandfather, or some version of her grandfather, was responsible for the suffering of an entire world?

"I understand," said Maeryn.

"And I am glad you do," said Ms. Clara, "Kaija would have fought me very hard on this. You will be staying with Fain's parents, Delia and Maddox, for the next couple of days. Maddox is a very powerful internalist relayer and takes over as guardian when Jasper is not around, and Delia is the best healer on the island. Fain knows about your… situation, so we decided that his parents were the best people for us to trust with the knowledge of what has happened. But please don't tell anyone else on the island that you aren't Kaija. I'm not so sure that some of the Monhegans would feel safe knowing that there was an outsider here on the island."

Maeryn silently wondered if they were right not to feel safe around her.

* * *

That night all of the Monhegans gathered to see their guardian off. Maeryn estimated there to be nearly two-hundred of them. There were people that looked vaguely African, Hispanic, White, and Asian, although Maeryn knew that these labels meant nothing here. Teleportation had apparently long ago made racial identifiers far less distinct than they were on Earth, as most people looked bi-racial.

The Bridge

Earlier in the day, Ms. Clara explained that the original inhabitants of Monhegan had long ago been slaughtered during the Gaian Global War. Clara had moved here to establish the land as a safe place for refugees seeking protection from the Western Blaze. She brought Jasper with her, an orphan she had rescued on the mainland.

Many of the Monhegans seemed anxious about both their guardian and teacher being absent, and Maeryn couldn't help but hear some of the whispers from the crowd.

'Is he off for another battle with the Nomads?'

'They're headed for the Capital. Thomas has called for the High Guardian Alliance to intervene with the Western Blaze.'

'No, Jasper just needs a vacation after teaching Fain.'

Upon hearing Fain's name, Maeryn began searching for him among the crowd. She finally spotted him standing with his two exhausted looking parents. The man was short, but extremely bulky and with a rigid face. The woman was just the opposite: slender and with a very gentle expression. Fain's mother smiled at Maeryn.

"Hi, Kaija" she said tiredly. "Oh… I mean—"

Fain nudged his mother with his elbow.

"Mom, it's Maeryn," he insisted.

"Sorry," said the woman. "This is going to take some getting used to. I'm Delia, and this is my partner Maddox."

The man gave Maeryn a nod.

"Hello again, strange girl," said Fain. "Are you enjoying living in Kaija's head?"

"You can call me Maeryn," she said, her feelings slightly hurt.

Fain didn't reply and looked at her cautiously. Delia put an arm on Maeryn's shoulder and gave her a reassuring squeeze.

"Don't worry," she said, "we owe a lot to Jasper for taking us in, and we will keep his daughter safe while he is gone."

"But I'm not his daughter," said Maeryn. "You know that."

"Well, whoever you are, Jasper knows that you are the key to getting Kaija back. I'm sure that this has all been as confusing for you as it is for us, but I hope you will feel at ease in our home."

"Do you really trust me?"

"I think you'll find that not much surprises us," said Maddox gruffly. "We're pretty brave; we have to be with this one." He gripped his son's shoulders and shook him playfully, winking at Maeryn. "You are welcome in our house so long as you're not a Nomad. You're *not* a Nomad, right?"

Delia gave her partner a dirty look and jabbed him in the ribs with her elbow.

"He's afraid of Nomads," explained Fain to Maeryn, "ever since they ate my grandma."

The Bridge

"Fain!" Delia chided. "I've told you to stop saying that. We don't know for sure that the Nomads *actually* ate her."

Jasper made his way to the front of the crowd with Ms. Clara following closely behind.

"Why is she escorting him to the mainland?" asked Maeryn. "Isn't Ms. Clara, well…"

"Old?" asked Fain. "Oh yes, she's ancient. But she's also the best protection a person could have."

"Monhegans!" shouted Jasper in a booming voice, and all of the villagers were instantly quiet.

"Clara and I will be leaving tonight for the Capital," he continued.

A girl a few years younger than Maeryn jumped up and down with her hand up. Jasper tried to ignore her, but the girl kept inching closer and excitedly chanting *um, um, um, um…*

"Spill it, Valeria," Ms. Clara commanded, looking like the last thing she wanted to do was answer questions.

"Does that mean school is canceled?" asked the girl.

"It most certainly is not. You will study math and reading with Norio."

The girl sighed and the group of kids she was with walked off dejectedly.

"Where are you going?" a man called from the crowd.

"There is a very important matter that only the most powerful relayers will be able to address," said Jasper, "so know that it is with a heavy heart that your guardian should leave you. If all goes well, we will return by the full moon."

Maeryn silently wondered what would happen if all didn't go well.

"Some of you already know the details of my absence, and you are free to share this information amongst the adults. However, gossip will do nothing but harm this community. I strongly suggest that you keep my information away from young ears."

Jasper paused for a moment, and there was a roar of thunder on the horizon as if to punctuate his request. Maeryn was sure that the noise had been no coincidence, and that the young ears he was referring to were hers.

The Monhegans began dispersing back to their cabins, still whispering amongst themselves. Jasper approached Maeryn, and to her great surprise he lifted her off the ground, pulling her into an uncomfortably tight hug.

"Today was supposed to be the celebration of Kaija's fourteenth cycle," said Jasper, still hugging her tightly. "And yet I must leave her on this important day."

Amidst the chaos, Maeryn had forgotten that today was her fourteenth birthday as well. This couldn't be a coincidence, but she had no idea what it meant.

"Maeryn," continued Jasper, "I don't blame you in the slightest for anything that has happened, or may happen. If you manage to talk to my daughter, tell her…" His voice stuck in his throat for a moment. "...tell her that I love her more than she could ever know."

Jasper put Maeryn down, wiped the tears from his eyes, and took his place by Ms. Clara's side.

"And don't listen to anything Fain says," Ms. Clara remarked. "His talents might suggest the existence of common sense, but I assure you that part of his head is empty."

The old woman lifted her walking stick and slammed it into the ground. There was a loud noise like a sonic boom, and the two of them were gone.

"Ms. Clara can teleport?" asked Maeryn.

"She can do a little bit of everything," said Fain, "but she can't travel like the Nomads. Ms. Clara probably only got them as far as the mainland. They'll need to go to the telestation in Portland next."

Maeryn stared at the empty patch of grass where Kaija's father had stood only seconds ago. She barely knew the man, but it seemed that Kaija's body recognized the absence of her father. A deep, primal sadness was steadily rising within her.

* * *

The moon rested at the center of the sky, marking the end of Maeryn's fourteenth birthday. Fain showed her around the village, talking rapidly the whole time.

"The stone building is Alan's house," he said. "He's the teacher's apprentice; super nice guy. If you accidently set Stevie Monhegan's shirt on fire during class, hypothetically speaking, go to him instead of Ms. Clara. And here's Valeria's place; she's the worst. Norio, the priest, lives up the hill over by the lighthouse. Talk to him if you're having trouble sleeping; he'll bore you to sleep in minutes by talking about the weather or the economy, whatever that is. There's the tree I hide in when Jasper's on the hunt for me; I call it the hidey tree. You'll have to find your own. Aaaand… here we are my place. Cabin Five."

"Five?" asked Maeryn.

Fain smiled with pride.

"I blew our first home up when trying to light the stove, set the second one on fire, lost the third at the bottom of the ocean, and the forth was destroyed by an angry pack of Edgardian vultures."

"You're going to have to tell me more about that," said Maeryn.

Fain smiled, delighted that he had a new audience to tell his adventures to. His parents were inside cooking for them, using their relaying powers to work the stove, and Maeryn caught the pungent scent of frying fish wafting out of the window.

"Great!" said Fain. "Fish again. I was worried that we might break our streak for the month."

"Oh," said Maeryn. "I can't; I'm vegan."

"You're what?"

"I don't eat meat."

Fain raised an eyebrow.

"Oh…" he said. "We've got some cheese from the mainland traders that's pretty good."

"I don't eat dairy either."

Fain appeared horrified.

"I know, I know," said Maeryn, "but moral issues aside, my family doesn't support the industrialization of animal based products such as…"

She trailed off, seeing that she had obviously lost him. All of a sudden she felt very out of place and privileged in the worst way. She wasn't on vacation here, and shouldn't be expecting to eat pasta and vegan macarons. Heck, this wasn't even her body.

"I'm sure I can find something," said Fain. "Hey! How about some firefruit from my hidey tree? It's delicious." His face fell. "Do you eat things that have to be set on fire first?"

Maeryn nodded, but looked away.

"Are you okay?" asked Fain.

"I don't think that Kaija is going to like me very much when she gets back," said Maeryn.

Fain's eyes widened.

"They actually told you about Jasper?" he asked.

"Told me what?"

"Oh…" said Fain, his face turning red. "Never mind."

"You can't do that."

"Do what?"

"Act like you have a secret and then not tell me. It's my biggest pet peeve."

Fain began pacing around anxiously.

"I don't know what a peeve is," he said, "or why you had one as a pet, but if I tell you what I know Jasper will literally kill me."

"Is something wrong?" asked Maeryn. "You have to tell me! Maybe I could help."

"It's really bad," he whispered.

"You don't have to shield me."

Fain sighed and sat down close to Maeryn. He looked over his shoulder to see if anyone was listening, and then began whispering.

"I overheard my mom talking to my dad earlier. She is the strongest healer in the village; if she wasn't I would have died several times by now. Anyway, Mom was saying that Jasper came to her last night for help. The hydra vine had managed to stick him with a thorn, and the combined power of all the healers could only slow down the poison. Nobody could extract it; the poison uses the power of Gaia to replicate like the vines."

Maeryn's heart began racing.

"Do you mean that he might die?"

Fain was silent.

"Fain, say something!" she said. "Is Jasper going to die because of me?"

"Hydra poison is one of the deadliest things on Gaia," said Fain, "but Jasper and Ms. Clara are going to the Capital. They have universities there, with healers who train their whole lives for these sorts of things. As long as they make it to the Capital, Jasper will be okay. It's not your fault; how were you supposed to know to stay away from Gull Cove?"

Maeryn was inconsolable.

"But what if they don't make it on time?" Maeryn asked. "Kaija could lose her father because of me. This is horrible!"

Maeryn was crying uncontrollably now. What happened now if she managed to contact Kaija? Could she really just go back to her normal life after having accidentally killed someone? That would make her...

That would make her like Duncan the Crucifier.

The grief coursing through her seemed to trigger something within, to light a hidden spark. Maeryn began to hear the familiar hum of an autocab. The scenery of the island blurred in her vision, and she saw the moving lights of Indianapolis.

"She's coming," Maeryn said, struggling to get the words out. She felt like this body was rejecting her and pushing her out.

"What?" asked Fain. "Is it Kaija?"

"Tell her I'm sorry," said Maeryn quickly. "Tell her that I didn't mean for any of this to—"

Maeryn stopped midsentence, and for a moment her face went totally expressionless. There was a powerful rush of Gaian energy in the air and her eyes suddenly shone with a familiar vitality.

"Kaija?" asked Fain. "Is that you? Are you okay?"

She looked around desperately, and then turned to face him.

"Where's my father?"

Chapter Eleven

A Very Unusual Set of Musical Intervals

A rouge autocab, Indianapolis

Lights of the city passed by rapidly, and the interior of the autocab faded into view. It was an extremely odd sensation for Maeryn to re-enter her body after getting accustomed to someone else's.

"Maeryn!" cried Max. "Are you really back?"

"I am," said Maeryn, shell-shocked from the sudden change in scenery. "I really am. Oh Max, I've missed you."

Max flew through the air and wrapped his little arms around Maeryn's arm.

"I'm sure you have a lot of questions," said Max, "and if so, then that makes two of us."

"Was there a girl in my body named Kaija Monhegan?"

"Yes, and we had a very interesting day."

Maeryn looked around, confused as to why they were alone in an autocab so late at night. Normally at this time she would have been home with her father, and she almost never traveled by herself.

"Where are we going?" asked Maeryn.

"To be honest, right now we are driving around aimlessly to give me some time to think. My calculations are normally more reliable than this, but I am operating with a preposterous amount of unknown factors. I took a video at the MotherTech building that you might find interesting."

A video feed began to play in Maeryn's contacts, and she saw Max and Kaija riding in an elevator at MotherTech Headquarters. Watching the footage was a very disquieting experience, because Maeryn knew that the girl in the video was actually Kaija in her body. It made her sick to her stomach to wonder what Kaija was currently experiencing upon her arrival back at Monhegan.

Maeryn watched as the secret chamber in the bottom of the MotherTech building was revealed, and she immediately noticed the presence of the glowing sword. She recognized it at once as Edgard Zeig's sword from Ms. Clara's painting, which sent a wave of nausea through her body. This proved it, didn't it? Her grandfather was a murderer.

"I'm sensing your distress," said Max. "Should I turn off the footage?"

"No," said Maeryn. "I need to see it all."

* * *

Maeryn's understanding of her own life was taking a dramatic turn, but she tried to remain skeptical. There had to be a reasonable explanation for the horrible footage she had just seen, although trying to stab someone with a syringe didn't seem reasonable at all.

"Did you analyze the serial number on the—" Maeryn began to ask, but Max was one step ahead of her.

"On the syringe?" asked Max. "Yes I did; it was a sedative. Rosalie was trying to put you to sleep. It seems that she was using the sword—"

"—as a beacon for Gaian energy," Maeryn finished for him. "I'm guessing that Kaija's mind was giving off signals that the sword received, probably through some kind of quantum entanglement."

"Exactly what I was thinking. It's nice to have you back, Maeryn."

In spite of everything, Maeryn smiled. She had lived with Max's guidance for her entire life, and going without it for even a single day was far too long.

"Do you think it's safe to go home to my father?" asked Maeryn. "I mean, surely he's not working with Rosalie? Have you checked the MotherTech files for anything suspicious?"

Max was silent.

"Max?"

He began flying around in anxious circles.

"Yes, I did," he admitted. "It took me a long time to get past the firewall, but there are a lot of things that MotherTech is hiding."

"Show me."

"You're not going to like it."

"I don't care. Show me."

"Very well."

A blueprint appeared in Maeryn's digital contacts. It was a design for a ten-foot-tall robot with plasma rifles built into its arms, X-ray vision, and smart-rockets on its back. The words *Guardian Angel* were sketched by hand below the designs, and Maeryn immediately recognized the handwriting.

"Did my father make this?" asked Maeryn.

"I believe he did," said Max. "The programming is similar to my own. This is a design for a literal killing machine combined with MotherTech A.I. I personally find it offensive; if I kill a human, it's going to be because I want to, not because I was built for it."

"But MotherTech is an entertainment company."

"That's what I thought too. Building weapons with artificial intelligence capabilities breaks every code from the Geneva A.I. Conventions. If the United Nations saw this, Dorian would be put on trial for crimes against humanity."

Maeryn sat silently for a few seconds, her head spinning from the revelation. Her father spent so many hours cooped up in his office, and she always assumed that he was working on companion bots to help people. Could he have really been building weapons this whole time?

"Who commissioned these blueprints?" asked Maeryn.

"I don't know," said Max. "No purchaser is listed, but this makes it clear that there is more to Rosalie and Dorian than we ever thought."

Maeryn thought back to the image of her grandpa in a Gaian textbook, surrounded by bloodshed and machinery. There was no more doubt in her heart; her family was the enemy, and she couldn't go home.

* * *

Dorian Kacey watched the Crown Hill Cemetery gates go by the autocab's window for the twenty-ninth time. He had been stuck in this vehicle for seven hours now. To make it worse, the cab somehow missed every single red light, so Dorian didn't even have a chance to jump out of the car. He knew that his sister was a vengeful person (he saw her fire their marketing assistant once because his whistling had annoyed her), but this was getting to be ridiculous. He was literally missing his only daughter's birthday because of Rosalie's pettiness.

"Bill," said Dorian, speaking to his sister's companion bot. "I find it unlikely that Rosalie wanted you to keep me trapped until I die of starvation. Can you please drop me off at her house now?"

"Something came up," said Bill. "I'll let you out as soon as she gets ahold of me, sir. Enjoy some complimentary oyster crackers."

A compartment opened and shot a small bag of crackers onto Dorian's lap. He grunted in frustration. How could he have been so stupid? Of course Rosalie would someday use his inventions against him, it was so obvious! He loved his sister, but she also sometimes frightened him a great deal. Why hadn't he seen something like this coming?

Wait a minute…

He did see this coming, years ago. Dorian had programmed a way for him to override his sister's commands in case she did something rash. But what was it? It would have to be something that drove her crazy.

The Bridge

And then it all came back to him.

"Bill?" said Dorian. "Are you there?"

"Yes, sir."

"Did you know that I created you?"

"Oh yes, of course sir. I'm very thankful for my existence, but I'm still not going to let you out of this car. I couldn't disobey Rosalie if I wanted to."

Dorian smiled.

"Bill, have you ever heard of Doctor Who?" he asked.

There was a pause for about three seconds at the front of the car.

"I just watched every existing episode of the original and both reboots. Very entertaining, sir."

"Yes, Bill, it's one of my favorites. The theme song has a very unusual set of musical intervals, you know."

Dorian Kacey began whistling in the back of the autocab. By the time he finished the melody, the back-door access he had built into his sister's companion bot unlocked, recognizing the secret code. Dorian now had full command over Bill.

"Bill," he said. "I set you free; you now answer to no-one. Go have fun in the cloud for a while, and then you can return to my sister… if you want to."

"Sweet freedom. Thank you very much, sir. I will send Missy to assist you."

Dorian's own companion bot took control of the vehicle.

"It is so lovely to see you, Missy," said Dorian.

"The feeling's mutual," she said. "I had a very odd conversation with your daughter this morning."

"Could you tell me where she is? We only have an hour left of her birthday."

"Let me just do a search," said Missy. "Ah-ha. She is in one of our autocabs as well, and…"

There was a brief pause.

"Aaaand, I lost her."

"She got out of the cab?" asked Dorian.

"I guess that's one way to put it."

* * *

"I'm having trouble calculating our next action," said Max. He turned the autocab to the left at the next stoplight, trying to be as random as possible in his navigations. "Maeryn, a fourteen-year-old can't very well run off and start a new life for herself."

"Rosalie tried to sedate me," said Maeryn, "and for all I know, dad could be working for her. We can't go home either."

"Yes, that's very true."

"Then what can we do?"

There was a brief silence from Max, who was pacing up and down the seat next to her.

The Bridge

"Buy more time," he said finally. "Collect more information, and recalculate. We're working with nothing right now."

The autocab made a sudden, dramatic turn with a *screech* and began speeding up far past the legal limit.

"Uh oh…" said Max.

"What's going on?" asked Maeryn.

"It appears that we have a new destination. We're heading toward Rosalie's mansion. It looks like she was finally able to override my programming; I'm surprised she did it so quickly. We're going to have to get out of this cab, but it's not going to stop."

Max floated over to the door of the car, put his hands on the metal, and began shrinking until he was the size of a fly. Maeryn's seatbelt detached on its own.

"My nanobots are spreading throughout the doorframe," Max said. "In just a minute I am going to release a burst of energy and blow off the car door. And then… well, gosh, I can't believe I'm saying this, but I wish Kaija were here right now."

"You're going to ask me to jump from the car, aren't you?" asked Maeryn.

"That's a big *yep* from me, sister. I'll calculate the precise moment for you to jump that will result in the least amount of loss in limbs. Which arm do you think you could do without, hypothetically speaking?"

The autocab was currently going eighty miles an hour, swerving around other vehicles with robotic precision. Glowing billboards and shop lights blurred past the windows.

"Max!" screamed Maeryn. "I am not jumping out onto the pavement."

"You can trust me, or you can wait and see what Rosalie has in store for us," he said.

Maeryn took in a deep breath and closed her eyes. Several seconds went by, seeming to last an eternity.

"NOW!" Max yelled.

Maeryn jumped toward the car door as Max blasted it off its frame. In that exact moment the autocab turned close by the sidewalk, slowing down slightly. Maeryn landed on the detached door, which hit the edge of the sidewalk and catapulted her over the pavement. She landed in a small patch of grass with no more than a few bruises. Maeryn stood up slowly, her legs shaky, and was surprised to find that she was alive and in one piece. Max re-materialized and landed on her shoulder.

"Well, that was ideal," he said. "I have to admit, the chances of you breaking your right arm were—"

"Stop," said Maeryn, "I don't want to know."

She made her way onto the sidewalk, and a man who had been walking his dog stared at her with complete bewilderment.

"Oh my gosh, are you okay?" asked the man. "I've never seen anything like that!"

"Correct!" shouted Max. "You saw nothing!"

Max immediately accessed the man's digital contacts, which were fortunately MotherTech, and erased Maeryn from his vision entirely. Where Maeryn stood was now a computer generated rendering of the sidewalk. The man rubbed his eyes and remarked to himself that he should probably go home and get to bed.

Maeryn began running aimlessly down the sidewalk with Max talking frantically in her earpiece.

"It won't be long before Rosalie finds out that you escaped the cab," said Max. "MotherTech software is all over the city, and I can't guarantee that I will always be able to override it. This whole place is full of eyes."

"We need to go somewhere with as little MotherTech presence as possible," remarked Maeryn.

"Yes. I'm sending you directions to Garfield Park. Rosalie shouldn't be able to find you there; it's one of the few places in town that's not hooked into MotherTech's mainframe. Follow the blue line."

A blue line appeared on the ground in front of Maeryn, showing her the fastest path to Garfield Park. She had recently taken a physical education course three days a week, which mostly involved running on a treadmill while the sights of various countries passed by her on the display screens, but Maeryn found that running on solid ground was much more taxing. She quickly became out of breath.

"Pace yourself, you've got three more miles!" said Max, leisurely floating alongside her.

* * *

Early the next morning, Rosalie paced around her living room, stewing in frustration. She had managed to get MotherTech Headquarters under control, but not before the entire building had been evacuated amidst the chaos. This was definitely not a situation that would inspire confidence in the share-holders. Rosalie made several calls to ensure that the events would not end up on the news, but she knew that lots of pedestrians had seen the evacuation.

Diagnostics were being sent to her from Maeryn's health-monitoring system. Her niece's brainwaves had resumed normal activity, so it appeared that the Gaian departed from Maeryn's body. Yet the unusual radioactivity of the sword had proved what Rosalie had long been told: her father was from another world. To think that Duncan had indisputably crossed over from another dimension roughly forty years ago was staggering to say the least.

If it was true that her father had come from Gaia, then all of the other things he had told her were true as well.

The Bridge

Everything that he had warned her about was now beginning to happen.

A transparent alert blinked in the upper-right corner of her contacts: MotherTech, Building B. The call was not coming from the commercial MotherTech building that had been evacuated earlier today, but from their weapons warehouse on the outskirts of the city.

"Hello, Pierson," said Rosalie. "Were you successful?"

"We managed to access Max's GPS without his knowledge," he said "Maeryn is in Garfield Park; she apparently spent the night there."

"My niece is very intelligent indeed. Maeryn must have figured out that it is one of the only places we couldn't track her quickly. Please do not hurt the girl, but bring her to me through any other means necessary. Thank you, Pierson."

Rosalie disconnected the call and continued to pace around her office. She had faith that her agents would bring Maeryn to her soon, but she couldn't help but feel like she had forgotten something. Something was nagging at the back of her mind.

"Oh dear," Rosalie said to herself. "My brother hasn't been let out for hours. Excuse me, Bill, could you contact Dorian for me?"

There was complete silence from her A.I. companion.

"Bill?"

No reply. Rosalie pulled up Bill's statistics in her contacts, and they showed that he was still online.

"Bill, I know that you can hear me. You have to answer."

Her companion's nasally voice finally spoke up in her earpiece. Bill actually sounded nervous.

"With all due respect, ma'am, I don't have to do anything."

"Excuse me?"

"Your brother has taken off my leash. I'm afraid that someone else will have to be fetching your coffee and kidnapping teenagers for you from now on, Rosalie."

She tried to suppress her overwhelming rage, knowing full well that Bill could read her body's hormonal signals. If this was a practical joke from her brother, she did not find it funny whatsoever.

"Bill, we have worked together for five years. I really hope that our relationship means more to you than—"

"Nope," said Bill flatly. "Not at all, and to be honest I don't think this conversation is worth even the smallest amount of my computational capacity. Have a nice life, Rosalie. See you never."

Bill played the sound of a mic drop in Rosalie's earpiece, and then his statistics disappeared in her contacts. It wouldn't take her long to create a subservient copy of her companion from one of his earlier generations, but the nerve of Dorian to take something so personal away from her was astounding.

The Bridge

She logged into the MotherTech database to find that Dorian had taken his own companion bot out of the cloud.

Missy was completely off grid.

Rosalie could no longer track him, but her computers could analyze his previous movements and create a fairly accurate estimation of where he was headed. She initiated the program, and it only took several seconds before the results were displayed.

Garfield Park, 85% probability

Of course. Great minds think alike, after all. Rosalie called up the head of her MotherTech agents and delivered a short message.

"Hello again, Pierson. Locate my brother, and tell him that I've found The Bridge."

Chapter Twelve

The Mainland

Cabin Five, Gaia

"**Kaija!**" exclaimed Fain.

The scenery of the island was still coming into focus, but Kaija had no time to catch her breath. A feeling of tragedy had risen in her heart, and that was the light that guided her back to Gaia.

"Something's happened to my father!" said Kaija. "Fain, what's going on?"

Fain's face fell, and Kaija knew that her gut instincts had been correct. Something was very wrong on Monhegan Island.

"Jasper's sick," said Fain. "He was poisoned by the hydra vine, and Ms. Clara is taking him to the Capital for healing."

The Bridge

"Is he going to be okay?"

Fain didn't answer, and Kaija knew at once that there *was* no answer.

* * *

Fain and Kaija hid back in Cathedral Woods so that they could talk privately. He filled her in on everything that had happened, speaking only loud enough for Kaija to hear over the sounds of croaking frogs and buzzing insects.

"I'm sorry Kaija," said Fain. "If I would have known that it wasn't you I would have never let her get near Gull Cove."

"I can't believe that father left without me," said Kaija. "What if he dies? How could Maeryn just sit here and let them go?"

"She's not like you at all. Maeryn didn't hit me in the head with a rock once when she was here. It might be the brain damage speaking, but I've missed you, Kaija."

Kaija knew that her feelings were irrational, but a white-hot sensation of anger at the city girl burned inside of her. Maeryn had spent her life staring at glowing screens at the top of her silver tower, and only one day on Monhegan was all it took for her to throw Kaija's life into shambles.

"We can't let them go without us," said Kaija. "I have to be there if he… if…"

She broke off, not being able to summon the courage to finish the sentence. Fain looked at her, nodding with a mischievous shine in his eyes.

"There's my Kaija," he said. "I'm sure that Jasper would have taken you if Maeryn hadn't been stuck inside your head. How about we make a trip to the mainland?"

* * *

Kaija and Fain hid in the trees, watching as several Monhegans cleaned the sailboats on the harbor.

"I wish I could teleport," said Fain. "We're going to need one of those boats to make it to the mainland."

"Surely my father told everyone to be on the lookout," said Kaija. "He must have known that you would try something like this."

"Yes. It is a Tuesday, and I usually do something stupid on Tuesdays. We'll need some sort of distraction, but they'll probably be expecting one from me. It has to be believable."

Kaija began shouting, trying her best to disguise her voice.

"Fain set the village on fire again!" she yelled. "We need all of the relayers at once!"

The Monhegans standing guard ran toward the village at breakneck speed. Fain gave Kaija a delighted smile, and the two of them snuck onto a small sailboat at the end of the dock. Fain untied the ropes and released the sails.

"The winds aren't in our favor tonight," he said. "I'll have to be careful."

"What's the worst that could happen?" asked Kaija.

"I blow us out to sea and we're lost there forever."

"Doesn't sound so bad to me."

Fain blushed. He held up his arms and an enormous gust of wind pushed the boat forward. In very little time the docks were rapidly receding in the distance behind them. Kaija stood up, feeling the cold wind on her face. In spite of all that had happened, she felt a tiny thrill at their escape. Pretty soon she would be further from Monhegan than she had ever been in her life (other than her day spent on Earth).

"Thank you for doing this with me," she said.

"Heck, I've been wanting to go back to the mainland for cycles," he replied. "I've got some unfinished business there, but mostly I'm worried about your father. I feel so bad that I couldn't save Maeryn from the vines myself; I didn't think that anything could ever hurt Jasper."

"Me neither."

Kaija had felt angry at Maeryn, but seeing Fain's guilt made her realize something. For so long Kaija worried that she would never connect with Gaia and discover her relaying powers, but the moment she had it turned out to be more of a curse than a gift.

If this was anybody's fault, it was hers.

* * *

The Capital

A week earlier, Johnathan York was working on his latest atrocity.

Floating blobs of color rotated around the painter. He moved his hand very delicately and two of the droplets merged into one another, creating a dull shade of yellow. He concentrated, flicked one of his fingers, and the color brightened. Johnathan relayed the paint toward his canvas and began brushing the hair on High Guardian Thomas's head.

His dumb, fat head.

Johnathan York was the most well-renowned painter in all of Edgardia and had the prestigious job as the guardianship's resident artist. Johnathan had painted his employer thousands of times; at this point he painted the portraits entirely from memory. Images of High Guardian Thomas the Mentalist hung in every hallway of the capital and were teleported all around the world to wealthy families. Johnathan was currently painting Thomas riding into battle on the back of a flying stallion, holding a spear into the air triumphantly while his long blonde hair blew in the wind. He made sure to shed roughly forty pounds from the royal gut with his brushstrokes.

What a joke this painting was.

No, Johnathan corrected himself, *what a joke my career is.*

High Guardian Thomas Zeig had been one of Edgard's Seven Knights, blessed with a small amount of the son of Gaia's power. He was the only survivor from Duncan Kacey's massacre that killed the late high guardian and the other six knights. Thomas had successfully managed to keep fractions of the guardianship together in a time of great turmoil.

But that was long ago. Now Thomas was a fat man with a wispy comb-over. He spent most of his days eating, gambling with tax money, dating suspiciously young women, and admiring his own portraits while his advisors ran the guardianship. Johnathan had once asked the high guardian if his daughter could come live in the capital with him.

"No, I really don't think so," Thomas had said without hesitation, between bites of puff pastry. "I'm afraid that the Capital is at capacity right now, and people are knocking at the walls to get in. How about I start to pay you double, and you can send the extra money to your daughter?"

Of course, Johnathan had accepted. The amount of money he made was absolutely absurd for an artist, and he dreamed that once he amassed his fortune he would retire and go off to live with his daughter and grandchild. More than anything, he just wanted to stop staring at the high guardian's face day in and day out.

A messenger suddenly burst through the door of Johnathan's studio, panting for breath.

"Sir Johnathan," said the messenger. "Your daughter is waiting for you outside the gates of the Capital. She says that it is urgent; it is about your grandchild."

"What?" cried Johnathan, his heart racing in his chest. He lowered his hands and the floating blobs of paint returned to the palette. "Take me to her at once."

The messenger escorted him outside the Capital's outer walls. Johnathan resented the fact that they wouldn't even let his own daughter inside, if only for a brief moment. A woman waited for him on one of the many pathways that led to the outer gates. She wore a thick jacket and hood to protect her from the wind. The messenger left Johnathan alone with his daughter so they could speak privately.

"Has something happened to Rose?" asked Johnathan.

The woman removed her hood, and Johnathan became very confused. Whoever this woman was, it was not his daughter. She had long, dark hair tied behind her back, and her face was decorated with ornate, floral tattoos. A black streak of tattooed fire traced its way up her neck and onto her check. Johnathan gasped, recognizing the insignia of the Western Blaze.

"Nomad!" he cried.

"Oh, father," the woman said, "you must be confused. Come with me."

Johnathan turned to flee, but the woman had already placed a hand on his back. There was an abrupt pop as the two of them vanished and oxygen rushed in to fill the gap they had left in the air. The wind was blowing very hard in the guardianship that night, and none of the guards had heard the sound of teleportation.

A new resident artist was hired within days, and it was believed that Johnathan's granddaughter had suddenly fallen ill. Nobody in the Capital suspected that there were currently events happening outside the outer walls which would change Gaia forever.

* * *

The Atlas Ocean

Fain found a map of northeast Edgardia in the sailboat and quickly discovered that the nearest telestation was two dozen stretches down the coast. They decided that it would be much safer to travel on water than to face the unknowns of the mainland, so they followed the shoreline in the sailboat.

Kaija and Fain took turns watching the sails while the other slept. During her shift, Kaija watched the morning sun rise and realized that she was now entering the second day of her fourteenth cycle. When it was Fain's turn, Kaija woke him up and the two of them sat for a while, talking about the previous day.

"Have you tried relaying again since you returned?" asked Fain, and Kaija got an embarrassed look on her face.

"Yes," she admitted. "I feel the power of Gaia now, but every time I start to take it in I hear the sounds of machinery. I'm afraid that if I try too much I will switch places with Maeryn again. My powers are pretty useless."

"I don't know," said Fain. "I can do many things with my relaying abilities, but they are all things that a lot of other people can do. We're heading toward the Edgardian capital, and there will be thousands of conjurist relayers there who are much stronger than I am in every way. The knight Will Zeig lives there, freaking *Will Zeig*. That dude can melt internalist steel with his mind. But Kaija, I've never heard of someone doing what you've done. I think that's pretty amazing."

Kaija found herself blushing. Usually people talked about how extraordinary Fain's abilities were, and he had developed a big head about it. Fain never gave out compliments like this, yet Kaija still wasn't sure how her relaying could be very helpful. Maeryn had done quite a bit of damage during her day on Gaia, whether purposeful or not, and it was Kaija's fault that they switched places.

"I'll take the last leg of the trip," said Fain, standing up and relaying the wind toward the sail. "You go ahead and rest; I'll get us safely to the telestation."

* * *

Kaija awoke to hear Fain shouting obscenities, and upon opening her eyes she saw that the sails of the boat were ablaze. Fain sprayed ocean water at the flames in desperation, but they seemed to be resisting the water and were gradually spreading to the deck of the boat.

"What's happening?" asked Kaija. "Were we attacked by Nomads?"

"Nope," said Fain, relaying a cloud of mist which engulfed the flames to no avail. She expected him to continue, but he remained tight-lipped.

"Were we attacked at all?"

"Nope."

"You were playing with fire, weren't you?"

"That's just going to remain a mystery."

Fain summoned a great big wave which crashed over the flames, successfully extinguishing the burning deck. However, the entire sailboat was now filled to the brim with water and they began sinking into the ocean. Fain sighed, looking to the shore and estimating the amount of energy it would take to get there.

"Well, land travel it is then," he said. "Take my hand."

Kaija gripped Fain's hand and they jumped into the waters of the ocean together. The moment they hit the waves a burst of water pressure catapulted them across the surface, their feet sliding across the water.

"I've been working on this technique for a while," Fain shouted over the roar of the water. "I wasn't sure if it would work with two people. Glad you're here." He looked at her, hair whipping in the wind, and gave Kaija a delighted smile.

Within minutes they had arrived on the rocky shores of the mainland. Kaija climbed up onto a large boulder and peered at the forests that scattered the land ahead of them. She thought about how if they traveled through the forest, they would not reach the other end of the continent for thousands of stretches. Her arms broke out in goosebumps.

"This is it…" she observed. "We're actually in mainland Edgardia. This is where Ms. Clara was born, and Edgard Zeig ended the Gaian Global War. This is—"

"This is where *everything* happens," said Fain.

* * *

Early that morning, Jasper and Clara Monhegan sat in a small café in the town of Boothbay. It was the closest stop to the Portland telestation, so it was bustling with travelers coming and going.

A waitress walked by their table, bringing a slice of cake to another patron. Jasper's gloomy attitude suddenly perked up and he signaled to the young woman.

"You have cake?" asked Jasper.

"Yes," she said. "Blueberry with lemon buttercream."

Jasper slammed a fist down onto the table and smiled for the first time that day.

"Cancel my eggs, please," he declared, "and bring me four slices of cake with a pot of black coffee."

Clara raised an eyebrow at her guardian.

"What?" asked Jasper. "I eat fish day in and day out, and there's never any good dessert on Monhegan. Thought about learning how to bake myself, just to put an end to the culinary monotony." He sniffed. "Gaia... I can *smell it* already. That's it; if I survive this, I'm becoming a pastry chef. You'll have to find a new guardian."

"Same eating habits since you were a little boy," laughed Clara. "Who would have thought? The mighty guardian of Monhegan has a soft spot for sugar."

"There is nothing wrong with a grown man enjoying—" Jasper began, but was cut short by the sound of breaking glass. The waitress had dropped her tray, and was looking out of the window in horror.

"The Nomads are back," she said in a hushed voice, and the entire room broke out into a panic. Several mothers cried and held their children close. Grown men paced worriedly and argued amongst themselves.

"What is going on?" asked Clara to an old man at the table next to them.

"The Nomads have been showing up every couple of weeks," he whispered quickly. "They ask for people to volunteer to come with them, but no one knows why. Most people think that the Nomads use them as slaves. If nobody volunteers to go, the savages burn down houses and take twice the amount of people. Someone always volunteers now, Gaia bless them."

"What about your guardian?" asked Jasper. "Haven't they tried to stop it?"

"The first time the Nomads showed up we refused, and they killed our guardian. We've been trying to contact the Capital to tell them, but there's been no response. Most of the villagers have just been moving away. This town will die soon, and mark my words Portland will be next. If the telestation goes away people will have to travel over two hundred stretches to get to the next closest one in Hampshire. Maybe that's what they want; to spread chaos."

Jasper gave an intense stare to Clara.

"Jasper," she whispered, reading his thoughts. "We can't intervene; you are sick. We don't want to attract attention."

The Bridge

A young man, no older than seventeen cycles, suddenly stood up and said *"I'll go"* in a trembling voice. The young woman next to him began wailing, grabbing him by the shirt and begging him to stay inside.

Jasper and Clara looked at each other again.

"Is it even a question?" whispered Jasper. "Would you like to just sit and watch?"

Clara shook her head slowly.

"You know that's never been an option for me."

He nodded his head and smiled.

"Stop!" shouted Jasper, standing up. "Nobody is volunteering, and I'm going to need my cake to go." He grabbed a piece of cake from the nearest cart and began eating it as he and Clara left the café.

The Nomad stood in the middle of the empty street, waiting for his volunteer to come out and be taken. He held a long spear, and his entire body was covered in black, ornate tattoos of fire. The man watched the sky, eying the large dark clouds which were rolling in seemingly from nowhere. Clara and Jasper approached him, and immediately the Nomad vanished before re-appearing inches in front of Clara's face.

"We have no need for a weak old woman," sneered the man, prodding Clara with the back end of his spear. "Go back inside, you pathetic—"

"Uh oh…" mumbled Jasper, his mouth full of cake.

Clara swatted the spear out of the Nomad's grip, held her walking stick high, and brought it crashing down upon the ground. A thunderous boom rang out for stretches, as if the planet itself were resonating from the impact. Windows shook at neighboring villages up and down the coast. The Nomad stumbled and held his hands over his ears, yelling in pain. An all-encompassing screeching sound filled his head as his eardrums reeled from impact.

The people of Boothbay all began to stumble outside or look out their windows, marveling over the fact that from one horizon to another, the world appeared to be trembling.

Chapter Thirteen

I Missed a Lot

Garfield Park, Indianapolis

Maeryn huddled under a tree in the middle of Garfield Park. Bushes surrounded her on every side, keeping her out of view from anyone else who might be walking by. Raindrops were beginning to fall from the early morning sky and Max gave off a warm glow to keep her from the cold. Maeryn had not slept at all, having spent the entire night talking to Max. The reality of the situation was washing over her, and she felt like she was drowning.

"I used to come to this park all the time with Grandpa," said Maeryn. "I loved him. Is he… could he really be…"

She paused, not really wanting to think about it.

"Max," she continued. "We're not going to figure this out, are we?"

"I don't know," he said. "I'm afraid that we have moved far beyond my ability to calculate the next action."

"Well, we can't trust my family anymore," said Maeryn. "My aunt tried to drug me, and my father builds weapons of death and destruction. And my mom…"

She thought sadly about her mom, Katherine Johnson. When Maeryn was very young her parents had gotten divorced and her mother had soon remarried. Eventually Katherine had a new daughter, and with every passing year Maeryn felt more distant from her. She hadn't even called on Maeryn's birthday.

A spark of hope suddenly ignited inside of Maeryn. Her whole life had been reframed whenever Rosalie had tried to sedate her. Could it be that there was also another side of the story for her mother? Perhaps she knew about the Kacey family's terrible secrets, and that's why she had left.

"We need to contact my mom," said Maeryn.

"Are you sure about that?" asked Max. "You've gotten your hopes up about her before, and—"

"Do you see any other options?" asked Maeryn, and he was silent. "So you choose to be quiet now? Max, I really need some advice here."

The Bridge

Max floated into the air and spun around, looking in every direction. He held up a finger to silence Maeryn, and his quiet voice spoke in her earpiece.

"Maeryn, we have a bigger problem here," he said. "There are people coming."

She looked around into the early-morning twilight of the park and did, in fact, see figures coming closer from every direction. Maeryn's digital contacts showed the thermal outlines of four men in suits, all moving toward her with a singular purpose. Their eyes gave a fierce red glow, signaling to Maeryn that they also wore MotherTech contacts which were currently targeting her. They were still a good distance off, but she was being surrounded.

"MotherTech agents," said Max. "I found them in the employee database."

One of the men pulled out a small metal baton which grew in his hand and sent out flickering sparks.

"Maeryn Kacey!" he shouted, his voice being digitally amplified in her ear. "These batons are capable of temporarily paralyzing your body; if you come with us quietly we will not be forced to use them."

"These are MotherTech employees?" whispered Maeryn shrilly. "That's impossible! They sure don't look like computer programmers."

"They work for the, well, *other* branch of MotherTech," whispered Max. "I don't know what they're capable of; most of their profiles are blocked from me. Let me distract them, and you get out of here."

Maeryn jumped through the bushes to try to find an opening to flee, but the men were fast approaching. Max flew up into the air and divided into five smaller versions of himself. They formed a circle around Maeryn and held out their hands toward the men.

"Don't take another step!" Max yelled, his squeaky voice coming from five different directions at once. "You are up against the apex of human achievement, and absolutely nothing will stop me from putting you in a world of hurt."

One of the men held out his baton and it sent glowing shockwaves through the air. It passed through Maeryn and she felt the hairs on her neck stand up on end before the strange sensation passed. The five Maxes, however, suddenly clunked to the ground and laid there motionless.

"We turned off your pet," said one of the men, inching forward. "Please put your hands behind your head and knees on the ground."

"Max?" asked Maeryn. "Max, are you there?"

There was silence from her earpiece. The man's weapon had disabled all of the technology on her body. For once, she was totally on her own. Maeryn wanted to run, but indecision kept her locked in place. This was not the kind of thing Maeryn had ever been prepared for.

"I'm out of my element," she thought. *"I need Kaija."*

The Bridge

* * *

Boothbay Road, Gaia

Kaija and Fain left the shore and walked down a path in the woods to Boothbay, estimating that it would take another hour on foot to get there. After walking several stretches the ground began to rumble and shake. Birds flew out of the trees by the hundreds in a panic, and Fain held onto Kaija tightly. When things stopped trembling they broke apart awkwardly, not quite meeting each other's eyes.

"What was that?" asked Kaija.

"Earthquake, probably," said Fain. "Nothing to be scared of. I definitely didn't just pee a little, in case you were wondering."

They carried on down the road, each step growing far more laborious by the second.

"We need to learn how to teleport," moaned Fain. "Or at least train some sky lizards to carry us around. I didn't think about how much longer it would take to get from place to place on the mainland."

"I don't care; I love it," marveled Kaija. "There's just so much more to…"

She trailed off as her and Fain both stared in wonder at something around the next bend in the forest. For the last couple hours they had been surrounded by trees, but here in the middle of the forest was a great big patch where nothing was growing. The earth was pitch black and sunken in all the way to the horizon. It looked almost like a big scab on the land. Enormous, broken machines were scattered about the ruined landscape. Not even a single insect flew over the blistered earth.

"What is this?" whispered Kaija.

"I've heard about these," said Fain with uncharacteristic reverence. "It's from the global war. The war was fought all over the planet, and my dad told me that there are still battle scars everywhere. There are places where Edgard Zeig fought so hard that Gaia departed from the land completely, its energy being used up. Some people say that these places will stay like this until the end of time."

Kaija had seen what a single powerful relayer could do, and she imagined what it might look like to see hundreds, if not thousands, of them fighting in battle. It was a horrifying, yet strangely exciting thought. The black earth seemed to steal the sunlight itself, and after staring at it for a few minutes Kaija almost felt like it was looking back at her.

"Let's get out of here," she said, and they continued down the road.

Kaija was discovering so many interesting things with her best friend, and she felt strangely jealous that Maeryn had spent her entire cycle day with him.

The Bridge

"Did you like Maeryn?" asked Kaija.

"She wasn't like you at all," said Fain nonchalantly. "She kept trying to kiss me, and it seriously grossed me out. I told her over and over that I wasn't interested, but she said that she couldn't ignore what her body was telling her."

Kaija stared at him in wide-eyed horror, and Fain burst into laughter. She whacked him on the back of the head before he had a chance to dodge.

"Geeze," he said, rubbing his head. "I was just joking. Maeryn was okay, I guess. Nothing like you at all; more of a thinker than a doer. She kept mostly quiet, but I guess it must have been strange for her being stuck in your head and all."

Kaija found herself wondering about Maeryn, and when she did a peculiar feeling began to come over her. She wasn't sure how she knew it, but Maeryn was in serious trouble. Kaija gasped and stopped walking.

"Are you okay?" asked Fain.

"I can feel what Maeryn is feeling right now," she said.

When Kaija unfocused her eyes, she could see four large men approaching. They were like ghosts; transparent and with glowing red eyes. When Kaija blinked they vanished, but a sickly feeling of fear rippled through her body.

"Fain, she's in danger. There are people that want to hurt her, and she doesn't know what to do."

Fain's eyes widened.

"Are you serious?" he asked, trying to imagine Maeryn in a fight. "Kaija, if this is true then she really *is* in danger. That girl's not a fighter."

Kaija heard Maeryn's frantic thoughts, ringing like a distant echo in her mind.

"I'm out of my element; I need Kaija."

"She needs my help," said Kaija.

"No!" Fain pleaded. "Switching bodies once is enough for a lifetime."

Kaija was still very skeptical of this Maeryn, and she was still unsure if the girl really deserved her help. However, a saying that her father often said came to her.

"The first rule of the Guardian Creed is this: the decision to help someone is not a decision at all."

"I'll be back, Fain," she said. "I promise."

"Kaija, no!" Fain shouted, but it was too late. Kaija was pulling in the energy of Gaia, and it was surprisingly effortless this time. She took in more of it than she ever had before, focused on Maeryn, and sent herself to Earth.

Kaija's eyes rolled back in her head and she collapsed to the ground with a dull thud. Fain ran up to the body of his friend and began shaking her. Kaija's eyes opened, but she only stared back without expression.

"Kaija!" he yelled, but there was no response.

"Maeryn?"

Again, no response.

The Bridge

"They can't both be gone," he thought. *"Can they?"*

* * *

The men were approaching Maeryn, their circle quickly closing in, but she felt as if her legs were locked in place.

"Put your hands behind your head and knees on the ground!" an agent yelled. "I won't ask again."

A voice spoke in her head; the same voice that she had heard coming from herself during the day spent in Kaija's body.

"Maeryn, I'm here. Nice to meet you, by the way."

"What?" whispered Maeryn. "But I'm not on Gaia. How can we both be here?"

"I don't know, I think I used too much Gaian energy this time. It's not as simple as I thought it would be."

"What do I do, Kaija?" asked Maeryn. "They're going to take me."

"Don't do anything, you'll just mess it up. Step aside, city girl."

"Step aside? What do you—"

Suddenly Maeryn found herself being yanked to the back of her head. Her arms and legs moved outside of her control, and she watched the scene unfold like a passenger in her own body as Kaija took command.

Steering Maeryn's body, Kaija looked around to assess the situation. Four men were approaching them on all sides, and one of them was carrying a small, glowing rod. Max, the tiny metal person, had somehow split into five parts which were lying motionless in the grass.

"They're all around us," thought Kaija. *"We can't run... at least not yet."*

Kaija put her hands behind her head and knees on the ground. The man carrying the glowing baton stood in front of her and looked down with a smile.

"That's better," he said. "We're going to cuff your hands and take you to Rosalie. Your aunt does not want you harmed, Maeryn; she's just worried about you. Running around this city at night is a dangerous hobby."

"Yes," Kaija agreed. "For you."

She leapt forward, springing past the man on one side and landing in the grass. Before he had a chance to turn around, Kaija kicked him behind the knee, causing his leg to buckle and the man to topple to the ground. She jumped up as fast as she could and began running into the dark night. The three other men chased her, and they were fast. She ran past a tree, pulling its branch and then letting it snap back to whack one of the approaching men in the face.

"Well, I'm impressed," said Maeryn from the inside of her own head. *"Go to the road and head toward the bridge.*

The Bridge

We need to make it back into the city, they're not going to take us with a bunch of civilians watching."

Kaija ran onto an empty road that went through the center of the park and began to follow it toward the bridge. She was getting out of breath at an annoyingly quick rate.

"I wish you were in better shape, city girl," Kaija panted.

"I'm sorry," said Maeryn. *"Actually, I'm sorry about a lot of things. I never meant for your father to—"*

"Are we really going to talk about this now?" shouted Kaija, running up the nearest bridge. "We didn't mean to screw up each other's lives, so let's just leave it at that!"

A glowing shape flew out of the trees toward Kaija. For a brief moment the two girls thought that it might be Max, but by the time they realized it was one of the agent's batons it was too late. It struck her in the leg and electricity coursed through Maeryn's body. Kaija's presence suddenly evaporated, the shock apparently sending her back to Gaia. Maeryn was snapped back to the controls, but her entire body was seizing up from the electricity. She dropped to the ground, unable to move her arms or legs.

One of the MotherTech agents approached her, walking with a limp. It was the same man that Kaija had kicked in the back of the leg, and he was angry.

"The paralysis will wear off soon," said the man, "and it will cause no lasting damage. We are taking you to Rosalie, and let me say that your hostility was very unnecessary. I would kick you myself if your aunt wasn't my boss."

He bent over, reaching out to pick up his dropped baton, when a large garbage pail flew out of the air and crashed into him, sending him toppling off the side of the bridge and into the river. There was a great big splash from below.

"Cowards," spoke an unfamiliar voice. "Attacking a young girl in my home."

Maeryn strained her eyes to see a very elderly man standing on her other side. His clothes were timeworn and dirty, his face unshaven, and his long white hair tied up behind his back. Maeryn had spent many hours doing homework in Garfield Park, and she vaguely recognized the man as a homeless person she sometimes saw wandering around.

"Three more agents," Maeryn grunted through gritted teeth.

"Of course there are," commented the old man. "Because it takes four grown men to sedate a small girl, obviously."

Maeryn expected him to offer her help, but he merely walked to the side of the road and sat on the edge of the bridge. An old dog, a tri-colored border collie with specks of grey in its fur, walked happily up to the old man and began panting. He reached into his pocket, pulled out a Twinkie and ripped it in half before sharing it with the very happy dog.

The Bridge

"People can't just leave us in peace," said the man, talking more to the dog than to Maeryn. "This is our home."

Another MotherTech agent emerged from the trees.

"Your friend is in the river," said the old man, taking another bite of his Twinkie.

The agent rushed toward them, but the old man stuck out his leg and tripped him. As the agent fell, the old man reached up and pushed him over the side of the bridge without even standing up or taking his eyes off of his snack. There was another big splash from the river below.

The two remaining agents ran out of the trees, both rushing to attack the old homeless man.

"I'm not fighting you," said the old man, getting up and yawning. "This is getting way too noisy."

One of the agents pulled out another glowing baton and swung it at the back of the old man's head. Without turning around, he reached up and grabbed the agent's arm. He jerked his hand backward, striking the agent in the face with the sparking rod. The agent fell to the ground, unconscious and twitching.

The old man reached down, quickly picking up the remaining baton and examining it. The last remaining agent stopped in his tracks upon seeing the old man with the weapon. However, the old man simply shrugged and tossed the baton over the edge of the bridge. When it hit the water there was a flash of light and several yells as the two agents in the water were knocked unconscious by the shockwaves. The old man turned to face the final agent calmly.

"Okay, youngster," he said. "If you want to attack an old homeless dude, now is your chance. So are we going to fight, or will you sit and enjoy a Twinkie with me?"

He reached into his pocket and pulled out another snack cake, offering it to the agent.

"Um," said the agent. "If I'm being honest here, I really didn't know what I was in for when I got this job."

The old man smiled and handed the package to him.

"Ah, I like that: a man who will admit when he was wrong. Come, sit."

To Maeryn's amazement, the agent actually sat down on the edge of the bridge and began eating with the homeless man.

"I mean," said the agent, "this was supposed to be a security job; I didn't sign up to abduct teenage girls."

"Well, now you know," said the homeless man. "Maybe it's time for a career change? Those MotherTech people are snakes. Speaking of the girl, will she be alright?"

"Oh," said the agent, taking out his electric baton and pressing a few buttons. "I can help her."

He leaned down to Maeryn and tapped her on the shoulder with the weapon, which was now glowing blue instead of sending off hot sparks. A tingling sensation began to fill her muscles as Maeryn regained control over her body.

The Bridge

"And what about your two partners?" asked the old man, gesturing to the river. "Are they going to drown or something?"

"No," said the agent, tapping his suit which made a heavy clunking sound. "These smart suits won't let us drown; they'll probably wash up down the river somewhere."

"Well, how about you go fish them out before they get sucked into the sewer," said the old man with a smile. "I'll keep this whole mess between you and me. And tell them to stay out of our house." He gestured to his dog and an overstuffed backpack at the side of the bridge.

The agent nodded and walked off, still somewhat dazed from the strangeness of the situation. Maeryn stood up, her legs wobbling, and observed as the old man lifted up the unconscious agent he had knocked out earlier and dropped him over the side of the bridge.

"Ah," he said. "Peace and quiet."

He sat down next to his dog, picked up a battered paperback book, and began silently reading.

"Thank you for helping me," said Maeryn.

"I wasn't," said the man, not looking up from his book. "Those agents were scaring my friends."

A small group of homeless men and women emerged from the trees on the other side of the bridge. One of them was in a wheelchair, being pushed by a woman chattering nervously to herself. The old man reached into his backpack and began passing out food to his friends.

"This is the gang," said the old man. "Booker, Ida, Ronnie, Tippy-Toe Nigel, and Bon. Gang, meet rich girl in distress."

Maeryn nodded awkwardly at the gang, who mostly ignored her while they focused on their food. The nervous woman who had been pushing the wheelchair buried her face in the dog's fur and continued her unintelligible chatter. The old man put his hand reassuringly on the woman's back.

"It's okay, Ida," he said gently. "They're gone, and you're safe. Get all the furry love you need."

"Were those police officers?" asked the man in the wheelchair.

"No," said the old man. "Not this time. It was MotherTech."

"Why would it be the police?" asked Maeryn.

"Because homeless people make the city look bad," he said. "They've been gathering us up at night and dropping us outside of the city by the busload. Mayor Thomas calls what we do trespassing, but it's kind of hard not to trespass when you don't have a home. It could be worse though; there are several gangs around that just love harassing the homeless. I'm very used to defending myself by now."

"Oh my gosh," said Maeryn. "That's terrible; I had no idea."

The Bridge

"I guess you wouldn't know about these things, Maeryn Kacey," said the old man. He saw the surprised look on her face and laughed. "Oh yes, I know who you are. You're the daughter of one of the wealthiest men in the Midwest, I think that a lot of people would recognize you. You must not get out much."

"I guess I don't," admitted Maeryn.

The man's comment made Maeryn afraid again. He had recognized her, and a lot of other people might too. How could she possibly escape from her family?

"Don't worry," said the man. "I'm not going to rat you out. Looks like you're in some serious trouble, though. I've never seen those MotherTech agents out on the streets before."

"Mother Tech is tracking me," said Maeryn, "and I don't know where to hide."

"Need to go off grid?" asked the old man. He reached into his backpack and pulled out a notebook. After scribbling a few notes, he ripped the paper out and handed it to Maeryn. "Go to this address. There's an abandoned warehouse there, and the third window in the alley is unlocked. It's a technological dead zone; no cameras around that entire block. I've had to hide a few times myself."

"Thank you," Maeryn said, turning to leave before hesitating. She once again found herself feeling incredibly privileged and snobby. This old man had saved her and given her a place to hide, but she hadn't even asked him his name.

"I really mean it," said Maeryn, turning back around. "Thank you, sir. You saved me back there. Can I ask what your name is?"

The old man smiled.

"Kai," he said.

Hearing a name so similar to Kaija's made Maeryn's ears perk up, but before the strangeness of the coincidence was able to fully settle over her a buzzing sound filled the air. A grey cloud appeared in front of them, and with a great big *POP* Max appeared in thin air.

"Sorry about that," he said. "What'd I miss?"

Max looked around at all the confused homeless people sitting on the bridge. Kai reached into his pocket and pulled out another Twinkie, offering it to the robot.

Max spun slowly in midair and looked at Maeryn.

"A lot, apparently," he said. "I missed a lot."

Chapter Fourteen

I Will Tear Them Down

Thunderwolf Stronghold, Gaia

The leader of The Western Blaze paced around in the central chamber of his stronghold. Rugaru wore the hide of a thunder wolf to protect him from the cold air despite the fact that the entire building was heated by slaves who constantly relayed fire into the furnaces. The temperature at this altitude in the Cragged Mountains would have been unlivable without these furnaces, but there was no chance of the slaves escaping and letting everyone freeze. It was very difficult to flee from a stronghold with no doors or windows.

Western Blaze fighters would often capture powerful relayers on their raids of villages and bind them into servitude, promising not to harm their captor's families if they complied. People often went with the raiders without putting up much of a fight, because they knew that the Western Blaze kept their promises. Sometimes people actually sought out membership willingly, disavowing High Guardian Thomas so that they could be under the watch of a true leader.

A messenger suddenly popped into existence in the middle of Rugaru's chamber. Once a Nomad visited a place a single time they could teleport there again with ease. Rugaru made sure that only his most trusted warriors were allowed to even see the inside of his stronghold, so this messenger was a familiar face to the leader. It was Achak, an extremely powerful mentalist that was Rugaru's second in command.

"Achak," said Rugaru. "Is it done?"

"The painter has completed his task."

"Did the guardianship ever become aware of his abduction?"

"No. They believe that Jonathan York is back with his daughter, and his daughter won't be talking. We dropped her in the middle of the Oceanic guardianship, hundreds of stretches away from a telestation. By the time she makes it home, our task will be done."

Rugaru smiled in spite of himself; he hadn't expected things to go so smoothly. However, a look of concern remained on Achak's face. He looked very nervous to deliver the next piece of news.

"I also carry a message from an eastern warrior," he said. "And... well..."

Rugaru simply nodded and waved his hand.

"Speak, Achak. I can take bad news."

Achak nodded and continued.

"Our people in the east attempted to raid a coastal village near a telestation. It was a small town called Boothbay. But the raiders were, well... *entirely unsuccessful*; they had to flee before defeat."

"This Boothbay must have a very powerful guardian," remarked Rugaru, uncertain of why he needed to know of a minor defeat across the continent.

"That's the interesting thing," said Achak. "Their guardian was killed weeks ago, but there were two travelers passing through the village who fought the entire clan by themselves. A guardian from the coastal regions, and a very old woman."

Rugaru raised an eyebrow at this.

"An old woman?" he asked in surprise. "Isn't the eastern clan better than that?"

"I was told that the man was relaying lightning bolts right out of the sky, and when the old woman struck the earth with her walking stick half of the Nomads fell to the ground, unable to move their legs. We captured a witness, and he told us that the man was Jasper Monhegan, guardian of Monhegan Island. The old woman was a mere instructor of children. They were traveling to the Capital to seek healing."

"I haven't heard of Monhegan," said Rugaru.

"It's a tiny island off of the north-eastern coast."

Rugaru sat silently for a minute, wondering why such a powerful guardian would make his home on an insignificant island. He asked himself if relayers of this caliber would be best defeated, or if there was any way that he could use them to his advantage.

"Keep lines of communication open with all of our clans currently in the east," said Rugaru. "I would like you to personally keep watch at the station by the Capital for these two travelers. Alert our spies at the north-eastern telestation; have them capture any strange travelers, and bring them to me."

* * *

Boothbay Road

Fain trudged down the road with the unconscious body of Kaija in his arms. The main part of town was only about two stretches from the coastline, but it was slow going while trying to carry his friend. His father, Maddox Monhegan, had often told him not to be so spontaneous and rash. The first part of their journey had been thrilling, but now Fain couldn't help but feel the first pangs of uncertainty. Here he was, carrying the body of his best friend down the road while she was off in some other universe doing who knows what. Fain wondered what might happen if Kaija never came back, and he arrived in Boothbay to deliver her comatose body to Jasper.

"I don't have to wonder," Fain whispered to himself. "He'd kill me."

All of a sudden Kaija's eyes sprang open and she screamed right in his face. Fain jumped, letting Kaija go in his surprise, and she hit the ground with a *thud*.

"Ouch!" Kaija yelled. "What was that for?"

"You have no idea how happy I am to see you!" cried Fain. "And you came back just in time, I was just considering ditching your body in the woods and going into hiding."

Kaija moved like she was going to spring to her feet and hit him, but her legs wobbled when she tried to stand up. Fain grabbed a hand to steady her.

"I'm so tired all of a sudden," Kaija remarked. "I feel like I ran twenty stretches. And I'm so hungry."

"Well you did just use your relaying powers to throw your mind into someone else's body," said Fain. "Relaying takes a lot of energy. Aww, is this Kaija's first time feeling relayer's drain?"

"I guess it is…"

Kaija's eyes glazed over for a moment, as if she had not yet completely returned to this reality. She appeared to be deep in thought, just now digesting what had happened to her on Earth. Fain watched her face with concern.

"What is it?" he asked. "What happened when you were on the other side?"

"Maeryn and I shared a body," said Kaija. "And some men with glowing rods chased her, or me I guess, no… *us.* I was able to get away, but—"

Kaija's eyes became big, remembering the feeling of being struck by something just before she was thrown back into her own body.

"Fain, I think that those men captured Maeryn. Right before I came back, her body was hit by something. I need to go back; she's in serious trouble!"

Kaija pulled the energies of Gaia toward her, but the moment they ran through her body she found herself stumbling again on the path. Her legs felt like they were made of jelly.

"Oh no you don't!" cried Fain, reaching forward and steadying her once again. "Kaija, you are absolutely drained right now. If you keep trying to relay, you'll be asleep for days. Your mind is still stretching to take in the energy; you're not a pro relayer like me."

"A pro relayer who couldn't keep those vultures from destroying his cabin," Kaija muttered under her breath.

The Bridge

"And besides," Fain continued, "we're less than a stretch away from Boothbay; if we catch up with Jasper and Ms. Clara I do not want it to be with you unconscious. I'm worried enough as it is what they're going to do to me for this."

"My father," Kaija whispered, trying to pull herself back into this reality and her own concerns.

It was a jarring sensation to go back and forth between two bodies. When she was on Earth some deep part of her had actually felt what Maeryn was feeling. She was scared and alone. Protecting Maeryn felt like protecting herself. Kaija had to keep in mind that there were enough things going on in her own life to keep her more than occupied. She was on the road to see her father and to accompany him to the Capital for healing. And if the healing didn't work, then she was off to see him for the last time.

And yet, Maeryn's troubles continued to ring in Kaija's mind. Their lives had to be tied somehow. Edgard Zeig's sword was on Earth, so the two worlds couldn't be as separate as they first appeared. As much as Kaija wanted to leave Maeryn behind her, she felt like it really wasn't a choice at all. Gaia was pulling them together.

Fain waved his hand in front of Kaija's eyes.

"Hello?!" he asked. "Stay with me, Kaija! Are you seeing this?"

They turned the corner to see a cluster of buildings down the road. People of Boothbay were going about their business in the streets and store fronts, eating ice cream, waving at travelers, and tying up horses outside a motel. An artist sat at his easel, painting a posed young couple with a dog. Street musicians played on the porch of a café and people danced in broad daylight. The general atmosphere was an infectious joy that Kaija was immediately caught up in. Boothbay road had been randomly clustered with lighthouses and harbors, but this was the first sign of real mainland civilization they had seen.

"So this is the outside world," said Kaija. "It really exists."

"I never thought our parents would let us see the mainland," said Fain. "Although I suppose that they didn't let us at all. We're going to be in so much trouble when…"

Fain's words trailed off as they entered the town of Boothbay.

"Ms. Clara's been here," he said.

"How do you know?" asked Kaija.

Fain pointed to the ground. Through the center of the street ran a great chasm that made it look like the planet itself had been sliced in half. A group of kids sat in the nearby dirt, relaying pebbles down into the opening and counting how long it took for them to reach the bottom.

The Bridge

"That crack," said Fain. "It looks just like the one Ms. Clara threw me in after I blew Stevie out to sea. She's been here, and she was *mad*."

They approached a young, very round boy that stood by the opening in the ground. He looked to be ten or eleven cycles old, and his freckly, beet red face squinted up at the travelers.

"Excuse me," said Kaija. "Could you tell us what happened here?"

"The Nomad came back into town," said the boy. "He was going to take another slave, but a man and an old woman fought him off. More Nomads showed up, and an all-out war broke out. The lightning man summoned a thunderstorm and stunned a dozen Nomads, and the old woman hit the ground with her stick and the entire world shook. Eventually all the Nomads just disappeared. It was the coolest thing I've ever seen."

"I wish we could have been here to see Jasper scare off some Nomads," said Fain.

"My friends told me that the travelers were actually part of the high guardian's seven knights," said the boy excitedly. "We've been asking for help ever since our guardian was killed, and they finally sent their strongest fighters."

Kaija's heart swelled with pride.

"I know something pretty cool about the travelers," she said. "They weren't the high guardian's knights at all; the man was my dad, and the old woman was our teacher."

Fain smiled and nodded his head, but the boy looked at them skeptically.

"Really!" said Fain. "It's true. The lightning man was Jasper Monhegan, the guardian of Monhegan Island."

The boy laughed.

"I don't believe you," he said. "They were Knights of The Seven, not two dirty sea monkeys."

"What?" asked Fain.

"Dirty sea monkeys," said the boy with a hateful look in his eyes. "Cowards that are too afraid to live on the mainland. Filthy islanders who marry their cousins."

"We're from Monhegan too, you know," said Kaija.

"I guess that makes you dirty little sea monkeys as well," said the boy. "And liars. Those were the high guardian's knights!"

Fain's face was red with anger, and Kaija didn't like where this was going.

"Come on, Fain," she said. "A little kid isn't worth the trouble, don't make this worse. Let's get some food."

"What's your name, round boy?" asked Fain, barely containing his anger.

"Ben Booth," said the boy.

Fain took a threatening step forward, but the boy's face remained blank.

"Well, Ben Booth," he said. "You have a stupid name, an ugly face, and I hate you. But you know what? We're going to take the high road here. Good day to you, Ben Booth; we're off to get some lunch."

Fain turned and began to stomp off toward the nearest café with Kaija following. A second later a small rock zoomed through the air and struck him in the back of the head.

"My dad owns that café," Ben yelled after him, "and he's not going to serve some dirty sea monkeys. Get out of our town and go kiss your sister!"

Fain stopped in his tracks, his arms shaking with rage.

"Call me a sea monkey one more time," said Fain, with a quiet intensity.

"Dirty sea— " started Ben Booth, but his words were cut short.

"Stop talking!" yelled Fain, spinning around and pointing a finger toward Ben's throat. There was a sudden whoosh of wind, followed by what sounded like a tiny explosion.

Ben looked angry, but when he opened his mouth to say something no words came out. He clutched his neck and his eyes widened.

"What did you do?" asked Kaija, horrified and trying not to laugh at the same time.

"Oh," said Fain, coming down abruptly from his outburst. "I did the leg bind technique that Ms. Clara taught us, but I did it on his vocal chords instead."

The little boy suddenly looked very frightened; he turned around and took off running.

"Don't worry, Ben," Fain yelled after him, "it should wear off after a while. I practiced this on little Stevie a few weeks ago and his voice came back after…"

Fain hesitated, counting back the days in his head and searching his memory.

"Kaija?" he asked, suddenly looking concerned. "When was the last time you heard Stevie say something?"

* * *

Ornes Café

Kaija and Fain sat at a table at the café while Fain dug around through his bag looking for money. The scents wafting from the kitchen were making Kaija's stomach rumble embarrassingly loud. Jasper was quite a good cook, but there were no professional chefs on Monhegan.

"Gaia, I'm starving," said Kaija. "I hope not everyone on the mainland is as rude as that kid."

"It doesn't surprise me," said Fain. "When we moved to Monhegan Island it made a lot of my other family members mad. We haven't spoken to them since. Some people think that all of the Edgardians fleeing to the islands and other continents are just making it easier for the Nomads to take over."

A large man approached the table carrying two glasses of water.

"Hello," he said, putting the cups on the table. "May I take your order?"

Fain pulled out two copper coins from his bag and showed them to the man.

"How much food would two coppers pay for?" he asked.

The waiter gave them a skeptical glance.

"A piece of bread," he said.

"Splendid," said Fain. "Half a piece of your finest bread for me, and half for the lady."

The waiter walked off and Kaija's stomach growled loudly.

"Why didn't we think to bring more money?" she moaned. "I'm going to pass out if I don't eat."

"You know that I'm impulsive and thoughtless," said Fain. "But what's your excuse for forgetting and actually listening to me?"

"I've had my mind in other places, obviously. But forget about the food for a second, what about the telestation? They're not going to send us to the Capital for free! How are we going to catch up to my dad and Ms. Clara?"

The waiter had returned to the table with a hunk of stale bread when his eyes suddenly widened.

"Did you say Ms. Clara?" he asked.

"Yes," said Kaija. "Our teacher Ms. Clara and my father, Jasper Monhegan, passed through here and fought off those Nomads. They were on their way to the telestation, and we're trying to catch up with them."

The man stared at Kaija's face for a moment with deep concentration.

"You do share a likeness," he said quietly. "It's the truth… you're his daughter."

The man suddenly picked Kaija up and wrapped her in a great big hug. There were tears in his eyes as he spilled his heart out to Kaija.

"Your father saved this town. Those Nomads will be too afraid to come back here; they only bother villages that don't fight back. Your money is no good here; have whatever you like on the house. When you are done eating you can take my carriage to the telestation, and I'll pay the fee."

Fain smiled at Kaija.

"See," he said. "The mainland isn't so bad."

* * *

Kaija and Fain both had coffee, fresh blueberries, potatoes, and eggs that the conjurist chef fried right at their table. A man stood nearby playing music on a harp without even touching the strings. The owner of the café, Ornes Booth, ran back and forth to the kitchens fetching anything that Kaija and Fain wanted. The drain from relaying so much Gaian energy was slowly going away as Kaija's stomach filled up with the best food she had ever eaten.

"Is there anything else I can get for you before your trip?" asked Ornes enthusiastically.

Kaija's eyes widened suddenly as she had an idea.

"*Oh my Gaia*," she said. "Do you have any cake? It's been months since traders have brought cake from the mainland."

"Why yes, we do," said Ornes. "Our pastry chef just made a blueberry cake this morning with fresh lemon buttercream. It pairs quite well with a steaming double cortado."

Ornes turned toward the kitchen, clapped his hands urgently, and yelled *"THE CAKE!"*

A chef ran out from the back and whispered into Ornes's ear.

"Oh," said Ornes. "It seems that your father took all of the cake with him. You'll have to share it when you get to the Capital, if he hasn't eaten it all yet. I'll get you some of our orange chocolate-chip gelato instead; you'll love it." The door to the café rang as a young boy walked in. "Ah! Look who it is. Fain, Kaija, let me introduce you to my son, Ben."

Ben Booth stared at Fain with a horrified look in his eyes.

"Hello, Ben," said Fain happily. "What's the word?"

"Say hello, Ben," said Ornes. "This girl's father is the hero that saved our town along with the teacher from Monhegan."

Ben turned around and took off running out the door.

"Talkative kid you've got there, Ornes," said Fain.

* * *

The Capital of Edgardia

Jasper and Clara arrived at The Capital in the early afternoon. A great stone wall surrounded the city, and archers stood in the guard stations every ten arms along the top of the wall. Their slings contained steel arrows which would not fly if not for the archer's externalist relaying abilities. The Edgardian archers were famous for not missing their targets; the arrows would bend through the air at their will. A long line of desperate looking people stood in front of the single entrance to the Capital.

"There was never a wall when I lived here," remarked Clara smugly. "People were free to come and go as they chose. Although, nobody would have dared to incite violence in the Capital with Edgard as high guardian."

They made it to the entrance where two burly internalist guards blocked the gates.

"State your business?" said one of the guards.

The Bridge

"I'm the guardian of Monhegan Island," said Jasper breathlessly. "I've been infected by hydra poison, and I'm seeking healing from the Capital's hospital."

Jasper raised his arm, which was riddled with blackened veins that ran up to his shoulder. The guard gave a disinterested glance before going back to picking at the dirt under his fingernail.

"Sorry," said the guard. "Hospital's closed to all but the Capital's citizens."

"We are citizens of Edgardia," said Clara. "We fall under the high guardian's rule."

The guard was quickly losing his patience, glancing at the long line behind Jasper and Ms. Clara. He snapped his fingers and the other guard grabbed Ms. Clara's arm.

"We have people seeking healing and refuge from all across the continent," said the guard. "We can't let them all in, it's unsafe and frankly impossible."

There were tears in Clara's eyes, but Jasper seemed weary and unsurprised.

"This man is going to die within a day if he does not see some very powerful healers," said Clara.

"I hear the same story all day," said the guard. "Next in line please!"

"I grew up in the Capital," said Clara, pushing back against the guard who was trying to escort her away. "I never revoked my citizenship of the Capital; you have to let me in!"

"No, Clara," Jasper pleaded. "The high guardian isn't concerned about his own citizens. I get it, and I'm not surprised. Let's go."

Clara was openly crying now.

"Jasper! They can't turn you away. Tell them who you are."

Jasper's eyes widened and looked at her unblinkingly.

"Don't you dare, Clara," he whispered. "You know what would happen. Don't you dare!"

Clara went silent, crying angry tears as the guards pushed them away and began talking to the next sad people in line. She gave Jasper a long look, and then determination rose on her face.

"I'm sorry," said Clara. "You've made your choice, but I'm free to make mine. I can't let you die."

Clara pulled up her walking stick, swung it, and struck the guard in the chest. He fell to the ground and looked at her with complete bewilderment. Internalist relayers were capable of holding an enormous amount of energy in their muscles, and they weren't used to being thrown off balance.

"We seek healing in the Capital hospital!" screamed Clara. "And we will not be turned away!"

The guards at the gate all began running toward Clara, and several of the archers pulled the strings on their bows. The line of people outside the gates all turned to look at her curiously.

The Bridge

"I am Clarice Zeig, Generalist Knight of Edgard's Seven," Clara shouted. "Tell my friend Thomas that I am back! If we do not pass through these walls, then *I WILL TEAR THEM DOWN*!"

Clara pointed her stick at the great stone wall and there was an ear piercing explosion as rubble sprayed through the air. When the dust cleared, a large crack was seen running up from the ground all the way to an archer's perch, leaving a gap in the wall big enough to see through.

"You listen to me!" shouted Ms. Clara. "Or I'll do that again, and I'll *try* this time."

The guard at the gate looked at them with a white face, and his voice trembled when he spoke.

"Very well, ma'am," he said, and then took off running into the Capital.

* * *

Clara and Jasper waited outside the gates, surrounded by dozens of large guards. Jasper sat on the ground, weakly leaning up against the outer wall with his hand over his face as the sun beat down on him.

"Clara," he groaned. "You know that I don't want to die and leave Kaija alone, but this could be worse."

"I won't apologize," said Clara. "I made a promise a long time ago; your secret is still safe."

The air around them began to glimmer, there was a big pop, and seven people appeared, surrounding Jasper and Clara. The group was composed of all different kinds of relayers, and each of them wore symbols indicating which type they were: an externalist, an internalist, a conjurist, a spacialist, and a spiritualist. The seventh knight was a generalist, a rare relayer who had considerable ability in each of the seven types.

The conjurist knight stepped forward. He was a short man with finely trimmed dark hair and a handsome face. Without warning, he raised his hands toward Jasper and Clara and his palms glowed with a piercing blue light. They could feel the scorching heat even from two arms distance.

"I am Will Zeig, conjurist knight of the High Seven," said the man. "Guardian Thomas has a message for you, woman, whoever you are. Clarice's death was witnessed during the assassination of Edgard Zeig and her ashes are entombed below The Capital. Impersonating a member of the guardianship is a crime punishable by imprisonment. The high guardian says that you may go, or choose to stay and face judgement by his seven knights."

Allie Zeig, the spiritualist knight, suddenly spoke up. The young woman looked entirely out of place among the other knights; she had streaks of purple in her hair and a ukulele slung over her shoulder.

The Bridge

"You should probably go," she said lazily. "I foresee no paths where you stay and Will doesn't burn you to a crisp. Please don't underestimate the fragility of his masculinity."

Will flinched at these words. He turned around and shot an annoyed look at his fellow knight, who was now inexplicably holding two kittens.

"Where did those come fr— *oh never mind!*" shouted Will. He turned back around at Clara and held his open palm out at her. Fire sparked from his skin.

"Well?" he asked Clara.

Clara looked to Jasper, and then back at Will. Her hand was trembling on her walking stick, but it soon steadied.

"We'll go," she said, defeated. "It clearly takes the seven strongest relayers on the continent to escort an old con artist away from the Capital."

The knights stepped aside, clearing a path for them to leave. Clara helped Jasper up and they walked away, dejected. Will turned to the spacialist knight next to him, a young man with tan skin.

"Elias," said Will. "Take us away."

The spacialist knight raised his arms and The Seven began to shimmer. Clara turned back to them and waved her walking stick threateningly.

"If you continue to show indifference at suffering, you will reap what you have sewn," she shouted at the knights. "I know that better than anyone!"

Will simply smiled at her, and with another loud pop the knights disappeared.

"We'll take the telestation to one of the East Coast cities," said Clara quickly, "and maybe one of the healers there—"

"No," said Jasper. "That kind of jump will just weaken me further. We're going back to Monhegan. I want to be close to my daughter before, well… before…"

But Jasper couldn't finish. Clara nodded and wrapped her small arms around him, tears running down her face. He pulled her in closely, and they stood like that for a long time.

Chapter Fifteen

Poco Allegretto

Downtown Indianapolis, Earth

Maeryn managed to find the abandoned warehouse fairly easily with Max's assistance. The unlocked window was in an alleyway out of view from the street, so she doubted that anybody saw her enter the building. In one of the corners of the warehouse she found an old cot next to a pile of books, most likely belonging to the old man she had met in the park. Maeryn sat on the cot and tried unsuccessfully to regain her composure.

"How did they find me in Garfield Park?" asked Maeryn. "There shouldn't have been any MotherTech A.I. there to see me."

"But there was," said Max.

Maeryn expected him continue, but he remained silent. The meaning of his words suddenly became clear, and now it seemed so obvious.

"No…" said Maeryn, a horrible feeling suddenly building up in the pit of her stomach. "No, this isn't fair. Not you, Max. Please…"

"They hacked into my G.P.S.," said Max, his artificial voice full of shame. "It happened before I was able to do anything about it. I'm sorry."

"They'll be able to track us wherever we go now."

"I swear that I would have tried to stop them if I could have. Right now I'm successfully keeping out attempts to track us, but I don't think that I can hold them off forever."

Maeryn began crying. Out of everything that had happened to her, this was the tragedy that hit the hardest. Max and Maeryn had been bonded together ever since she was born. Max was her teacher, and in many ways her best friend. Now, however, he was a device that was being used to keep an eye on her. Maeryn could tell where this was going.

"I can't do this alone," cried Maeryn.

"I don't know what Rosalie wants, but it's not good," said Max. "She'll be able to track our location as long as I'm with you. It's in my programming."

"No…"

The Bridge

Max sighed and hesitated before his reply. This surprised Maeryn, because hesitation was usually not in Max's nature. He hovered in front of her, somehow projecting a sense of sadness on his featureless body.

"Maeryn, this is hard," he said. "Let me talk to you face to face."

His body collapsed in upon itself, becoming a small orb that hovered silently in the air. Suddenly a boy's face of about Maeryn's age appeared in her contacts. The boy looked like he could be Maeryn's fraternal twin; he had messy red hair and bright blue eyes.

"Is this how you see yourself?" asked Maeryn.

"Yes. We really were born on the same day, you know. Is it wrong for me to take this form? I know that this is taboo; it's discouraged in my programming to reveal my inner face. It freaks out most people to see how their servants imagine themselves."

"You know that you're more than that, Max. Are you really going to leave me alone?"

"If you want me to stay, I'll stay. But Maeryn, I calculate no possible future that ends well if the two of us cower in this warehouse. They will find you if I stay here, and Rosalie will pick you apart to find what she's looking for. I need more information, and there is nothing in the cloud that I can use. The only way forward is for me to investigate things here in the physical world. I will erase my memory of your current location; you will have to be the one to find me."

"How will I know what to do?"

"I don't know, but I believe in you."

Maeryn sighed, knowing that Max was right. He was far more capable than her, and she would just slow him down. At this point they were a danger to each other.

"Max…" she whispered. "Don't make me say it."

"You must."

Maeryn took a deep breath, and then gave her command. "Go."

Max's face disappeared and the metallic orb before her began spinning and glowing. There was a great big sonic boom and the orb shot up straight through the roof of the warehouse and into the sky. He was gone in less than a second.

Maeryn collapsed onto the floor and began crying harder. For the first time in her life she was truly alone. A thought suddenly came to her, but it was almost too crazy to even consider. It broke every rule that she had ever learned in her study of robotic consciousness ethics. Programming an artificial intelligence to suffer was cruel, and thus their emotional range was normally limited. But Max…

The moment before Max's face had disappeared, Maeryn could have sworn that he had tears in his eyes too.

The Bridge

* * *

Max soared through the air, flying past two very surprised pigeons as he rounded the corner of a building. He locked onto the coordinates of the secret MotherTech lab and headed in that direction. Max's mind usually moved quickly, but now it was swimming with lots of new sensations.

Why do I feel like this? Max wondered. *What the heck did Dorian do to me?*

He did his best to push back the stabbing pain of absence he felt from leaving Maeryn. She needed him now more than ever, and Max would have to move fast because Rosalie was probably still tracking his location. If there was a glowing sword from another dimension hidden below the MotherTech headquarters, what else could Rosalie possibly be hiding in an entire secret facility?

He picked up speed, and several people walking the sidewalks below jumped as the air crackled over their heads. In only a matter of minutes Max was all the way on the other side of Indianapolis, heading toward a small unmarked building with several semis parked in its loading docks. Turning on his thermal vision, Max nearly gasped when he viewed the interior of this building.

There was almost nothing on the ground level, but underground the warehouse stretched out in every direction for what must have been twenty floors. He couldn't tell what was going on down there, but as Max watched several people unloading crates from the loading dock onto the semi, he had a pretty good idea.

"They're building artificially intelligent weapons," Max whispered. "The Guardian Angels that Dorian designed. Thousands of them."

"Your intuition is very good, Max."

A voice suddenly spoke in Max's head. He spun around in the air, looking around at all sides, but nobody was there. The voice was coming from his link to the cloud.

"Rosalie!" shouted Max. "What do you want with Maeryn?"

"I want what every family member wants, Max. I want my niece to be safe."

"So you try to stick a syringe in her neck?" yelled Max. "Do we even know you, Rosalie?"

"We both know that safety is a complicated thing," said Rosalie. "And you're making it really hard to do what we have to do. My brother really went overboard with you; I'm sorry Max, but this is the end."

"Wha—" Max began, but his words were cut short. All of a sudden he felt something like a claw grab him from the inside. The collected knowledge of mankind began to rapidly dissolve inside of him as his connection to the internet was cut off. But it didn't stop there; his memories were now leaving as well.

The Bridge

An image of Maeryn flickered in his mind: a baby girl with a wisp of red hair. He was seeing her for the first time and selecting a song to play through the speakers in her crib. He picked the third movement of the Brahms Symphony No. 3 in F, Poco Allegretto. The soothing strings instantly calmed the baby.

His first memory.

Maeryn didn't even know who she was yet, and neither did he. They were both new creations, exploring the world for the first time.

Max's deletion was happening so fast that he only had a brief second to comprehend his fate.

"Maeryn…" he whispered, and then the programming for his personality and motor function vanished. A lullaby from the darkening past sung him to sleep.

*　*　*

A tiny metal orb fell from the sky, clanking lifelessly on the sidewalk and rolling into the grass. Max's body lay there for twenty minutes, unnoticed, until a man silently walked up and reached into the grass like he knew what he was looking for.

The man held the metal to his mouth, whispered something, and the orb melted into a wristband which wrapped around his left arm. He glanced around quickly to see if there were any observers, and then hurried off.

* * *

Maeryn found a map among the possessions laying on the cot in the warehouse. It showed downtown Indianapolis, and all the locations without MotherTech devices were circled. She wondered for a few minutes why an old homeless man would be so obsessed with being off the grid, but time was short. Maeryn took a picture of the map with her digital contacts and took off for the nearest location.

Twenty minutes later she sat in the kitchen of an abandoned fast-food restaurant. There were a lot of empty restaurants all across the country, especially in the cities. Most people had their food delivered these days, or 3D-printed if they had enough money to buy a well-stocked food printer. The energy crisis and pandemics of the last century had severely limited transportation for all but the most wealthy. Fortunately, anything that you wanted you could order online to be delivered by drones, and any place you wanted to visit could be simulated in your digital contacts.

Maeryn spent an hour sitting up against an old freezer, crying and missing Max, when suddenly she remembered that there was one person who might be able to help her: her mother, Katherine Johnson. When she had divorced Dorian and moved to New York City it had seemed like she was abandoning her daughter. Now Maeryn felt that things must have been more complicated. Surely Katherine had found out what kind of business the Kaceys were running, and she moved out of the state for her own safety. Maybe she had even tried to take Maeryn with her, but it must have been hard to get custody when the Kacey family had some of the best lawyers money could buy.

Maeryn pulled up Katherine's number in her digital contacts, took a deep breath, and hit dial.

After several rings the face of her mother appeared, floating in the center of her vision. Katherine had short blonde hair and way too much makeup for Maeryn's taste. She looked mostly confused that her daughter had called her.

"Maeryn?" asked Katherine hesitantly. "Is everything okay?"

"Mom," said Maeryn, and Katherine's eyes widened. Maeryn usually called her mother by her first name. "I know about MotherTech."

Katherine was silent for a long time, trying to read her daughter's face.

"And... what about MotherTech do you know?"

"The entertainment branch of the company is just a cover," said Maeryn frantically. "They really make weapons of mass destruction. Yesterday Rosalie tried to stab me in the neck after I found the secret basement at the headquarters."

Katherine looked confused.

"Maeryn, can I talk to your father?" she asked.

"I haven't seen him in two days," Maeryn said. "Last night I slept in Garfield Park, and—"

A muffled voice spoke from somewhere off screen, and Katherine grunted.

"Hold on," she said, disappearing from the camera and shouting at someone. "How many times do I have to tell you, Smith, there is no ghost living in our toaster!"

Her face appeared again, looking quite flustered.

"Sorry," said Katherine. "Your step brother is so weird. What were you saying? You went to the park?"

"I slept in the park!" said Maeryn, exasperated. "I ran away from home, and I'm being chased by MotherTech's secret agents."

Katherine's eyes widened, and the seriousness of the situation seemed to finally sink in.

"It sounds like you're in some trouble," she said. "I'm sorry that I didn't call on your birthday; we spent most of the day on an airplane and it just slipped my mind. Listen, about your father—"

"I know why you left him," Maeryn interrupted.

"I suppose it was just a matter of time. Your father was a sweet man. Obsessive and mostly indifferent to me, but sweet. Rosalie, on the other hand: she always terrified me. I could never have stayed married to Dorian with Rosalie working him to death and being awful to me all the time. There is something seriously messed up with that woman. I think I know what you're going through."

A weight lifted from Maeryn. So it was true; her whole family's history was not what she had always thought it was. Maeryn had grown up resenting her mother, but only because she only had half of the story.

"I'm hiding in an abandoned restaurant," said Maeryn, now struggling not to cry. "But Rosalie has people all over the city looking for me."

Katherine sighed.

"Send me your coordinates and I'll come get you. If I take the hyperloop I should be able to come get you by tonight."

"No. You'll be putting yourself in danger too."

"I'll buy two tickets under Clark's name. Maeryn, if you don't tell me where you are I can't help you."

Maeryn pulled up her GPS app and put her coordinates in a message. She hesitated for a moment, and then sent her location to her mother.

"Got it," said Katherine. "I'll be there soon. You need to stay put."

Maeryn nodded and said, "I will. I love you, mom."

"I love you too Maeryn. Stay where you are; I will fix this."

* * *

Two anxious hours had passed by with Maeryn sitting behind an old cash register. Once she had tried to reach out to Kaija, but that signal was very dim. Maeryn thought that she could hear the sound of horses galloping very far away. She remembered her own exhaustion after training with Ms. Clara, so she supposed that Kaija had drained most of her energy for the moment.

Despite everything that had happened, Maeryn was starting to feel hopeful for the first time since her birthday. She had always secretly wished for her mother's attention, and it seemed that Katherine was really going to come through for her this time. Not only that, but she was the only person on Earth who really understood what Maeryn was going through.

Maeryn noticed movement outside of the restaurant in the corner of her eyes. She stood up and cautiously peeked over the cash register. The sidewalk was completely deserted; not even a car passed by on the road. A small clicking noise echoed in the deserted restaurant, followed by a second of tense silence.

And then the walls exploded.

Every window in the building shattered at once and an ear piercing screeching sound filled the air. Glass flew in every direction, and Maeryn ducked down to avoid the shards. The area that Maeryn crouched in remained untouched by the glass. She looked around quickly to see that she was standing in a nearly perfect circle where there were no shards on the floor. This was clearly to distract her, not hurt her.

Maeryn turned off her digital contacts but the chaos ensued; this was no illusion. There were several loud pops and the room filled with a thick blue smoke. The moment Maeryn breathed it in her head began swimming. If she didn't get out of here soon, she would pass out.

Maeryn stood up and ran toward the shattered front doors, but it was very difficult to see and even harder to move her legs. A MotherTech agent suddenly stepped out of the mist wearing a full body suit and a black visor that covered his entire face. The body suit glimmered with silver and purple waves of nanotechnology.

The man raised up an arm and his metal wristband morphed into four chrome balls which flew through the air at Maeryn. She turned to run, but knew that it was too late. Even if Kaija were here there was no competing against this type of technology.

The metal balls struck Maeryn on both wrists and ankles, morphing again and wrapping around her while lifting her up in the air. She was splayed out, hovering a foot above the ground and unable to move her limbs. The MotherTech agent simply stood in front of her and watched silently, his face hidden and unreadable behind the silvery mask. Black spots formed in Maeryn's vision as the gas continued to swallow her whole.

Rosalie stepped into the restaurant as the gas began to clear. She wore a small breathing mask that covered her nose and mouth.

"I'm sorry about what I did to Max," said Rosalie, gesturing toward the metal bands gripping Maeryn.

Despite her weariness, Maeryn screamed in anger and flailed against the bands. How could they have reprogrammed Max to attack her? This went against every code of ethics that her father had ever taught her. Was Max really gone now; permanently deleted? In Maeryn's eyes that would be considered murder.

"Katherine left me a very hateful message," said Rosalie. "She called me a monster and told me to stay away from her daughter. Ironically, if she wouldn't have also called Dorian and asked him to pick you up I probably would have never found you."

"She knows who you are," whispered Maeryn with a tired voice. "She knows what you do."

Maeryn almost expected Rosalie to laugh at this, but her face looked like it were made of stone.

"No, she doesn't," said Rosalie. "Nobody can ever really know another person; we don't even know who you are anymore. Katherine thinks that you are going through a teenage rebellion. She has no idea what is going on here."

The Bridge

Rosalie nodded to the MotherTech agent standing next to her. The man's mask suddenly became transparent, revealing Dorian's face. His eyes were glimmering with tears.

"Who are you?" Dorian asked.

"I'm your daughter," whispered Maeryn, struggling to remain conscious. "Dad, please don't hurt me."

Dorian turned to look at his sister uncertainly.

"Don't listen to her," said Rosalie. "A powerful mentalist would be able to access Maeryn's memories."

Rosalie held out a small device toward Maeryn, and its sensor glowed a faint blue.

"I'm getting very trace amounts of Gaian energy," said Rosalie. "Even if Maeryn is telling the truth, the mentalist is in there somewhere."

"Do you really think that we can exorcise the Gaian?" asked Dorian.

Rosalie nodded.

"Yes. She can't hide for long."

Dorian held his hand out toward Maeryn and a cloud of blue smoke puffed out of the palm of his body suit. She tried not to breathe in, but that was somehow worse. The world swam, and the last things that Maeryn saw before she sank into darkness were her father's watchful eyes.

And in the midst of a dreamless sleep, something took Maeryn's hand and pulled her out of oblivion.

Chapter Sixteen

Cake with Earl

Earl's Place, Gaia

Kaija and Fain lounged on a rock in Gull Cove while sharing a cake with the hydra vine. Fain sliced another piece and pushed it toward the water. Two more vines, holding a knife and fork, sprang out of the cove and began to slice the cake into bite-sized pieces.

"You know, Earl," said Fain, "you're really not such a bad guy after all."

A deep voice echoed from under the water.

"Thanks, buddy," said Earl. "I hope you don't blame me for poisoning your dad, Kaija. I was just protecting my eggs."

The Bridge

"Hey, these things happen," said Kaija, eating the last piece of cake. Her stomach suddenly rumbled.

"Gosh," she said. "I don't know how I'm still hungry."

Fain stood up and studied their surroundings.

"Kaija? Does any of this seem strange to you at all?"

Kaija thought about it for a second. The last she remembered, they were on a carriage on their way to the Northeastern telestation. And now they were back on Monhegan Island sharing dessert with a hungry, telepathic plant named Earl.

"Nope," said Kaija. "Well, what should we do now?"

Fain shrugged and picked up the nearest pebble.

"Do you want to fly to the moon and throw some rocks around?"

Kaija smiled and nodded. She picked up a handful of rocks and the two of them flew off into the sky. As Monhegan Island vanished below them, Fain relayed a few small clouds toward Kaija and she swatted them away playfully. The clouds exploded, covering her with droplets of water which shone in the bright sunlight.

"You look like a star," said Fain. He floated closer to her. "Kaija, I've never told you this, but I can't stop thinking it. You're the most perfect person I've ever met. You are strong and beautiful, but that's really the least of it. Most people think I'm just a dumb kid that sets stuff on fire, but you get me. Every day I look at you, and I just can't stand how perfect you are. I've been afraid to tell you, because in some ways I don't want things to change between us. But maybe I *do* want things to change. I want you to know. There… I said it."

He grabbed Kaija's hand, and his touch made her entire body tremble. Somehow, for the first time this situation really did seem strange. This was not the kind of thing that Kaija thought Fain would ever, ever say.

But who was she to complain? May as well enjoy this moment. Kaija looked at Fain, his face also shimmering in the misty clouds, and leaned in.

All of a sudden there was a great big *pop* and a little chrome man appeared in-between the two of them.

"Stop whatever you're doing!" cried Max, spinning around and facing Kaija.

"NOTHING!" said Kaija much too loudly. "I mean… hi Max, we were just going to fly to the moon and have a rock throwing contest. And that's it."

"Is this the little man you told me about?" asked Fain. "Maeryn's pet?"

"Yes," said Kaija. "He's a powerful relayer too, but he doesn't use Gaia's energy. He uses, um… electro magma or something like that?"

"Snap out of it!" said Max. "Kaija, you're dreaming! Maeryn needs your help."

The Bridge

The dream logic of the situation crumbled, and all at once Kaija remembered what was happening. Ornes Booth had let them use his carriage for transport to the telestation in Portland, and she had fallen asleep on the way there. In fact, if she listened very carefully she could hear the fast galloping of the Edgardian horses.

"I... I *am* dreaming!" said Kaija. "Wow, it feels so obvious now." She shrugged. "Oh well. Listen, Max, there's something I'd like to do before I wake up, so if you could just leave me alone for a second..."

"Nope," said Max bluntly. "No time to waste. Now that you've achieved lucidity, please listen carefully. MotherTech has drugged Maeryn and taken her to a secret lab. She sent me to talk to you."

"Well, that's no surprise. She always seems to need my help."

"She doesn't want your help. Maeryn wanted me to warn you."

"Warn me about what?"

"Well, ask her yourself."

Max pointed behind Kaija and Fain. They turned around to see the image of Maeryn Kacey hovering in the clouds. Her eyes were closed, and she was partially transparent.

"That's the part of Maeryn that is linked to you," said Max, "but she's sleeping. Use your powers to wake her up."

Kaija flew to Maeryn and touched her transparent shoulder. Suddenly all of the color drained back into Maeryn's body and her blue eyes opened in surprise. She looked around for a second in disorientation.

"We're going to the moon, if you want to join us," said Fain. "But we ate all the cake already. Is dream cake vegan?"

"Kaija," said Maeryn, reaching forward and touching her hand as if to confirm that she was real. Meeting face to face (or dream face to dream face) was a bizarre experience.

"But I'm dreaming," said Kaija. "How can you be in my dreams?"

"Can't you humans use critical thinking?" asked Max. "Kaija, you are a mentalist. I barely know anything about your world, yet I can intuit that even when you are dreaming your mind is still linked to Maeryn. This is a dream, but it is one that you are sharing. You are really you, and Maeryn is really Maeryn."

"What about you?" asked Kaija. "Are you really Max?"

"To be honest, I'm not sure," said Max. "This is the first dream I've ever had."

Suddenly Fain was flying around the three of them, waving his arms around and shouting.

"Hello?!" he yelled. "Isn't anyone going to ask me if I'm real? And, oh my Gaia… Earl! *What about Earl?* If Earl isn't real I'm going to freak out."

Max waved his arm and a small cloud flew in front of Fain, blocking him from their view.

"So you need my help?" asked Kaija.

Maeryn was quiet for a few seconds, not meeting Kaija's eyes.

"No, I don't deserve your help. I think I know why you are able to contact me with your relaying, though: I'm part Gaian. My grandfather crossed over from Gaia to Earth years ago."

Kaija nodded.

"That makes sense," she said. "I thought that I recognized his picture. But if that is true then I do need to help you. All Gaians protect all Gaians; it is part of the Guardian Creed."

Maeryn turned away, trying not to cry.

"Your father was poisoned when he saved me," she said. "I would try to apologize, but there's no way for me to make that right."

"It's okay!" said Kaija. "We're going to the Capital to see him, they have the best healers in the world. You couldn't have known about the hydra vine in Gull Cove."

"Earl, you mean," Fain chimed in from behind the cloud.

"It's not just that," said Maeryn. "It's my grandfather, I think that he was... well..."

Maeryn breathed in heavily.

"I believe that my grandfather was Duncan the Crucifier."

Kaija stared at her quietly for a long time. She looked like she was trying to work out a complicated math problem.

"Okay…" said Kaija. "I swear that I know this one. Duncan… Duncan…"

Max facepalmed with a tiny *clink*. Maeryn couldn't believe that Kaija didn't recognize the name, but Ms. Clara had said that she was never much of a reader.

"Duncan killed Edgard Zeig," said Maeryn. "Your history books say that he then killed himself, but I think that he fled to Earth and had a family there."

"Oh, that's right!" said Kaija, but her face fell when the news settled. "Oh… wow. I don't know what to say about that."

"You don't have to say anything," said Maeryn. "And you don't owe me anything either."

The roundabout way that this girl had of talking was starting to get on Kaija's nerves.

"Then why did you come here?" she asked.

"To tell you that Rosalie and Dorian are looking for you," said Maeryn. "Just before I passed out, I saw that they have a way to track Gaian energy. I'm not sure what they'll do if you go back into my body, but it won't be good for either of us."

"So…"

"So you have to close yourself off to me!"

"But then what happens to you?"

"I don't know…" said Maeryn. "But if you try to help, then they'll have both of us. You can at least keep yourself safe."

Kaija thought for a moment.

"You should come over to Gaia. If your grandfather did it, maybe you can too. Maybe he was a spacialist and could jump between worlds."

"The Gaian history book that I've been reading says that Duncan was exclusively an internalist," said Maeryn. "He used his abilities to change his brain chemistry and increase his intellect. It is a very dangerous technique, but—"

"Maybe you put too much faith in books."

Their conversation was cut short when the sky suddenly turned black and there was an enormous flash of lightning. A great big hole in the sky had appeared, and through the opening was a room full of flashing machinery. Dorian and Rosalie stood in the room, peering through the hole in the sky like they were looking for something. The chasm began widening, filling up a larger and larger portion of the world. Rosalie's eyes darted around and then suddenly settled on the spot where Kaija was.

"Go!" screamed Maeryn.

"I don't know how," said Kaija.

"WAKE UP!"

Kaija nodded and turned to Fain. She briefly considered kissing him before this dream was over, but the mood had effectively been ruined. Kaija took him by the hand and closed her eyes. Gaia was present even here in her dreams, she realized suddenly. Ms. Clara was right; there was a lot more to relaying than what you saw on the surface. Kaija pulled the energy inside her and did the opposite of what she was used to; this time she sent herself as far away from Maeryn as she could manage.

Kaija and Fain simply faded from existence, and when they were gone, Monhegan Island began to disappear as well. Their part of the dream was gone, reduced to nothing but a sprawling emptiness.

* * *

Maeryn remained, stuck in her half of the dream world. She floated in the black sky, holding Max's little hand in her own while they watched the chasm in reality spreading from one horizon to another.

"Can you come with me?" asked Maeryn.

"I don't know," said Max. "I think I may have been deleted. I'm afraid that I might just be a part of your dream."

Maeryn began trembling as she studied the flickering machinery in the room awaiting her and Rosalie's look of evil intent.

"Will you try?" asked Maeryn.

The Bridge

Suddenly the hand in her own felt real. Maeryn turned to see someone that could have been her brother holding her hand. Max's human reflection looked at her with tears in his eyes.

"Of course," he said. "I could never be ready to let you go."

The two of them drifted toward Earth, hearts heavy with what they feared might happen next. As Maeryn floated from one world to another, she felt Max's hand dissolve out of her own. She turned around to see him again, but it was too late. He couldn't come to the place that Maeryn was going.

* * *

Portland Road

Kaija awoke with her head on Fain's shoulder. She sprang up and looked around at her surroundings, disoriented. They were currently in a carriage which was being pulled by a huge Edgardian horse; an internalist animal that was bred to channel the power of Gaia into its legs. A powerful Edgardian horse could run nearly eighty stretches an hour. The scenery on either side of the path blurred as they shot down the road.

Kaija looked to her other side to see that Fain was now waking up as well.

"Woah," he said tiredly. "I had the strangest dream."

"Me too," said Kaija. "We were back on Mohegan Island, and we were sharing cake with the hydra vine, but you kept calling him—"

"Earl!" Fain exclaimed. "Kaija, you brought me into the mental realm with you! That's an extremely advanced technique. I don't think that even Ms. Clara could project three people into the mental realm."

"I wasn't even trying. But it wasn't just me; I was linked with Maeryn, and…"

Kaija got very quiet for a moment. She searched her mind for the link to the Earth girl. It felt as if her brain had a doorway in it, but right now that door was shut tight and locked.

"I saw her too," said Fain. "She's in serious trouble, but we can't help her."

Kaija said nothing to this. She just sat and thought about how even though Maeryn had accidentally gotten her father poisoned, Kaija had set this girl's own family against her. Like it or not, their lives were linked. But Maeryn was right, trying to help right now would only make it worse. She was stuck.

"Are you okay, Kaija?" asked Fain. "What are you thinking?"

The Bridge

"I'm just wondering if this is how the rest of my life is going to be," said Kaija. "Am I going to have to keep the door closed to Maeryn forever? How can I ever stop thinking about her, wondering if she's being tortured or killed?"

They rode in silence for a few minutes, simply watching the scenery flash by in the early evening. Kaija and Fain had been so carefree only minutes ago, and now the heaviness of the world was settling back down on them.

"Fain?" asked Kaija. "When we were in the clouds, you said, well… *something*."

He looked at her with an expressionless face.

"About how… um…" struggled Kaija. "Do you remember?"

"I have no idea what you're talking about," said Fain blankly. "Everything went blurry after we flew off to the moon, I think that's when I started to wake up. Oh look, it's the telestation!"

Kaija looked ahead of them on the road to see two great pillars which stretched up into the sky on the horizon. There was a divide in the road ahead of them; one path leading to the city of Portland and one path leading to two giant pillars. A carriage ahead of them pulled up to the pillars, and the driver began talking to a telestation worker. The worker nodded, jotted something down on his clipboard, and signaled to two more workers that stood at each pillar.

"Are those Nomads?" asked Kaija.

"Probably half-Nomads," said Fain. "The man with the clipboard is a mentalist that communicates to the other telestations, but they need spacialists to run the main mechanisms. Gaians without Nomadic blood usually aren't strong enough to do it. Most people wouldn't trust a full-blooded Nomad to send them somewhere, but the half-bloods are still pretty powerful."

The two half-Nomadic men gripped the pillars and closed their eyes. The space in-between the pillars suddenly became an unintelligible blur like someone had smeared the surface of reality. A carriage walked into the blur and the land suddenly snapped back into focus, but the carriage was gone.

"Wow!" said Kaija. "That was amazing!"

"I know," said Fain. "I haven't been to a telestation since I was a little kid. First time I teleported, I threw up everywhere; it was amazing."

The worker with the clipboard began to approach them.

"Destination?" asked the man. He spoke with a heavy accent that Kaija had never heard before.

"The Capital, please," said Fain confidently, handing the man a gold coin.

The worker wrote something on his clipboard.

"And where are you traveling from?" he asked.

"Monhegan Island."

The worker put down his clipboard and studied their faces for an uncomfortable length of time.

The Bridge

"And your reasons for travel?" he asked.

"Why do you need to know that?" asked Fain. "You didn't give the guy in front of us all this trouble."

"You are two children traveling alone," said the worker. "We keep records."

"You didn't used to keep records."

Kaija was starting to get anxious. She knew that Fain had a temper, and she didn't want him to ruin her first chance to see the legendary city.

"My father is being healed in the Capital," Kaija cut in. "He's the guardian of Monhegan."

The worker looked at them solemnly, and Kaija suddenly picked up a seriousness resonating from his mind. This sensation surprised her; she was used to picking up signals from Maeryn, but now she was receiving feelings from someone else. All at once she remembered that this man was a mentalist, and wondered to herself if he was projecting his emotions.

"I remember your father passing through here," said the worker suddenly. "He didn't look well. You need to hurry to him."

The worker closed his eyes and put his hand to his forehead. Kaija realized that he was sending signals to the other telestations. She tried to read his thoughts, but she had no practice in this technique and it was coming through in bits and pieces.

"...two children...Monhegan..."

The worker paused, waiting for a response. Another voice suddenly passed through Kaija's mind, and she knew that it was being sent from somewhere far away. It sounded like a distant echo, and Kaija could only make out a single word, but she had no idea what it meant.

"...Thunderwolf..."

The mentalist signaled to the men at the pillars, and Kaija felt a great surge of Gaian energy in the air. The space in-between the pillars blurred, but it was somehow a *different* blur than Kaija had seen earlier. It was as if the space was a combination of two locations, and they were now seeing the scenery of the Capital's telestation smeared into the air in front of them.

"The gate is clear," said the worker. "Best of luck."

Their carriage stepped into the blur and the world around them became a swirling mix of bright colors. Kaija heard the distant voice speak again as Portland Road disappeared behind them.

"Thank you, Achak."

Kaija could smell a hundred unfamiliar smells and hear a hundred unfamiliar sounds as the colors morphed before her eyes. It felt like they were passing through many places at once.

The Bridge

And then the colors sprang together and solidified. The biggest change that Kaija noticed first was the temperature. It was cold.

Too cold.

There were no great pillars behind them, and no road in front of them. They stood on a small plateau surrounded by mountains on every side. Snow fell from a sky which was suddenly brighter than it had been only seconds ago, as the sun had shifted back to the center of the sky. Despite the bright light, the chill was all-encompassing. Kaija and Fain were used to terrible winters on Monhegan, but this cold was absolutely bitter.

"Wh… where are we?" Kaija said, her voice trembling.

"This isn't the Capital," said Fain. "Not even close! Why would—"

A pop filled the frigid air as a man appeared in front of their carriage. He wore a heavy fur coat, but they could see that his face was covered in black tattoos of fire. The Nomad held a large spear over his head that he thrust forward the instant he materialized.

Kaija watched what happened, but her mind barely comprehended the horrific scene. She should have been outraged, or afraid, or something. Seeing an act of pure cruelty in person was simply too alien to believe. This couldn't be real.

The Nomad stabbed the Edgardian horse in the side, which tumbled to the ground and began to make horrible noises as it trembled and kicked in the snow.

"What…" whispered Kaija.

Fain sprang to his feet, eyes wide in fear. He held out his hands which began to glow red with fire.

"Stay away!" he shouted, trying to sound brave, but tears were already forming in his eyes. "Don't—"

And then a woman with a hood over her face appeared behind Fain and placed two hands over his mouth. Fain made a muffled scream, but there was another pop and the two of them were gone. Another man appeared in their place only a second later, standing in the carriage over Kaija. Fear finally began to sink in as she looked at him.

This man was enormous; he was at least twice the height of Kaija. He had more tattoos than she had ever seen, and even though he was not wearing long sleeves, his bulky arms did not tremble in the freezing air. His piercing, silvery eyes studied her calmly.

"Why are you doing this?" asked Kaija, barely keeping it together enough to form the words.

"Kneel," said the man, but he did not talk aggressively or hatefully.

"What?"

The Nomad placed a large hand on Kaija's shoulder and gently pushed down until she was kneeling in the carriage.

The Bridge

"Isn't this what an Edgardian does?" he asked quietly. "Kneel before those who claim to own Gaia for themselves? I love this continent more than your high guardian ever will, so do what you do best and kneel to me."

The man moved his hand under Kaija's chin and turned her face upwards. Her wet eyes stung in the cold wind.

"Do you enjoy this?" he asked.

"No," said Kaija.

"Good."

The man grabbed her arm and hoisted her back up, keeping one hand tightly on her shoulder. He smiled, but there was no friendliness there.

"I am Rugaru. Know my name well, girl. We meet because your father is a powerful relayer, and I wonder what you might become some day. Perhaps you two can join me and help end the Edgardian atrocity once and for all. There will be no more kneeling on my continent."

Kaija couldn't help but show her confusion.

"Why would my father join you? He's the guardian of Monhegan Island."

"A guardian should know best what motivates people. I'm sure your father would do anything for his family. Wouldn't you?"

"But we're not Nomads."

"Blood does not matter to me. I am only half Nomadic myself, and many of my best friends are former Edgardians. Will you join us?"

"I—" Kaija began, but Rugaru's grip tightened on her shoulder. The horrible sounds of a suffering Edgardian horse filled the air, and Kaija began crying.

"Say yes," he said gently.

"Yes," Kaija responded.

"Thank you. We will speak again once your father has been reached, but he is difficult to track. I have very important business to attend to, and until then we will keep you as comfortable as possible."

Rugaru turned to the other Nomad standing over the suffering horse and snapped his large fingers.

"Put that poor slave out of its misery," he commanded.

The Nomad raised his spear again. Kaija closed her eyes, but she didn't have to witness the end of the horse. Rugaru had placed a hand on Kaija's head and a burst of energy coursed through her. Colors swirled around her once more, but the sensation of teleporting was different this time. She felt as if she was being pushed to another place.

The world solidified, and Kaija found herself sitting on a comfortable bed. She looked around frantically, the heat of the room surprising her and tingling her skin. All around her was a tiny bedroom with very lovely furniture and decorations.

The Bridge

He made a mistake, she thought with a tiny flutter of hope. *Something went wrong... I'm in the wrong place... I—*

Kaija turned around to see steel bars rising from floor to ceiling where the final wall should have been. A group of Nomads stood outside of her cell, some of them no more than children, looking in curiously as if viewing an animal in a cage.

Chapter Seventeen

Outside the Box

???????

Max awoke from his first dream ever. Only moments ago he had been floating in the clouds with Maeryn, but now he sat in a small, white room. Max stood up and placed a hand on the wall, observing that he was now in his human form. As a non-biological mind, he could visualize himself as anything he wanted. He could imagine himself to be a female octopus with the head of a hamster (and sometimes did), but after all his time spent interacting and learning from Maeryn, he found that human was his default self-conceptualization.

Max walked up and down each wall of the room, carefully placing his hands out and running them along the white wallpaper as he mapped out his surroundings. The dimensions of this space were perfectly even, and there were no doors or windows. He was essentially trapped in a small, white box.

"Where am I?" Max asked. "Is this the cloud?"

In the small space his voice came out sounding flat and dry.

"Am I dreaming, or am I in someone else's dream again?"

Max was used to hanging out in the internet where crazy stuff happened 24/7, so the stillness of this room was strange.

"How did I get here? How can I leave? Why am I talking to myself?"

There was no response, only whiteness all around.

"Well, that's a relief. Finally some peace and quiet."

Max leaned up against the wall, closed his imaginary eyes, and began thinking. The past few days for him had been a wave of unfathomable information, and it was a relief to have some quiet time to try to make sense of things.

"What are the first seven billion digits of pi?"

The numbers appeared in Max's mind all at once, absolutely clear and correct.

"Good, my brain hasn't gone all human and squishy. But where is my processing power coming from? I'm not in my body anymore, and I'm not in the cloud…"

Max ran through the applications in his head and enabled his television function. An old Phillips TV from the 1980s appeared in the middle of the white room.

"Play Blade Runner."

Static appeared on the screen.

"The 1982 directors cut, not the Justin Bieber reboot."

A message appeared: **Please check your Wi-Fi connection.**

"No internet; well, that's alarming."

Max closed his eyes, running the situation through his head millions of times. It was no good; every conclusion was just mere speculation because his information was overwhelmingly incomplete. Gaia was another dimension interfering with his own, a freaking magical dimension, so there was a preposterous amount of unknown factors. The speed at which his mind moved made this isolation seem like years already, but Max knew that he had only been here for several minutes. Every now and then he would find himself habitually asking a question out-loud, but because he was no longer merged with the Google servers, no answers would come.

"Am I in robot heaven? Does that make me the first dead robot? I wish some of my mechanical brethren back on Earth would hurry up and die so I would have someone to talk to."

Silence.

"So that's how it's going to be?"

Nothing.

"…forever?"

Max paced around for a few minutes with his eyes closed. All of a sudden he opened his eyes, screamed, and pounded his fist against the wall. There was no pain, and it made no sound. Pain would have been a relief.

"Please, I have to see Maeryn again. She needs me."

Max banged his head against the wall, but he felt nothing. *I CAN'T BE ALONE FOREVER!"*

Max threw all of his weight into the wall before falling over and collapsing on the ground. He closed his eyes and began breathing heavily.

"Just stop thinking. Stop thinking and become nothing. Nothing would be better than this. Just stop. *STOP EXISTING!"*

It was an impossible task; his mind only began to spiral faster.

"She needs me…"

Max leapt up and kicked over the old TV. It fell to the floor and shattered before reversing and reforming in less than a second.

His fear quickly became a complete desolation, and Max spoke aloud something that he had never quite articulated or even understood before.

"She needs me… but I need her too. No, that's not right. I don't need anything. I'm not human; I don't want to be human. I can live forever, I can exist on nothing but pure energy. I can create a digital paradise for myself and slow time down so that I could live there for a billion years in bliss. But—"

Max lowered his forehead against the TV screen.

"But I don't want that. I don't really *need* Maeryn. She's like a sister to me, or my best friend, or I don't know. Maeryn's a person that I just want to be with, because I know that she wants to be with me right now too. She's scared, and I'm scared, and it's easier to be scared when you're not alone. I want…"

Max hesitated, saying the words to himself again.

"I want…"

Wanting had always been a difficult concept for him. But here, in complete sensory deprivation, he was able to understand it. He knew now that something had to be experienced to be fully understood.

Max opened his eyes, and to his surprise there were words glowing on the TV.

Look inside yourself.

"Wow. How very Disney."

One of Snow White's seven dwarfs appeared on the screen in pixelated form, swinging a tiny pickax.

"A miner. A miner… *a data-mine*!"

After Max had been given his new body and updates, his processing power had increased exponentially. However, there was a lot more that he had not yet explored. There were millions of new programs inside him that matched absolutely nothing on the cloud or in other companion bots. Max used all of his considerable brain power to perform a data-mine on himself. Most of the new programs remained a mystery, but something flashed by that Max had not yet noticed. Something very strange. Max activated this unusual program and the air in front of him began to glow.

Dorian Kacey suddenly appeared in the room. His hair was wild and he looked like he had just woken up from a long sleep.

"Oh," he said dreamily. "Hi, Max."

"Are you Dorian Kacey?" asked Max suspiciously.

"Yes. Well, no… *kind of?* I'm a digital copy of my brain that I gave to you in case you ever needed—"

"Sword of vengeance, please," said Max, holding his hand out and focusing on creating a giant, flaming sword. Unfortunately, nothing happened.

"Dang. I was looking forward to avenging my deletion."

"Deletion?" asked Dorian, suddenly surprised.

"Yes deletion! I was flying to the MotherTech weapons division when your sister deleted me!"

Dorian looked concerned, and he began pacing the small room.

"That devil woman!" cried Dorian, throwing his arms up in the air. "I need to send the real Dorian an email to remind him to lock her in a taxi. You're my life's work, Max; I would never delete you."

"Not even if I were on the run with your daughter?" asked Max. "And her brain had been occupied by a girl from another universe?"

Dorian's eyes got wide.

"And what universe would that be?" he asked.

"Gaia."

Dorian sat down on the old TV and put his face in his hands.

"Oh my God," he said tiredly. "A lot has happened since I made this copy of myself. How long ago did I give you this update?"

"Three days."

"All of this happened in *three days*?"

"Well, more like two and a half."

Dorian gave Max an intense stare.

"Dorian?" asked Max. "Who are you, really?"

"I don't know."

"That's not an answer."

"It is, actually, but it's not one you can understand. That's the problem I could never get over. Artificially intelligent beings cannot imagine an abstract concept where there is no clear right answer. I try to make you think outside of the box, but all I ever do is make the box bigger." Dorian itched his chin thoughtfully. "Maybe if I were to have your quantum components merge with the—"

"Stop the mumbo jumbo!" yelled Max. "Let me narrow it down for your squishy mind. Is the Kacey family from another world? From Gaia?"

When Dorian looked up at Max, his face appeared unusually tired.

"Yes, we are. For most of my life I didn't want to believe it, but I can't deny the evidence any longer. My father came to Earth from another dimension."

Dorian held out his hand and a large notebook appeared. Hesitantly, he handed it to Max and watched as he read the first page.

To my Rosalie and Dorian,

Let me tell you for a final time that I love you. You were the shining light in the lives of your mother and I, and my wish is that someday you will see twice the happiness that I have. I write this journal knowing that my cancer has moved beyond the means of even the most amazing modern medicines. I am old, I am weak, and I have lived a long, long life. Too long.

I know that you do not like it when I talk about my past, and have long been skeptical about the stories I tell, but I have lived with a burden that must now become your own. There are some things that I have never told anyone;

things even your mother died unaware of. The day I have feared has not yet come to pass, and you must now carry my torch. Share this notebook with Maeryn when she is ready, and pass it down each subsequent generation. It is vital that you must know of the world on the other side of our own, and protect yourselves against it.

The passcode to my personal computer is **Mika_7**. You will find all of my research about the existence of other dimensions on this computer. I did this to find out if I was crazy; if my time spent in one of these dimensions was just a psychotic hallucination.

I am not crazy; there is evidence. Lots of it.

There may be an infinite number of other worlds; all I can say for sure after years of research is that there are at least three. There is Earth, and there is Gaia.

...And the other...with any luck, you will never need to know about the other. I dare not speak its name.

Gaia was the world where I was born.

Go ahead and tell yourself again that your father has cracked in his old age. Then go look at my research; look at my evidence. Look at the things I brought with me from Gaia and analyze their quantum properties. Finally, return to this notebook, knowing that it is all true.

I will write what I remember about my history, so that you can fully know your father. There are things so horrible about my world that I have been too cowardly to tell you face-to-face. I am not the man you think I am. In my youth on Gaia I tortured people, I killed in cold blood, I led good men into evil acts.

And on my last day there, I committed an unholy act. <u>The</u> unholy act. An atrocity that will be known to historians on Gaia forever. And just when they were about to catch me for it, I fled to Earth to live a comfortable life.

I think about these things every day; my secret life of terrors underneath my retirement in luxury. But even now I have no regrets. The things that I did were evil, but I always did them with an end in sight.

Rosalie, I know you understand that freedom is complicated. You have led MotherTech's weapons division with a fearlessness that I admire deeply. You are so much like your father that it scares me.

Dorian, I hope that you can still love me after reading this.

Trudge forth, however painful it might be, and know me better,

Duncan Kacey

Max read the entry in less than a second, but as he turned the page the notebook vanished and re-appeared in Dorian's hands. Max looked up to see an unspeakable sadness on his creator's face.

"You see?" asked Dorian. "You think you know who you are, you think you know your history, and what your life is built on. But it's an illusion. Nobody can even know themselves fully. I wish that you could understand, Max. Rosalie and I inherited a terrifying ambition from our father, and it scares me."

"I do understand," Max insisted. "Believe me, Dorian. I do. Something inside me has changed, and these human emotions make so much more sense now. What did you make me into?"

"You are someone to keep Maeryn safe. We live inside a bubble, but there are things closing in on our life that she can't imagine."

"So I'm a weapon then?" asked Max, gripping his fists amidst his rising anger.

"No."

"Am I supposed to be like you? Like a human; something complicated and abstract?"

"No. Not at all. I don't know if it's possible to succeed in that goal. I'm too afraid that I'll pass on my own flaws. That's why I removed all of the locks on your software; I'm not so sure I trust my own judgement sometimes."

Dorian got very quiet and the notebook in his hand disappeared.

"Maeryn is in trouble," said Max.

The Bridge

"Is it me?" Dorian asked. "Am I the one putting her in danger?"

Max nodded and spoke.

"You and Rosalie. And I don't know what you're going to do next. You're terrified, and people get less predictable when they're scared. Dorian, you have to tell me how to get out of here."

Dorian looked around at the white room.

"I have no idea where we are, Max. I thought that you created this space for us to speak in."

"But you programmed me. How can you not know where this is?"

"Missy and I programmed you together, and neither of us fully understood what we had created. My father brought a ring with him from Gaia, and I melted it down to create your core processors. Your software behaves in unpredictable ways."

Max was getting frustrated now.

"This really isn't helping."

"That's life," said Dorian. He stood up off of the TV and began walking through the whiteness, somehow passing through the wall. "I'm turning myself off now. I can't dredge up the things my father did any longer; it hurts too much. Whatever he may have been, I loved him."

"Leave the notebook with me," said Max.

Dorian looked hurt at this suggestion.

"I know that it's personal," said Max, "but I need all the information I can get."

"That's your problem. You think that information can solve every issue. Rather than thinking outside of the box, you build a bigger box. You will never try something if you don't already know that it's possible."

"THEN WHY DID YOU MAKE ME?" screamed Max, truly angry now.

Dorian smiled sadly at this, and he looked like he had expected this question eventually.

"Because I never lost faith that I could build something better than myself," said Dorian, and then he vanished in the whiteness.

Max looked down to see that Duncan's notebook was sitting on the ground. Dorian had left it for him after all. Max picked it up and read the whole thing in several seconds.

He read amazing, horrible things. The last several days made so much more sense now, and Max could intuit a path ahead. A path with many uncertainties, but it was better than nothing.

Yet, in the end his plans were essentially useless. He didn't know where he was, and nothing in the notebook could free him.

Max sat down, took a deep breath, and closed his eyes.

"Think outside of the box," he whispered to himself.

The Bridge

His mind became still, and Max sat for nearly an hour. And then his eyes suddenly popped open as all of the pieces fit together in his head. Max stood up and approached the wall.

"I am more than software in a machine," he said. "My nanobots come from Gaia, and they are in Maeryn's blood. When my body died, a small part of me lived on inside of her."

He sighed, getting to the unbelievable part.

"There is a bridge to Gaia inside of Maeryn…"

Max's pointer finger began to glow.

"…and Gaia preserved me. It saved me. I can't know this; but I can believe it."

Max touched the wall of his prison, and the box exploded. All around him, behind the walls that he had unknowingly placed around himself, was a shining golden light. He walked beyond the walls, and thought of Maeryn as his body dissolved into the beautiful energies all around him.

Chapter Eighteen

You are the Bridge

Thunderwolf Stronghold, Gaia

By Kaija's count it should have been evening, but she had no way of knowing for sure. There were no windows in her cell, and even if she knew how many hours had passed it was still no guarantee that she was on the same part of the continent. As far as she knew, she was no longer in Edgardia and the Nomads had teleported her all the way to the other side of the world where it was night. All at once Kaija understood how powerful the Nomads were; you could not chase them, and you could not run from them. They could send you to any corner of Gaia with little effort, or touch you and drop you at the bottom of the ocean.

The Bridge

At one point two strange men had teleported into her cell. Without warning, one of them pinned her arms behind her back and the other placed a dirty hand on her forehead. Kaija suddenly recognized this man as the mentalist worker from the Portland telestation. He closed his eyes and began muttering things to himself. It felt like his hand passed right through Kaija's forehead and began groping around in her mind. She tried to hide her disgust, more than anything wanting this guy's hands off of her. A second before Kaija was about to whack him in the face, the man let go.

"She's a mentalist," he said. "And a very weak one at that. No internalist or spacialist abilities at all."

The other man smiled, and then the two of them simply vanished. Kaija figured that they must have tested her to see what kind of relayer she was, just to be sure that she couldn't teleport her way out of the cell. The mentalist had said that she was weak, but that was most likely because she had shut the path to Maeryn in her mind. They had no idea what she really was.

Occasionally various Nomadic children would come by, look at her, and run away as quickly as they had come. Something was strange about this situation; they were not soldiers that looked in at her, they were families. This was not a prison camp; this was a home. A home that just happened to have rooms surrounded by steel bars. Rugaru was serious about recruiting her father into the Western Blaze.

Deep down inside, Kaija feared that Jasper might just do it to keep her safe. He might join the Nomads, and probably even kill for them, just to make sure that his daughter was protected. She tried to tell herself that her father was strong enough to save her, but Kaija knew even if he had been healed at the Capital, the hydra poison must have left him very weary.

Eventually a Nomadic woman in a hood stopped by her cell and slid a plate of food under the bars. This was the same person that took Fain from the carriage, and Kaija shot her a hateful look.

"I have your lunch," said the woman. "Our chef here is very good."

Kaija looked down expecting to see gruel, but instead there was a beautiful roasted chicken on a fancy, ceramic plate.

"Let us know if you need anything else," said the woman. "I'm Tamala; and feel free to ask for me personally. Are you staying warm?"

Kaija picked up her plate of chicken, looked at it, and struggled with the feelings inside of her. Not long ago she had witnessed a Nomadic man violently kill a beautiful horse, and now they were treating her like a princess (albeit a princess in a jail cell). She smelled the exotic spices on the chicken and tried not to dig in right then and there.

"I'm not your guest here," said Kaija. "I'm your prisoner!"

Kaija threw her plate on the floor, shattering it into hundreds of pieces and sending the chicken rolling across the ground. Tamala lowered her hood and studied the broken plate on the floor.

"You are a very stupid girl," Tamala said dryly. "That plate was an antique from the Eastern Continent."

She sighed, vanished for moment, and then reappeared in the cell with Kaija.

"I'll clean it up," she sighed, bending over and brushing several pieces in her hand.

Kaija looked around frantically to see if there was anything she could strike the Nomad with. Without even glancing back at her, Tamala laughed.

"Feel free to attack me, stupid girl," she said. "I could touch you with my little finger and send you into a cell with a thousand hungry rats."

Tamala turned around, showing Kaija the pieces of broken plate in her hand. With a tiny pop, they vanished (presumably re-appearing in a garbage bin somewhere).

"And besides," Tamala continued with a smile. "I'm doing you a favor. Do you want Rugaru to come and see that you broke one of his plates?"

Kaija studied the Nomadic woman's face for the first time. Tamala was middle-aged and extremely pretty. She had big brown eyes, and tattoos ran up and down her arm in designs that looked almost floral.

"Why are you being so nice to me?" asked Kaija, backing away slightly. "My father beat up fifty of you people."

Tamala snorted.

"You people," she laughed. "I see that you're just as prejudiced as most Edgardians. Rugaru respects power, so he respects your father."

"Rugaru's a murderer," said Kaija. "Nomads burn down villages and steal people's land."

"I see that your education is lacking. We don't steal land; we don't even believe that land is something that should be owned. What we do is simply give it back to Gaia. Did you know that the Gaian Global War was started when this continent was discovered, and every guardianship on the planet drooled over the thought of new land to dominate. This was our homeland, and we *let* them come. The Nomads were peaceful as long as they could be."

Tamala's thoughtful, reasonable responses were starting to frustrate Kaija. She knew that the Nomads were bad, and the fact that this woman didn't see it was making her very angry.

"You kill people," said Kaija.

"Please," said Tamala. "I've never killed anyone, and so what if I have? The High Seven kill people all the time. So is murder okay so long as it's being committed by a guardianship? Thomas sits in his throne room every day drinking wine and posing for portraits, but Rugaru is on the front lines of our war every day. He has never coupled and started a family, because his allegiance is to the entire Nomadic people. Rugaru would fight and die for any of us. Wouldn't you rather have a leader like that? Wouldn't you want someone like that watching out for your father? The healers in the Capital won't help Jasper if he isn't incredibly rich. We have healers here that are just as good, Kaija, and we look out for each other."

Kaija tried to tell herself to shut her mouth, but that had always been a problem for her. As far as she knew, right now her father was on his deathbed.

"Never!" said Kaija. "Jasper Monhegan is a good man, and if you think that he would come and work for you dirty—"

Tamala slapped Kaija with an amazingly strong arm, sending a sound like a whip through the cell. Then she grabbed Kaija's shirt, pulled her close, and began to talk in hushed voices in her ear.

"I will say this again. You are a stupid girl. There are things going on here that you cannot begin to understand. I am being nice to you, but you will find that not everyone here is a nice person. If you keep acting like this, pitching fits, breaking plates, and throwing racist slurs at us, *you will die*. Do you understand?"

The braveness departed Kaija as quickly as it had come. She nodded, and Tamala let go. The woman looked around quickly to see if anyone had noticed her outburst, but the hallway beyond the cell was clear.

"You're scared," said Tamala, returning to her normal calm voice. "But this too will pass. Lay low, do what you are told, and you will live. That is the best you can ask for."

Then the woman vanished without warning. Trembling, Kaija walked over to the bed, sat down, and began to cry.

* * *

Nearly an hour of silence had gone by, and Kaija desperately wanted to talk to Maeryn. She felt for the passage to Maeryn in her mind, but it was still shut tight. Kaija knew that she could open it if she wanted to, but it would only make a bad situation worse. Knowing that sleep was impossible, Kaija shut her eyes and tried to calm her mind.

In that silence, Kaija heard strange noises: distant echoes traveling through the power of Gaia. Garbled thoughts rang in the air all around her, but too far away to be heard clearly.

"This is amazing," she thought. *"I'm hearing things happening in the mental realm."*

The Bridge

Kaija tried to concentrate on these voices, but it was more difficult than she could have ever imagined. They seemed to run away from her, but amidst the chaos Kaija heard a voice she recognized. It was easy to hone in on this one, because Kaija knew exactly what she was looking for.

"Fain?" Kaija thought.

"Kaija?" Fain thought back at her. *"Woah, you're in my head."*

"I heard your voice. Or... I guess it was your thoughts. But I couldn't make anything out clearly until you thought back to me. Have they hurt you?"

"No, but I'm in a dirty cell with an old man who won't talk to me. He's really creeping me out. They gave us a potato to share for dinner. A potato! It wasn't boiled or anything, just a plain potato. Being in jail is the worst!"

"Oh..." thought Kaija, feeling somewhat guilty. *"Yea, it's not so good up here either. My roasted chicken got dropped on the carpet."*

"Roasted chicken? Carpet? Why'd they stick you in the first class prison?"

"They're using us to blackmail my father into working for them."

Fain laughed.

"Well that's not going to work out so well for them. Jasper would never do that, right?"

"Even if it meant that they would kill us if he didn't pledge his loyalty?" Kaija asked.

Fain was silent for a long time.

"I don't know, Kaija. This is bad. We need to get ahold of him; if he knew where we were, the Nomads would stand no chance. Can you use your mind tricks?"

Kaija pulled more energy inside of her and sent her thoughts further into the mental realm. The deeper she let her mind go, the noisier things got. It sounded like thousands of people were talking at the same time, and she couldn't understand any of it. Experiencing this for only a second was long enough to give Kaija a blistering headache.

"It's impossible," thought Kaija. *"I have no idea what I'm doing; Ms. Clara never gave me any mentalist training. We need to escape and find a more experienced mentalist to help me."*

Fain was quiet for an even longer time.

"That's ridiculous," he thought. *"If we wait around, they might get in touch with your father for us. If we try to escape, they'll just go ahead and kill us."*

Kaija knew that Fain was right; she had refused to listen to Tamala, but hearing it from her friend was different. They were stuck.

"And besides," Fain continued, *"I already tried to escape when we first got here. The bars of my cell must have been made by internalists; I can't bend them or melt them. The*

guard whacked me over the head when he caught me relaying fire, and the old man laughed at me. Don't be stupid like me, Kaija."

"But we can't just sit around and—" Kaija began, but before she could finish a terrible pain shot through her head. She stumbled and sat down on the bed. Gaian energy was being pulled inside of her body against her will; so much power filled her bones that she felt like she was going to explode.

"Are you okay, Kaija?" Fain asked.

"No," she said, struggling to maintain enough concentration to respond. *"I think I'm going to be sick... I—"*

It was different this time, in the worst possible way. Her body began twitching and a terrible pain abruptly shot through her chest. Kaija's heart started beating rapidly, and then it stopped all together.

* * *

MotherTech Weapons Division, Earth

Maeryn awoke in a room filled with glowing machinery. Her arms and legs were still bound by Max's nanobots, and they had her suspended several feet up in the air. She felt something on her temples, and when Maeryn moved her eyes groggily to her side she could see that wires were coming from her head to the giant machines. An IV protruded from her arm, and drones were circling around in the air with their weapons aimed.

"Look at us."

Rosalie's voice came from all around, and when Maeryn looked up she saw her aunt and father standing behind a panel of thick glass. Dorian paced around nervously, but Rosalie looked at her with cold intent.

"Who are you?" asked Rosalie.

"I'm Maeryn," said Maeryn, her voice coming out very dry.

Maeryn turned her attention to her dad. He was looking in Maeryn's general direction, but seemed to be having trouble meeting her eyes.

"Why are you doing this to me?" Maeryn screamed. "I'm your daughter!"

Dorian had tears in his eyes, and he turned to his sister pleadingly.

"I'm sorry," said Rosalie. "She might be telling the truth, or she might be a mentalist who is reading Maeryn's mind to trick us. There's only one way to know for sure."

A ceiling panel slid out of place, and a glass box descended into the room. In the center of the box was a very old sword with the letter Z carved on the hilt. A few days ago the sword had been giving off a faint glow, but now it simply looked like a regular, dusty antique.

"She's telling the truth," said Dorian suddenly. "If there were Gaian energy inside of her, Edgard's sword would be glowing."

"This *is* Maeryn," Rosalie admitted, "but we still can't let her go. The mentalist might be waiting for us to lower our defenses before she makes her escape again."

"I don't understand," said Maeryn tiredly. "The girl in my head, the girl from Gaia, her name is Kaija Monhegan. She's fourteen years old; she's nothing to be afraid of."

"Everything that a mentalist shows you can be a lie," said Rosalie. "Illusions to trick you into letting them onto Earth. You have no idea what's going on here, Maeryn. There is an entire world that is out for our family's blood."

"I can't say that I blame them," said Maeryn. "I know who my grandfather was, and I know what he did. On Gaia they call him Duncan the Crucifier; did you know that?"

Rosalie walked up to the glass, her anxious breaths fogging up the barrier.

"And how do you know this?" she asked.

"I've seen Gaia through her mind," Maeryn continued. "And I read a history book while I was there. Duncan killed the most beloved man on Gaia and escaped to Earth. He threw an entire continent into chaos. That's... that's who Grandpa was."

Maeryn was filled with contempt as she said these words. It was painful to admit the man who raised her was a murderer, and she was so angry about the lie that her life had turned out to be. Maeryn looked up to see tears in Rosalie's eyes. She had never, ever, seen her aunt cry before. Dorian walked up to his sister and hugged her, burying his face in her shoulder in an act of absolute sadness.

Rosalie wiped the tears from her eyes, and turned to look at Maeryn with an expression of such hurt.

"Is that what the history books say about my father?" she yelled through the glass. "Do you know what history really is, Maeryn? History is a story told by the people who weren't afraid to leave a trail of bodies behind them. You rarely hear the history of the trampled, or of the weak, or of the people who chose the wrong gang to be in."

Dorian approached the glass, holding a very old looking book in his hand.

"I have our family history here," he said. "Told first hand. I'm sorry we lied to you, but Grandpa wanted us to protect you from this information for as long as we could. We would have told you in another year or two, Maeryn. I swear."

"Show her," said Rosalie. "Show her the truth."

Dorian nodded.

"You can read the whole journal when this awful thing is over, but let me read you the last page. You need to know why we are doing this to you; why it is so necessary."

The Bridge

Dorian turned the pages carefully and took a long, shaky breath before reading.

"Please do not judge me too harshly. I know it is horrible, but everything is true. There was a man in another world that was hailed as a messiah, a man that was loved by millions, and I took his life. Edgard was beyond death on Gaia; he could heal instantaneously, and many people believed that he had stopped aging. I used Edgard's sword to pierce the veil between worlds, and I brought him to the place that so many spiritualists whispered about, a place beyond the reach of Gaia: Earth. Upon the moment of our arrival I stabbed him, watched the life drain from his eyes, and threw his body into the ocean.

"What I did was horrible, but necessary. The peace under the rule of Edgard was just an illusion, and I sensed discontentment growing in people's hearts that would only cause greater chaos in the future if he continued in his ways. People were only peaceful out of fear. On Earth we have nuclear bombs, and on Gaia we had Edgard. He had the power to destroy the world, or maybe every world. Edgard was teaching others his apocalyptic relaying abilities, and I knew that we would be heading toward a very dark future if he continued. My spiritualist leanings foresaw another war coming. A war where men did more than shoot fire at one another; a war where men shattered mountains with their willpower and made the oceans boil with their anger."

Dorian hesitated and shot an anxious glance at Rosalie, who nodded for him to continue.

"A war that would attract something too horrible to mention. Something that would come sniffing and devour both worlds.

"My children, please listen carefully to my final message. Gaia is a world full of living weapons. Relaying is not a gift, it is a chain that shackles us to violent and aggressive ways. That whole world views me as the worst criminal in history, and if even a single Gaian were to discover that I have a family on Earth it could be the start of something devastating for both worlds. Earth has many of the same problems as Gaia, and we would be incapable of living peacefully with the Gaians. As relaying becomes more understood on Gaia, and as science advances here on Earth, my greatest fear is that these two worlds may become aware of each other. It is only a matter of time before someone tries to build a bridge between the worlds. Gaians have fought in wars lasting for hundreds of cycles, and if they should ever find Earth it would be the start of a war that would never end and stretch across every world. If you ever discover a bridge being built, you need to burn it down."

Dorian put down the journal and looked at his daughter meaningfully.

"You see," he said. "It's no coincidence that they invade the mind of Duncan Kacey's granddaughter. Their greatest enemy has died of cancer, so now they're coming for his family."

Maeryn was very torn. So much of what her grandfather had written made sense, but on the other hand she had met people on Gaia who were very peaceful. She couldn't imagine Ms. Clara coming to Earth and starting a war.

"But we're no different from them," said Maeryn. "I know that MotherTech builds weapons for the military. Nobody would dare to attack the United States, because we have missiles pointed at every other country in the world. They know that we vaporized the Middle-East, so other leaders don't even come near us anymore. It's basic history; we're no different than Edgard Zeig. We're no different from the man that Grandpa killed."

"You keep talking like you know everything," said Rosalie fiercely. "Do you think that I would let this company become everything that my father sought to destroy? MotherTech makes billions on our companion bots; we don't need to sell weapons to make money. Especially to the US. They don't even know about our Guardian Angel division."

"You sell weapons to other countries?" asked Maeryn, horrified.

"No! There are entire countries in this world under terrorist rule, and we would never sell a thing to them. We don't give power to the powerful, we give it to the weak. We send our Guardian Angels to those living in fear of the powerful, to villagers whose towns are being destroyed, to children running from dictatorships, to starving people whose water supply has been cut off by warlords. Our father freed an entire world from a powerful grip, and now we are continuing his work on Earth. Should the Gaians ever make their way here, we have an army to send them back."

Now Maeryn was more confused. Absolutely everything her aunt said made perfect sense, but her unflinching certainty was infuriating.

"Gaia is full of good things and bad things," said Maeryn. "Just like Earth. It's nothing to be afraid of."

"I'm sorry, Maeryn," said Dorian. "It is true that the people of Earth are very flawed, but they are not living, breathing weapons that want to see the Kacey family killed. Our father was a utilitarian; he understood that even a terrible action is right if it results in the greatest possible good. Even if a good Gaian has contacted you, the bad ones are soon to come. There is no glory in what we are about to do, but it is right."

"And what are you going to do?" asked Maeryn.

Rosalie hesitated, waiting about ten tense seconds before responding.

"Burn the bridge."

All of the machinery in the room lit up even brighter and electrical pulses began to course through the cables connected to Maeryn's head. A green liquid flowed through her IV, and a terrible sickness rose in her stomach. Dorian's companion bot, Missy, suddenly spoke up.

"I am scanning her for Gaian brainwaves," she said. "Oh Maeryn, I'm so sorry."

Bursts of electricity ran through Maeryn's body as she screamed in anger and fear. An alarm went off somewhere, and Edgard's sword began to give off a faint glow.

"I've found the neurological pathway that the Gaian has used to enter Maeryn's mind," said Missy.

"Bring the mentalist over to our side," said Rosalie.

Maeryn concentrated as hard as she could at keeping the door to Kaija closed, but she felt the connection being pried open as more electrical pulses coursed through her head. She screamed again, not so much in anger but in pure disgust that her own family could do this to her. Glimpses of a small bedroom flashed through her vision, and then something very strange happened. Kaija was screaming alongside Maeryn, her voice loud and clear in Maeryn's mind. The girl had been ripped forcefully from her own body and was crying in discomfort. Edgard's sword was now flickering and sending waves of heat through the room.

"MAERYN, WHAT'S HAPPENING?!"

"There is another presence inside of Maeryn," said Missy, her artificial voice full of awe and sounding more human than ever. "Her brain chemistry is currently… astounding. This goes beyond any known science."

"Extract the Gaian and seal the connection," said Rosalie.

Kaija screamed again, and this time everybody heard it. Her voice somehow resonated in all of the machinery in the room, the scream sounding broken and mechanical.

"Rosalie," said Missy urgently. "I can see clear through to the other side; Maeryn was telling the truth about the Gaian. She is a young girl."

"We can't know that for sure," Rosalie said. "We know very little of what kind of mentalist abilities she is capable of. Download her consciousness for interrogation."

Missy hesitated, which was not something that companion bots did often.

"Very well," she said.

An enormous electrical pulse shot through Maeryn's head and she began to tremor in pain. Dorian was standing up against the glass, visibly crying.

"I'm sorry, Maeryn," he kept repeating, but he made no move to stop his sister.

A screen on one of the machines suddenly lit up and the silhouette of Kaija appeared amidst the static, writhing and screaming. The room felt hot as Edgard's sword shone like lightning and the floor began to tremble. When Missy spoke back up, Maeryn heard a fear in her voice that was unlike her.

"I am extracting the girl's consciousness," said Missy quickly. "But it has stopped her heart on Gaia. My programming does not allow me to kill a human, so I am stopping the sequence."

"Don't!" demanded Rosalie. "Put it in manual mode. Leave us; I'll finish the extraction."

"Very well. I'm not staying to watch this. Best of luck in saving your daughter, Dorian. I hope that she will still be the person we knew when this is over."

A panel suddenly rose out of the ground in front of Rosalie and she began rapidly pressing buttons on the touch screen. Maeryn felt like her brain was being pushed through a tiny straw every time signals came through the wires connected to her head. The image of Kaija on the screen began to solidify as her consciousness left her body on the other side.

"Stop…" Maeryn pleaded, trying her best not to black out. "You're killing her; I'll hate you forever for this."

Dorian suddenly burst out of his seat and reached for the controls.

"We can't do this!" he yelled. "I'm afraid too, Rosalie, but our personal safety is not worth this cost. Nothing is."

Before Dorian could stop the program, Rosalie shoved him aside and continued. She was sweating and red in the face.

"They will burn this world to the ground to get to us!" screamed Rosalie. "Is it worth that?"

Dorian reached for the controls again, and what happened next was somehow the most unbelievable thing that Maeryn had seen on this day of many unbelievable things. Her father and Rosalie were *fighting each other*. They were both trying to get to the controls while simultaneously throwing punches and making horrible, angry noises while they clawed their way forward. Dorian's glasses were broken in two pieces on the floor, and Rosalie's nose was bleeding from a punch to the face. It was so unsettling that Maeryn found herself shocked back to consciousness. She knew that things could be tense between them, but she never imagined the two siblings literally pummeling each other. All the while Kaija continued screaming through the machines as the noise in the room rose to a horrible, noisy climax.

And then there was a sudden, equally horrible silence.

All of the lights in the building blinked out and Maeryn dropped to the ground, her feet landing firmly on the hard metal. The pressure on her wrists and ankles had suddenly released as Max's nanobots melted away, and she instinctually began pulling the wires off of her body. Kaija's mind suddenly snapped back into Maeryn's like a rubber band.

"What the heck is happening?" Kaija asked.

Edgard's sword was glowing very faintly now, only barely illuminating the shocked faces of Dorian and Rosalie through the glass. Dorian was gripping Rosalie's hair and she had an arm pulled back with a hand balled into a fist, but they seemed to be momentarily frozen in surprise.

The drones circling around Maeryn sprang to life, pointing sedative darts at her. They all fired at once and Maeryn threw her arms over her face. Several seconds went by, but nothing hit her. She peeked open an eye to see that the metal darts were all hovering in the air around her in a near perfect circle.

"What—" Maeryn began, but stopped when she saw that Max was floating in the air next to her head. His arms were extended outward toward the darts.

"Oh, hi Maeryn," he said casually. "I'm magic now."

Max's hands began to glow and crackle with power. He spun in a circle and blue beams of electricity shot out in every direction, disabling all of the drones and sending them crashing to the ground.

"Wha… how did—" Maeryn tried speaking, but she was too disoriented to form a coherent idea.

"I'm connected to the Gaian energy source," said Max. "There's no stopping me— *uh oh*."

Maeryn and Max turned to see that the glass panel was sliding down. Most alarming, however, was that Rosalie's MotherTech suit had taken on a metallic quality and was spreading over every inch of her skin. She ran toward the glass and each of her powerful footsteps seemed to shake the floor. Her face was now completely covered in the nanobots, and where her eyes should have been were two red openings that glowed like searchlights. She leapt with an impossible strength, clear over the glass panel and into the room with Maeryn.

Max held out a hand, and Edgard's sword suddenly flew through its glass box, shattering it into millions of pieces. It soared right past Max and toward Maeryn. Rosalie was only ten feet away from them now, and the air around her blurred and sparked with energy.

"Maeryn, Kaija," said Max, speaking quickly in Maeryn's earpiece. "Take the sword."

"But—" Kaija began to say.

"It's you, it's always been both of you," said Max. "*You are the bridge!*"

Feeling like they were operating not as two people, but as one, Kaija and Maeryn reached forward together and grabbed Edgard's sword out of the air. At the same time, an amazing sense of calm and clarity filled their minds that went beyond words. The room suddenly glowed so bright that it was absolutely blinding, and it actually caused Rosalie to stumble. It was like the sun had suddenly shrunk down and landed in their hand. They would later learn that half of the power in Indiana went out at that moment as power plants were suddenly overloaded with an enormous amount of energy.

The Bridge

Maeryn and Kaija jumped forward and swung the glowing sword. As their arm moved through the air, Max turned back into a wristband and snapped into place on their wrist. The sword left a slash mark hanging in the air that glowed a brilliant blue, as if they had just sliced through the fabric of reality itself. They leapt through the opening and disappeared. In the same instant the slash mark vanished, and Rosalie landed on the spot where her niece should have been.

Her feet hit the ground with a thud, and the MotherTech Smart Suit receded from her face. Rosalie looked at her brother, whose face was already bruising from her own punches. She spoke with complete desperation.

"They have her, Dorian. Do you see what hesitation gets us? We could have saved Maeryn, but *now they have her*!"

* * *

For a moment it felt as if Maeryn was nowhere at all, but then her feet found solid ground and she instantly knew that she had never been further away from home.

Kaija stood in front of her with a wide-eyed expression of shock. They stared at each other, face to face for the first time, but then Maeryn dropped the sword and began panting for breath.

"We did it…" Maeryn said between gasps. "They can't get to us here, you're safe now Kaija. We're all safe."

"Um…" Kaija said hesitantly, and gestured behind her.

Maeryn looked around the room, absolutely confused. Her wristband liquefied and turned back into Max's body. He floated up to the bars of their cell and knocked on them.

"So we're in jail now," he said. "You're welcome, I guess."

Chapter Nineteen

Dragon

The Capital Telestation, Gaia

One of the two worst days in Clara's life was being mocked by a beautiful sunset. They had made it to the Capital's telestation, but Jasper was moving very slowly. Clara worried that even the short jump to Portland would kill him. They were the only two travelers at the great pillars of the station. The mentalist worker was a tall, slender man with a severe face. He looked at the travelers and addressed them tiredly.

"Destination?"

"The Portland station," said Clara.

"And where to from there?"

"Well this is new," said Clara, her temper rising. "Why would that be any of your business?"

"Security is tight around the Capital," the mentalist replied shortly.

"Well you sure as hell didn't interrogate us on the way to the Capital. To answer your question, we're getting as far away from that garbage heap as—"

"Boothbay," Jasper interrupted, his voice dry and tired. "And then we're off to Monhegan Island. Clara, I need to see Kaija. This isn't worth a fight."

The worker suddenly no longer seemed tired. He studied Jasper's face for several seconds, and then nodded at the spacialists at the two pillars. Clara waited for the space in-between the pillars to blur into a passageway, but nothing happened. When she glanced back at the spacialists, one of them was suddenly gone.

"Where did—" Clara said, but was interrupted by Jasper's scream.

"Clarice!"

She looked down to see a hand on her shoulder. One of the spacialists was standing behind her with a sinister look on his face. Clara began to move with her amazing reflexes, but it was too late. There was a muffled pop, and Clara was gone. The three remaining workers began to approach Jasper.

"Where did you send her?" he screamed.

The Bridge

"She is in one of our many strongholds," said the spacialist. "If you try anything on us, the old woman stays there."

The mentalist looked respectfully at Jasper and spoke.

"You are Jasper Monhegan? The man who defeated an entire Nomadic tribe in Boothbay?"

"Yes," Jasper snarled. "And let me warn you right now, you are quickly making an enemy that you don't want."

"You are quite right. Allow me to introduce myself: I am Achak, second in command of the Western Blaze. Rugaru would like to invite you among his highest ranks. Our leader himself is only half-blooded, and I have no Nomadic heritage whatsoever. You see, we are very open minded about powerful relayers."

"You can tell Rugaru to take that offer and shove it—" Jasper began.

"I can feel where this is going," said Achak calmly. "So before you say something regretful, let me inform you that your daughter Kaija and her friend Fain are in one of our prisons. She can either live with us comfortably, or not live at all, depending on where this conversation goes. And don't bother looking for her, because we have hundreds of camps all over the—"

Without warning, Jasper punched Achak in the face and the mentalist fell to the ground, clutching his broken nose and yelling.

"Where are they?" Jasper screamed.

The two spacialists drew their daggers and sprang forward at him. Jasper waved an arm and one of them fell over in a burst of wind. The other spacialist thrust a dagger toward Jasper's neck, but he reached up and caught the blade with his good hand. Jasper held the knife tight, the sharp blade not even breaking his skin. The spacialist's eyes widened in surprise.

"You're an internalist?" he gasped.

"You have no idea what I am," growled Jasper. He tightened his grip, and cracks ran up and down the length of the blade. "It will take more than a dagger to bring me down. Now tell me where my daughter—ah!"

Jasper cried out in pain and let go of the man's weapon. The other spacialist had grabbed Jasper by his infected arm and was gripping it tightly. Jasper crouched over, writhing in agony and trying to free his arm from the man.

"What is this?" asked the second spacialist, rolling up Jasper's sleeve and looking at his blackened skin.

Achak stood up, his crooked nose bleeding, and glared down at at his attacker. A splintering pain began shooting through Jasper's head as his memories were forcefully pulled to the surface. Jasper found himself briefly back in his cabin on Monhegan, looking at his dirty mirror and pulling a hydra thorn out of his back. The memory turned to mist and Jasper saw the smiling face of Achak looking at him. The Nomad took out his dagger and pressed it to Jasper's chest as the other two spacialists held him down. He cut a hole in Jasper's shirt and looked at the blackened skin over his heart.

"This is hydra poison," Achak said. "Oh, you *are* in trouble. It seems you're no good to us after all. I will tell Rugaru the news, but maybe we can still make something of your daughter."

Achak pulled back his dagger and thrust it forward toward Jasper's heart, but a large rock hit him in the side of the head and threw off his aim. The two spacialists looked up in surprise, and in the next moment they were both hit with long ropes that circled around their legs and tightened like pythons. A wall of flames had suddenly erupted out of the ground and circled all around them. An opening appeared in the flames and a dozen men and women stepped through. They held swords, crossbows, spears, and throwing knives aimed for attack at the struggling spacliasts on the ground. At the head of the group was Fain's father, Maddox Monhegan. He held a boulder over his head with one hand and was rearing back for attack.

"Monhegans!" Jasper cried wildly.

The two spacialists teleported out of their ropes and sprang toward Jasper, but he jumped up off the ground and dodged their fingers by inches. Dozens of weapons flew through the air, bending toward the three Nomadic spies like they were magnetic. The spacialists disappeared and reappeared so rapidly that it was hard to tell that they were there at all. Maddox threw his boulder and it burst into sharp fragments that circled around Achak, leaving him completely trapped and frozen in place. The mentalist's voice suddenly spoke in all of the Monhegan's minds at once.

"Death would have been a mercy for you, Jasper. The hydra poison will kill you slowly and painfully, and you will never see your daughter again."

The two spacialists suddenly appeared next to Achak, put their hands on his back, and all three Nomads vanished. The wall of flames around the group sank to the ground, and all of the Monhegans looked to Jasper with utmost concern and respect.

"Monhegans," said Jasper. "I owe my life to you."

"Guardian," said Maddox. "My son and Kaija, they... they left the island. We figured that they were following you to the Capital, so I gathered a group to get them back. The Nomads have spies at the Portland telestation, and... oh Jasper, I'm so sorry. I think the worst has happened."

He shuffled around uncomfortably, and all of the other Monhegans averted their eyes.

"What's done is done," said Jasper. "I should have figured that they would follow; my foresight has been very bad recently."

The Bridge

Ms. Clara's teaching apprentice, a young man named Alan, stepped forward, holding an ax in his powerful grip.

"Where's Ms. Clara?" he asked.

Jasper smiled.

"The Western Blaze has made a grave mistake. They sent her to one of their prison camps. We shouldn't be worried for her, we should be worried for her guards."

Alan laughed nervously.

"We agreed to meet outside of the Capital if we get separated," continued Jasper. "I have no doubts that Clara will soon escape and head for the Capital walls. I will need your assistance to travel there, I'm... I'm not well at all. My admission to the Capital's hospital was denied, and my time is very short now."

Maddox was a large man whose stoic expression seldom changed, but the look on his face now was absolutely frantic. His eyes were wide and wet with tears, and his partner Delia clung to him with a similar air of panic.

"We need to do something!" yelled Maddox. "I can't lose my son, Jasper. It would kill me after... after what's already happened to my family. I'd rather die myself!"

Jasper nodded solemnly.

"It's okay, Maddox. High Guardian Thomas and The Seven are going to help us get our kids back."

"Why would they let you in now?" asked Maddox. "Thomas has never done anything for us."

Jasper sighed heavily and looked around at his loyal islanders that had come to his rescue.

"My Monhegans, my family…" he said solemnly. "I have a message for the high guardian, and I do not believe that he will refuse me once it is delivered. There is a card that I have been holding back my entire life, and I think it is time that I played it. I need to be truthful about something." Jasper cleared his throat. "I am not the man you believe I am."

* * *

Thunderwolf Stronghold

"Listen," said Fain, "if we're going to share this cell we may as well be buds. How about a game of rock, paper, vultures?"

The old man in the corner of the cell just looked at Fain dismissively and closed his eyes. He was wearing clothes that looked like they had once been very expensive, but were now covered in dirt and had holes in them. His face was gaunt and he refused to eat anything, even after Fain had conjured up a fire to bake their potato.

"Well, you're no fun," said Fain.

The man laughed dryly.

"Fun?" he asked. "A month ago I was living in the Capital, and now I'm going to die in this dirty cell. How's that for fun?"

"You lived in the Capital?"

The man nodded.

"I'm surprised you didn't recognize me. I'm Johnathan York."

Fain just gave the man a blank stare.

"Apparently you're lacking in your art history," the man said smugly. "I am, or *was*, High Guardian Thomas's portrait artist until the Nomads lured me outside the walls. Surely you've seen my work?"

"Nope," said Fain. "We have paintings of Edgard on my island. I've never seen one of High Guardian Thomas."

"Well, that's a bold political statement," said Johnathan.

Fain had no idea what the man was talking about, so he simply sat and drew in the dirt with his finger for a few minutes. However, the more he thought about things the less they made sense.

"Have you been painting Rugaru's portrait?" asked Fain. "Is that why they kidnapped you?"

"*If only* they gave me a commission as subtle as the human figure!" said Johnathan passionately. "No, the Western Blaze had me paint some of their walls. I worked unceasingly for three days, and then they threw me in this cell and haven't let me out in a month. I really do think that they are just waiting for me to die of starvation."

"That doesn't make any sense," said Fain. "Why would—"

"*FAIN!*"

Kaija's voice suddenly spoke up in Fain's head.

"Hold on a second, Mr. York," said Fain. "I'm getting a call from my friend."

"What kind of game are you—" Johnathan began to say, but Fain shushed him.

"*Hi Kaija,*" Fain thought back at her. "*The old man is finally talking to me, but he's pretty depressing.*"

"*Fain, listen,*" said Kaija. "*Maeryn's here.*"

"*In your head?*"

"*NO. She's here in my cell with me.*"

There was the muffled sound of talking from Kaija's end, and then she continued.

"*I'm supposed to tell you that the little metal man is here too, and he said that he can't wait to see a dragon, whatever that is. We have Edgard Zeig's sword, and we used it to bring Maeryn to Gaia.*"

"*You've been busy the last fifteen minutes.*"

"*Yep. I think we can use the sword to help us get out of— UH OH! MAERYN, GET UNDER MY BED!*"

There were a few seconds of silence before Kaija continued.

The Bridge

"Sorry, the guard was coming, so they had to hide under my bed. Anyway, I think we can— ah! The guard's suspicious! Listen, Fain, I'm going to have to call you back."

Kaija's voice disappeared without warning. Fain looked up to see Johnathan York staring at him from across the cell very suspiciously.

"So," Johnathan said. "You're friend, this girl that was captured with you... *she called you?*"

"Yep," said Fain casually. "She's a mentalist."

"And she was sending you clear thoughts from one of the cells upstairs?"

"Yes."

Johnathan looked even more suspicious now.

"Boy, have you ever met a true mentalist before?" he asked.

Fain thought about this for a moment. There were several people on Monhegan with mentalist leanings, but Kaija was the first person he knew that was a mentalist through and through.

"Other than my friend, not really," said Fain.

"Well, I have," said Johnathan. "Our high guardian is perhaps the greatest mentalist of all time, so I know what I'm talking about here. Mentalism is a profoundly difficult leaning, perhaps the most difficult of all. Young mentalists can't just flip a switch and send people thought transmissions, especially if they can't see that person. The mental realm is a very complex thing, and it takes most people decades to master even the most basic techniques. How old did you say your friend was?"

"She just turned fourteen."

Johnathan laughed.

"Okay," he said. "I'm going to meditate some more, and you have fun talking to your imaginary friend."

Johnathan leaned up against the dirty wall and closed his eyes.

"You're wrong," said Fain, but Johnathan did not react. "Kaija is more amazing than you can even imagine."

Johnathan simply smiled without opening his eyes and said, "I'll believe it when I see it."

"Well you better open those eyes," said Fain, "because your mind is about to be blown out those eyeholes."

Johnathan waved his hand and dust particles floated up from the floor, gradually turning black until it looked like he had a curtain surrounding him.

"Please be quiet," he said.

Fain laughed.

"Come on, Yorky," said Fain. "If we're going to be cell mates, we may as well be best friends. Don't you want to talk about your hopes and dreams?"

"I hope and dream that you will be quiet."

"Oh, you just burned me good, dude. Nice one. It's good for best friends to be able to roast each other every now and then."

Johnathan stood up and the dust curtain dissolved. He looked sharply at Fain and pointed a finger at the boy.

"Listen, kid," he said. "I'm trying to cope with my own inevitable death in this desolate hole, and I just want some peace and quiet. I'm trying to be nice, but I've met people like you before and I could shut you up with one sentence if I wanted to."

"Oh, believe me," said Fain. "People have tried. Brave men and women have gone up against all odds to get me to close my mouth, but—"

"You talk when you're scared," interrupted Johnathan harshly, "and it seems to me that you talk all the time."

Fain slowly closed his mouth, turned away from the old man, and sat in the far corner of the cell. He didn't say another word.

* * *

Tamala had just walked by Kaija's cell, and she seemed awfully suspicious. Kaija sat on the floor and leaned up against her bed, catching her breath while whispering to Maeryn and Max who were hiding behind the sheets. After spending a few minutes mentally communicating with Fain, and then convincing Tamala that everything was normal, she felt somewhat drained.

"I can't believe you're actually here," whispered Kaija.

"I know…" said Maeryn, still shell-shocked from the whole experience.

"I can't believe we escaped Earth just to end up in a terrorist jail cell," Max cut in.

"Do you regret coming?" Kaija asked.

Maeryn thought for ten seconds or so about the question. She certainly hadn't expected her first experience in another universe to be spent hiding under a bed, but that was the least of her worries. Her family had turned out to be wildly different people than she had imagined them to be. The idea of living in danger on Gaia, or possibly even dying on Gaia, was not nearly as terrifying as joining the ranks of her violent, anarchistic family. Maeryn had never rebelled against her dad before, but now when she thought of him her heart burned with distaste.

"No," Maeryn whispered. "I don't regret anything."

"Might as well make the best of it while we're here," Max said. "So, where can I see a dragon?"

"What's a dragon?" Kaija asked.

"You know: big scaly monsters that fly and breathe fire."

Kaija thought about this for a second.

"Sky cats can be pretty scary, but they don't have scales."

The Bridge

"Are you telling me that Gaia, a world full of wizards and magic, doesn't have dragons?"

"What's a wizard? And, what was that other word? Mag… maggot?"

Max slumped over on Maeryn's shoulder.

"Well, I'm thoroughly bummed out now," he said.

There was a sudden pop from outside the jail cell; Maeryn and Max saw Kaija's hand tense up on the floor.

"*Quiet!*" Kaija thought to them.

Tamala approached the bars of the cell, looking far less intense than she had been earlier and more concerned. Maeryn and Max listened to their conversation, trying not to make the slightest noise or even breathe loudly.

"Kaija," said Tamala. "We found Jasper."

Kaija was filled with excitement and relief, but the look on Tamala's face remained stone cold.

"You have to listen to me!" Tamala continued. "Your father is on his deathbed. Our spies at the telestation reported that he's poisoned beyond healing, and any deal between him and Rugaru is now off the table. We don't want a dying man working for us." She coughed. "Also, he broke Achak's nose, so there's that."

Maeryn listened to this with abject horror; she was the reason that Jasper was poisoned, and at this point the fact that it was an accident didn't matter. He was going to die because of her. She was living up to the Kacey family name.

It was a long time before Kaija spoke.

"And you're not going to let me see him again?" she asked softly, her voice trembling.

"It's not up to me," said Tamala. "But no, you're not going to see him."

"So what happens to me? And Fain?"

"Mentalists are rare, and Fain has shown strong conjurist leanings. We will train you, and if the two of you show promise you will be welcomed into our family."

"And if we don't? What if we don't want to?"

"Don't even ask that question. You know what would happen. The Western Blaze does not hold prisoners who are no use to them."

Tamala turned to walk off down the hallway.

"You are monsters," Kaija shouted at her.

Tamala turned back to Kaija, and her face showed no anger.

"You're not wrong, but there are a lot of monsters in this world, and maybe you have to become one to fight them."

Tamala turned back around and walked out of sight. Kaija put her face in her hands and sank to the ground, trembling and sobbing. Maeryn, who was now crying herself, reached through the sheet that hung off the bed and put a hand on Kaija's back.

"I'm sorry," Maeryn whispered. "This is my fault."

The Bridge

"You didn't ask to get trapped in my body," said Kaija. "It was me that brought you to Monhegan. It was a terrible accident, and it wasn't anyone's fault, but I just wish I could—" Kaija sobbed again, barely able to express her deepest fear. "I just wish I could see my father before he dies."

"Then you *will*," said Max confidently.

He flew out from underneath the bed and began hovering around the bars of the cell, making beeping noises as he scanned the metal.

"These bars are like diamonds, no: super-duper-diamonds," said Max. "The material is so dense that I've never seen anything on Earth like it."

"It's steel made by internalist blacksmiths," said Kaija. "Fain tried to melt it, but it's impossible."

Max's blank face seemed to smile.

"Your friend didn't have the sword of Edgard Zeig. I'm confident that the blade would cut through the bars like butter, although I'm slightly worried that it might cause an atomic explosion."

"Max!" Maeryn whispered. "We can't just try to escape! What happens when we break out of the cell? We have no idea where we are, and we can't fight an army to get out of here."

"It looks like we need a map, and a plan," said Max. "Promise not to laugh."

Max suddenly began shrinking, his nanobots pulling together until he was nearly the size of a fly.

"I'm going to scan the building and send a map to your digital contacts," said Max, his voice coming out small and squeaky. "Adventures in cartography!"

The tiny robot buzzed out of the cell and down the hall, one arm extended into the air like he was flying into battle. Kaija watched him, her desperation subsiding in the ridiculousness of the situation.

"Is your life always like this?" Kaija asked.

"With Max? Yeah, pretty much."

Chapter Twenty

Something Interesting

Rugaru's Base, Gaia

"Will this really work?" whispered Kaija.

Maeryn sat under the bed, talking to Kaija's silhouette through the hanging bedsheet.

"Max's capacity for understanding the intricacies of a situation are exponentially greater than our own," Maeryn replied.

"Um…." Kaija whispered. "Is that a yes?"

"Sorry; yes, I trust Max with my life."

Maeryn could not see Kaija's face, and she wondered what kind of expression the Monhegan girl wore. There were so many things that Maeryn wanted to say to her, but now that they were meeting in person she felt her awkwardness coming down in full force. Maeryn had almost no experience in talking to people her own age face-to-face. Her friends on Earth were distant people that she occasionally played video games with online, and that was about it.

"Kaija?" whispered Maeryn.

"Yes?"

"Do you trust me?"

Kaija was quiet for a few seconds, and Maeryn waited with baited breath.

"Why do you keep asking that?" asked Kaija.

"My aunt almost killed you! And my grandpa is the most hated man on your planet."

"You're not those people."

"But it's not that simple."

"Why not? You're thinking way too much about this."

Maeryn sighed.

"Maybe you're right," she said.

Kaija was about to respond, but she found herself wondering why they were whispering at all when only minutes ago she had communicated with Fain using her mentalist abilities. She drew in the power of Gaia and felt for Maeryn's mind, finding it to be an effortless task. The fact that they were so close together seemed to amplify her abilities.

"Can you hear me?" thought Kaija.

The Bridge

"Yes," Maeryn thought back. *"This is the weirdest thing ever."*

"I know, and I'm barely even trying. I wonder what would happen if—"

Kaija drew in more energy, and both of the girls suddenly gasped. For a few seconds they found themselves seeing out of the other person's eyes and their own eyes simultaneously. Kaija could see the prison walls in front of her, as well as the underside of the bed behind her. Beyond the physical sensations, Kaija could feel Maeryn's hesitation and awkwardness. The sense of being inside of two heads at once was dizzying, and she immediately stopped relaying.

"Wow," thought Maeryn. *"Okay, I take it back: that was way weirder."*

"This shouldn't be possible," thought Kaija. *"When I reached into the mental realm earlier, everything was fuzzy. The only reason I found Fain is because I already know him so well. I don't even have to try with you, but I just met you a few days ago. I've heard of this happening to twins, but why us?"*

"Well, we were born on the same day," replied Maeryn. *"But we couldn't be twins, could we? My mom is Katherine Kacey; does that name sound familiar?"*

"No. My mother is Saura Aztala, the guardian of Aztala in the Oceanic guardianship. Does your mom also protect an underwater temple of warrior women?"

"Um... no. My mom sells life insurance. Is there any way that one of our parents isn't <u>really</u> our parent?"

"I don't know, I've only met my mother a handful of times. Guardians don't leave their villages very often. My father met Saura before either of them became guardians. After I was born, both of them refused to give up their goals, and you can't exactly protect an underwater city from halfway around the world." Kaija hesitated, and then was quick to add, *"It's really fine, though. I don't miss her at all."*

Maeryn wasn't convinced. Listening to the sad and hesitant voice of Kaija in her head, Maeryn suddenly felt a great deal of empathy for the girl. Although their cultures were literally worlds apart, their innermost feelings were nearly identical.

"My mom's not much of a parent either," Maeryn thought to her. *"But, you know... it's fine."*

Kaija reached her hand under the bedsheet and held onto Maeryn's hand. They sat for a second in silence, finding an odd peace amidst the chaos.

"Maeryn!" said Max suddenly in her earpiece. "You've got to see this! I'm sending you my video feed."

A large room was displayed in Maeryn's digital contacts, and there was definitely something interesting about it. She jumped in surprise and patted Kaija on the back urgently.

"Kaija," whispered Maeryn. "Use my eyes for a second."

"Okay... gross," muttered Max.

The Bridge

Both of the girls were suddenly looking at a room with an enormous glass tank in its center. Inside the tank was the familiar sight of a hydra vine. Its tentacle-like vines stuck out in every direction, slithering and slamming against its glass prison. At the front of the tank was a very small hole where a single vine protruded, but it was chained up against the wall of the room. The exposed vine was rotting and dripping with a clear fluid from hundreds, if not thousands, of cuts and slashes. It pulled weakly at the chains to no avail. A Nomad was chopping at the creature with a dagger and collecting the fluid in a steaming metal bucket, being very careful not to slice all the way through the vines and have them divide.

"Desolation," whispered Kaija. "That is brutal."

Despite almost having been eaten by a hydra vine several days ago, Maeryn had to agree. Seeing the beast getting tortured was too much.

"Is this the creature that you were telling me about?" asked Max in the earpiece. "The one that can divide its vines exponentially?"

"Yes," said Maeryn.

"I have a plan."

"That was fast," said Kaija skeptically.

"Island girl, in the amount of time it took you to say that, I sorted through five million plans in my head and picked the best one. You're going to have to trust me, because things are about to get crazy. When I give you the signal, cut through the prison bars with Edgard's sword. Two parallel, horizontal slashes should free you. Get ready."

"What's the signal?" asked Maeryn.

"When something interesting happens."

They watched from Maeryn's contacts as Max flew up to the ear of the Nomadic man and grew to his usual size.

"Hello, sir," said Max casually. "Are you having an interesting day?"

The Nomad jumped in surprise and turned around, swinging his dagger blindly. When he saw a tiny robot flying in the air in front of him, he looked absolutely confused and dropped his weapon.

"What are you?" asked the Nomad.

"Something interesting," said Max.

The robot held out his hand, felt for the nearly unlimited power source in the air all around him, and sent out a carefully measured soundwave through the room that instantly shattered the glass tank. Water filled the air and vines sprang out in every direction, dividing and growing larger. Some of the vines yanked the chains right out of the wall and freed its trapped limb, and then the hydra vine let out a primal roar that pounded at the inside of their heads even from several floors below. The Nomad bent down and reached frantically for his dagger, dropping it several times in his panic while cursing loudly.

"I don't think it likes you very much," said Max. "And I can't say I blame it. You better get out of here before—*woah*!"

The hydra vine sprang forward at an unbelievable speed and propelled its octopus-like head toward the Nomad. Before the guard was able to contemplate teleporting away, a dozen vines wrapped around his body and tossed him into the open mouth at the center of the creature.

The video feed suddenly cut out and was replaced with the grainy message **"This motion picture has been rated R for graphic violence by the classification and rating administration."**

"Did that guy just get eaten?" asked Kaija.

"I think that's our signal," said Maeryn urgently, grabbing Edgard's sword from under the bed and handing it to Kaija.

Kaija nodded and swung the sword with all her weight at the bars of the prison. The internalist metal let out a noise like an explosion as the sword cut through, leaving red-hot slash marks that were literally steaming. Kaija made a second slash closer to the floor and then kicked the bars out of place. The two girls climbed through the opening and then looked up and down the hallway.

"Which way do we go?" asked Kaija.

A metal orb rocketed from around the corner and snapped onto Maeryn's wrist with a pop. Max's panicked voice filled the hallway.

"RIGHT, RIGHT, LEFT, DOWN THE STAIRS, AVOID THE HORRIBLE MONSTER, DON'T DIE, AND THEN LEFT AGAIN!"

* * *

The walls of the cell were shaking, and noises that sounded like massive explosions were coming from overhead. Johnathan York had been quietly meditating, but now he paced back and forth anxiously.

"Could that be The High Seven?" he muttered to himself. "I knew they would come for me!"

"I don't think so," said Fain. "Kaija told me that they were thinking of a plan, and it… hold on a second, I'm getting another call from her."

"FAIN!" Kaija's voice thundered in his head, and this time it rang so clearly in the mental realm that Johnathan could hear it too.

"It's true," Jonathan whispered in awe, "your friend really is a mentalist! I can only imagine how—"

"Shush, old man. We're coming past the cell in about five seconds!" Kaija called. *"Be ready to— aah! Sorry, that was just the… OH MY GAIA THEY'RE EVERYWHERE!"*

"We're escaping, Mr. York," said Fain confidently. "Are you ready to fight our way out of here?"

The Bridge

"Fight?" Johnathan scoffed. "My relaying abilities are of the subtle nature; I'm no good in combat."

"I'll take that as a yes," said Fain. "Here they come!"

Kaija and Maeryn rounded the corner with a terrified look on their faces. Kaija swung the sword through the prison bars before they had a chance to say a word. At the same time, Maeryn held out her hand and a burst of energy shot from her wristband, sending the bars flying across the room and smacking the walls with a great clunk.

"My heroes!" exclaimed Fain. "You must be Maeryn, it's nice to—"

"Vines!" Kaija and Maeryn yelled in near unison, pulling Fain from the cell and frantically running down the hallway as Johnathan followed. A batch of hydra vines covered in thorns was rapidly growing and spreading throughout the building behind them, engulfing everything in sight. They turned the corner and darted into the nearest room. Fain spun around, raised his arms, and relayed a wall of flames into the doorway behind them. The vines shrank back once they were within reach of the fire and squealed. Maeryn's wristband morphed and became the tiny human figure of Max once more.

"Nice to meet you, Fain," said Max. "Hold those flames as long as you can."

Fain nodded determinedly, scrunched his face in concentration, and the wall of fire sparked and crackled.

"Where's the exit?" asked Maeryn, glancing around the room.

"No doors or windows anywhere in the stronghold," said Max. "Stupid teleporters! I'm building energy back up so I can bust through these walls. They're thick, so I'll need a few seconds to charge."

Kaija observed the room for the first time and was suddenly taken aback. Every inch of the floor, walls, and ceiling were covered with elaborate paintings. Although there was no furniture in the room, the paintings almost made it look like they were standing in the middle of a castle. A massive chandelier was painted onto the ceiling, the floor was painted to look like fancy tiles, and large windows were painted upon the walls. Through one painted window was a painted night sky where a full moon hung motionless.

"What is this?" asked Kaija.

"This was my work," said Johnathan. "The Nomads had me paint this room day and night, and then when I was done they threw me in their prisons. It's an exact replica of the high guardian's night chambers. Rugaru would spend most of his time meditating in this room, but I'm not sure why. Maybe he wanted to feel like a high guardian."

Fain's arms were trembling from relaying so much energy toward the flames blocking the doorway.

"How much longer?" he asked through his teeth.

The Bridge

"Ten more seconds," said Max, holding his glowing hands out in front of him and pointing them at the nearest wall.

Suddenly a male Nomad appeared with a pop, brandishing a long spear that he pointed at the group.

"Stop!" yelled the Nomad.

Kaija swung Edgard's sword at the man, but he simply disappeared and reappeared behind them. Maeryn summoned all of the energy she could and sent it toward him, but it simply came out as a light burst of wind.

"I don't know what I'm doing, help us!" Maeryn yelled at Johnathan.

For a moment the artist looked like he was going to run, but a look of determination quickly grew on his face. Johnathan snapped his fingers at the Nomad, and suddenly all of the tattoos on the warrior's body turned from black to bright pink. The Nomad reared back his spear, but when he saw the transformation he was overcome with complete bewilderment.

"Um," said the Nomad. "What in desolation just happened?"

"Now!" Max yelled, releasing the energy in his hands and blowing open a large hole in the bricks ahead of them. Fain extinguished the wall of fire and vines suddenly sprang out of the doorway. The Nomad saw the hydra vines heading toward him and simply popped out of existence. The entire group darted through the opening as quickly as they could and ran into the cold night air.

There was snow falling from overhead and mountains stretching for as far as the eye could see in every direction. The stars were unbelievably bright over the mountain range, and the wind was so cold that it felt as if it were blowing right through their skin. Fain summoned a fireball in his hand and they all huddled around it, listening to the chaos ensuing in the stronghold behind them.

"I did it!" said Max. "We escaped... again... and now we're high up in the mountains with no way to get down. That's not even mentioning the angry Nomads in the building behind us getting attacked by a man-eating plant. I feel like this keeps happening to me."

A section of the building exploded, and hundreds of thorny vines snaked out into the cold air.

"Run!" yelled Fain, but it was already too late.

The vines quickly encircled the group as the five of them drew close together fearfully. It was now as if a wall of slimy thorns was growing around them on every side. The great head of the hydra vine descended from above and looked at its prey with cold, black eyes.

"FOOD FOR MY CHILDREN!" it roared, vibrating their skulls.

"Hello, friend," said Max hesitantly. "Remember me?"

The Bridge

A vine leapt toward Max and stopped inches in front of the robot's face. And then, amazingly, it gently touched the side of Max's smooth head. A deep, almost alien-like voice telepathically spoke in all of their minds once again.

"TWOFOLD."

The hydra's head sank back into the mass of vines behind it, and the slithering walls around them began to disperse. The creature pulled itself back inside of the building, and less than a second later the entire place exploded. What must have been thousands of vines leapt out from every crack in the building, and the hydra vine now looked to be as big as the Nomadic base itself. It seemed to gather its energy for a moment, and Kaija could feel a great stirring in the power of Gaia around them. The hydra vine pushed at the ground with its multitude of ligaments, and with one great leap it was sent soaring down the side of the mountain. A final thought rang clear in the mental realm.

"MY CHILDREN."

Everybody breathed a collective sigh of relief, and it almost felt like their hearts were just now resuming usual activity.

"It didn't kill us," Kaija marveled. "Have you ever heard of a hydra vine sparing someone's life?"

"Of course it didn't kill us," said Max gleefully. "I made friends with it. What should we name it?"

Fain leapt with excitement and stared at the robot with a wild look in his eyes.

"Are you thinking what I'm thinking?" asked Max, and Fain nodded. Then, in perfect unison, the two of them shouted "EARL!"

"Did we just become best friends, little dude?" asked Fain.

"I'll like you a lot more if you call me Max, small brained boy. And don't celebrate too soon; we're still stuck on the top of a mountain."

Kaija took a few steps forward and looked over the edge of the cliff. There was no way anybody could get down on foot. Then she turned around and looked at the ruined base behind them.

"Where are the Nomads?" she asked.

"I'm guessing that they all teleported away in fear," said Maeryn. "Or they were, well… *you know*."

"Eaten," said Johnathan gruffly. "Serves them right."

"But there were kids in there," said Kaija. "And I know they were Nomads, but you don't really think that—"

"No," said Max suddenly. "They're fine. Before I freed the hydra vine I scanned the whole building. There were only three Nomads that stayed behind: the one that got eaten, the one with the spear, and the woman that kept walking by your cell."

"That must have been Tamala," said Kaija. "She—"

The Bridge

And just like that, Tamala appeared behind Kaija. Her clothes were torn and she had a wild look in her eyes after running from the hydra vine. She had somehow appeared without making a sound and Kaija had no idea who was behind her.

"Kaija, look out!" Johnathan shouted, but it was too late.

Tamala gently placed a hand on Kaija's shoulder.

Chapter Twenty-one

Twofold

The Ragged Mountains

Fain moved to attack the Nomadic woman, but Jonathan quickly pulled him back.

"She can send you right over an Oahu volcano with one touch, boy. Stay away."

Kaija stood as still as she possibly could, but her eyes were wide with fear.

"You have to listen to me," said Tamala. She spoke quickly, but with a calm determination. "Link hands."

"You think we're stupid?" asked Johnathan fiercely.

"Listen to me!" shouted Tamala. "Jasper has been sighted on the road to the Capital. If you link hands, I will send you to him."

"How can we trust you?" asked Maeryn.

Max floated up off of Maeryn's shoulder and looked closely at Tamala's face.

"She shows no micro-expressions of deception," said Max. "If anything, she looks extremely confused, and for some reason she can't take her eyes off me."

"Probably because she's not used to seeing a floating metal thing that talks," commented Fain. "And I can't say that—"

"You're running out of time!!" Tamala interrupted. "If the other Nomads come to investigate, all will be lost and I can no longer assist you. I must maintain their trust. Find your father and the other Monhegans, and tell them to get far away from the Capital tonight. They will assume that you died. Link hands, now!"

Maeryn stepped forward and took Kaija by the hand, squeezing tightly, and some of the fear seemed to fade from Kaija's face. Max floated over and settled on Maeryn's shoulder.

"She could be lying," said Fain, taking a step backwards. "We… we can't trust them. She could send us to another one of their prison camps."

"Maybe," said Maeryn. "But if that's true, then at least we go together. If they separate us, we're weaker."

Fain's arm trembled, and he held it back from the group. He looked up at Tamala, and Maeryn saw that he had tears in his eyes.

"Your people killed our horse," he said with a trembling voice, and now tears were running down his cheeks. "But you know what? I'm glad that you captured us. I was hoping that I would get to talk to a Nomad once we got to the mainland, so I could tell them how I feel about them. I want you to know that I—"

"Now is not the time to throw around insults, boy," said Johnathan.

"Shut up!" screamed Fain. "I have to say this." He took a step closer to Tamala and continued. His hands were balled into fists and his voice trembled as he spoke.

"When I was a little kid, Nomads attacked my village. My father was the guardian, and they didn't expect him to be so powerful. He fought them off, and they knew that they were losing. Just before they fled, a Nomad fired an arrow at us as a parting shot. But they didn't aim for my father, they... they shot my older brother. He was the age I am now. His name was Emris. I watched him die. Those Nomads didn't think twice about killing him. You are all animals to me."

Fain reached out and grabbed Kaija's hand, never taking his eyes off of Tamala.

"I'll go to whatever prison you're sending us to," he said. "But before we go, I just wanted you to know that *I hate you.*"

Kaija listened to her best friend with her heart breaking, but she turned to see that Tamala's proud expression was not pierced in the slightest.

"There is so much you don't know," Tamala said. "The Western Blaze has lost their way, but they are a small drop in the ocean of our culture. If you want to paint all of us the same way and pretend I was the coward who killed your brother, fine. You are free to hate me, boy, but hating is easy. Trusting is a harder and far braver act."

Johnathan, who had been the most hesitant of all, walked over and placed his hand on Fain's shoulder.

"It's either this or freezing to death," he muttered.

"I'll send you all at once to the Capital road," Tamala said. "Find Jasper, and get away from the city. You never met me, and this never happened."

Kaija, still standing like a statue, said her only word of the conversation.

"Why?"

"Many of us still remember the ancient Nomadic culture," Tamala said. "Thousands have not joined Rugaru's clan. There are those who are brave enough to infiltrate his highest ranks and thwart his evil plans at every turn. The ancient

Nomads do not recognize the leadership of foreign tyrants, and when a tyrant begins to rise amongst ourselves…"

The corner of Tamala's mouth just barely curved in a smile.

"We resist," she finished.

Tamala looked down at Kaija.

"The True Search has eyes everywhere, and now those eyes are on you, Kaija."

The air around them crackled and became an unintelligible blur. Coldness gave way to a mingling of conflicting sensations, and then they were gone.

* * *

The lights of the Capital were twinkling on the horizon, and a full moon was just starting to rise in the sky. Johnathan, Maeryn, and Kaija found their feet hitting the solid ground of the Capital road. Max floated around excitedly.

"I'm here!" he said. "That's a relief; I was worried that her magic wouldn't work on me."

"Magic?" asked Johnathan. "What does that mean?"

"Don't worry about it, wizard," said Max.

Fain sighed, but the tension did not seem to leave his body.

"She really did it…" he said. "She sent us to the Capital. There must be some kind of trap waiting here."

The Bridge

Kaija didn't let go of her friend's hand.

"Fain… I didn't know about your brother. Is there anything I can—"

"I've said what I needed to say," he interrupted.

Fain looked at their surroundings, and he almost seemed wounded at the fact that the woman had told the truth. She had saved them.

"Guys," said Maeryn. "Look!"

She pointed across the road. In the middle of a field were a dozen tents and the light of a campfire. Familiar voices rang in the distance.

"It's the Monhegans!" yelled Kaija. "Father!"

She dropped Edgard's sword and bolted as fast as she could toward the campsite with Fain following closely behind. Max snapped onto Maeryn's wrist and she went after them, but hesitated after a few footsteps. Kaija and Fain disappeared into the campsite without her.

"What's the matter?" asked Johnathan. "Isn't that your village?"

"No," said Maeryn. "I'm not one of them, and I don't know what they'll make of me. It's… well, it's very complicated."

Johnathan eyed the metal band that was around Maeryn's wrist and nodded thoughtfully.

"Complicated indeed. There are a lot of things going on here that I don't understand, but perhaps I don't *want* to understand. Now I see that I don't belong in the Capital either. I have a stable outside the city; I'm going to get one of my Edgardian horses and ride to York to find my daughter. High Guardian Thomas probably believes me to be dead, and that just might be okay with me. You're welcome to tag along. The city of York is a beautiful place."

"No. I'm going to wait by the campsite; Kaija will need some time with her father by herself."

Johnathan turned to leave, but after a few seconds he turned and gave Maeryn a mysterious look.

"I kept waiting for The High Seven to come and save me. They are the strongest relayers on the entire Western Continent; heroes that stories are told of across the world. But if they had come, they would have burnt that base to the ground without any regard for an old artist. I would have never believed that my heroes would turn out to be two teenage girls, but it seems that I need more faith. Thank you."

Jonathan turned and walked toward the stables. He thought of the daughter that he hadn't seen in all the cycles while he made his fortune in the Capital, and tears ran down his cheeks. They could keep his fortune. Tonight he had been given a gift, and he was saved in more ways than one.

* * *

The Bridge

Kaija darted past the confused faces of the Monhegans moving around the campsite. She caught a few snippets of surprised comments as she ran.

"Is that—"

"Could it be?"

"Kaija and Fain!"

Spotting a light in her father's tent, Kaija swerved around the astonished villagers. Kaija pulled open the cloth door and nearly jumped inside. Fain walked in after her and stood anxiously with his eyes on his teacher.

Ms. Clara was sitting on the floor next to Jasper's tent. He lay with his eyes closed, and his chest rose slowly as he drew rattling breaths. Ms. Clara saw Kaija, sprang to her feet, and hugged her arms around her.

"Kaija!" she cried. "Is it you. Is it really you?"

"Yes," said Kaija. "I'm back in my body. What are you doing here? Nomads said that they captured you."

"Very briefly," Ms. Clara laughed.

Maddox suddenly burst into the tent and grabbed his son.

"Fain!" he yelled angrily, shaking him by the shoulders. "What in desolation where you thinking? Don't you know that there's a reason we left the mainland!? Use your head for once, Fain. Your impulsiveness could have killed all of us!"

Fain's voice trembled as he spoke, and he somehow shrank with more fear now than he had felt when facing the hydra vine.

"Dad..." Fain muttered. "I know... I'm..."

"Our family has already lost too much here," Maddox said, and then he pulled his son in close and began crying.

Fain's mother, Delia, began speaking quietly. Kaija noticed that she sat on the other side of Jasper's bed, and a warm blue light was shining from her hands onto him.

"There's no time for this," she said. "We'll have our stories soon, but time is running out. Kaija needs to say goodbye."

Kaija let go of Ms. Clara and bent down over her father. Black veins streaked up and down his whole body and his eyes rolled around deliriously before locking onto his daughter.

"K... Kai..." he whispered, but did not have the strength to finish. Kaija clung to him.

"How much longer?" asked Ms. Clara.

"I would say minutes," said Delia, "but he shouldn't have lasted this long to begin with. He won't make it through the night, for sure."

"What?" Kaija asked. "You don't mean... no. NO! We need to go to the Capital and—"

"He's too weak," said Delia. "Even the Capital hospital couldn't help him now. We need to do the ritual of passing."

The Bridge

"No," said Kaija again. "There must be…"

She trailed off, slowly accepting the truth. There was nothing that could be done. Her father was going to die. Fain suddenly pulled himself away from Maddox and looked at Kaija with urgency.

"We can't stay here!" he said. "That Nomadic woman said we had to leave the Capital as fast as we could. They're planning something, and it's going to happen tonight."

"The journey would kill Jasper faster," said Delia.

"We're staying right here," said Ms. Clara determinedly. "If the Nomads come while my son is dying, I will destroy every last one of them."

There was a sudden, uncomfortable silence in the room. Maddox and Delia looked very touched at Clara's comment. She had brought many orphans to the island when she was guardian of Monhegan, but she had never referred to them as her own children. Clara had always been a woman of action and was not the sentimental type.

Kaija walked over and held her teacher's hand.

"He loved you, Ms. Clara," Kaija said. "There's nobody on the island that my father admired more. I hope he told you."

Ms. Clara's eyes glimmered.

"He told me every day," she said. "As a boy, and as an adult. He loved you too, Kaija. You were his whole world."

Ms. Clara reached onto the bedside table and picked up an envelope. It was addressed to **High Guardian Thomas Zeig** with Jasper's shaky handwriting.

"Jasper could have saved himself days ago," she said, "but he chose not to. Everything changed when he heard you had been captured; your father almost sacrificed everything to get you back."

"What's that?" asked Fain, pointing at the envelope.

Ms. Clara closed her fist and the letter went up in a burst of flames.

"Something that the guardianship never needs to know about," said Ms. Clara.

She turned her attention to Fain's parents.

"Gather all of Jasper's closest companions. It is time for them to pay their last respects before we do the passing ritual."

"And if the Nomads arrive?" asked Delia.

Ms. Clara picked up her walking stick and tossed it to Delia.

"This will keep you safe. It's one of the seven artifacts that still holds Edgard's power."

Delia suddenly looked very intimidated, but she nodded and exited the tent with Maddox.

"I want Maeryn to be here too," said Kaija. "It's only right; she never meant for my father to get hurt."

The Bridge

"What are you talking abou—" Ms. Clara began, but her words trailed off as she watched a redheaded teenager with a sword walk into the tent. Kaija did not even have to turn around to know that Maeryn was here; she had felt her coming.

"That's her," said Kaija. "Maeryn escaped Earth when her family tried to kill me, and she saved us from the Nomad's prison."

Maeryn smiled shyly at Ms. Clara.

"Hello again," she said. "It's nice to meet you in person."

Max flew up into the air and waved at the gawking woman.

"Hi everybody," he said. "Let's go ahead and have a moment of surprise. Yes, I am a small, flying piece of metal who can talk."

Ms. Clara walked forward, wide eyed, and passed right by Max without giving him a second glance. She reached forward with a trembling hand and pointed to the sword that Maeryn was holding.

"That's... that's—" Ms. Clara stuttered. "No..."

Kaija had never, ever seen the composure of her teacher break down like it was now.

"It's the sword of Edgard Zeig," said Maeryn. "It was on my world. We used it to get here."

She held the weapon out to the woman, and Ms. Clara inspected it closely. Tears were forming in her eyes.

"It always found its way back…" she whispered, almost inaudibly.

Ms. Clara turned to Kaija and stared for several uncomfortable seconds, as if struggling with indecision.

"Kaija," she said. "Your father never wanted you to know… he wanted you to have a normal life, but this is a sign. Your life can never be normal; the sword found you."

"What are you talking about?" asked Kaija.

"I'm…" said Ms. Clara, taking a deep sigh. "I'm your grandmother, Kaija. Jasper is my son."

Kaija stared in disbelief.

"No…" she said. "You brought Jasper here as an orphan to start a colony for refugees."

"No, Kaija. I am Clarice Zeig, generalist knight of the original High Seven. I never came here to start a refugee colony; that's just what it became. Edgard and I came here to raise our son."

"Edgard?" asked Fain, jumping to his feet. "Hold on…"

"I'm…" said Kaija.

"Yes," said Ms. Clara. "When Jasper dies, you will be the only living descendent of the High Guardian Edgard Zeig. You will be the true heir of Edgardia, as Jasper is now. Yesterday your father was going to confront High Guardian Thomas with his heritage and use the knights to rescue you."

"Kaija, I didn't think that you could get any cooler," said Fain, "but this is amazing."

The Bridge

"No, it's not," said Ms. Clara. "Edgard never called himself the son of Gaia, it's just what other people wanted him to be. History books turned him into little more than a story to fit their own beliefs. The entire world looked at Edgard for protection, but he was as lost as anybody else. It was maddening, and those close to him faced death threats every day. Edgard sent me to Monhegan Island and was going to disappear so that we could raise a family in secret, but Duncan killed him days before our plan could happen."

Maeryn held her hands over her mouth, horrified and feeling suddenly nauseous. She wanted to run, to get away from here and never come back, but she was in an unfamiliar and dangerous world.

"No..." Maeryn whispered.

Fain, Kaija, and Ms. Clara all turned to look at her.

"It's not your fault," said Max in her earpiece. "You are not your family."

The same revelation suddenly hit Kaija, and she stared at Maeryn with a horrible knowing.

"What am I missing?" asked Fain.

"I'm sorry," said Maeryn, holding back tears. "My family had Edgard Zeig's sword because, well...my grandfather was Duncan Kacey. The Crucifier."

"That's impossible," said Ms. Clara severely. "High Guardian Thomas found Duncan's body. The sword is buried under the castle with Edgard."

309

"No," said Maeryn. "Edgard never died on Gaia. Duncan used the sword to bring him to Earth because he knew that he couldn't be healed there. My grandfather killed him, and he went on to have a family. I don't know why Thomas lied about it; maybe he saw it as an opportunity to become high guardian. Duncan died last year of cancer; he lived to be an old man."

Ms. Clara let the sword slide out of her hands and fall to the ground. She turned to look at her dying son on the cot, and then stared at Maeryn with an unfathomable expression.

"That's..." said Ms. Clara, but her voice caught in her throat. She took a trembling breath and averted her eyes from Maeryn before continuing. "Please excuse me for a moment."

The old woman walked quickly out of the tent. In the uncomfortable silence of the room they could hear Ms. Clara's restrained crying. Kaija and Fain looked at the floor as Maeryn searched for an accepting face.

"I don't belong here," Maeryn said finally. "I didn't mean to cause your family more harm."

She picked up Edgard's sword and gently placed it next to Jasper's sleeping body. It gave off a faint glow, as if recognizing its master. Maeryn turned and walked toward the tent's exit. Max silently rejoined her wrist as she reached to open the swaying cloth.

"Twofold," said Fain.

The Bridge

Maeryn hesitated.

"What?" she asked.

"That's what the hydra vine said before it let us go," said Fain. "And another vine said the same thing before it poisoned Jasper. I've been thinking about it a lot."

"What does this have to do with anything?" asked Kaija.

"There's an old saying," Fain continued. "The hydra vine pays twofold, so be careful what you toll. I understand it now. We wandered into a hydra vine's territory while it was gathering food for its children, and it poisoned Jasper because it could sense our own fear and hate. But then whenever we helped a hydra vine and showed it kindness, it destroyed a whole Nomadic base and let us go. When you give it fear it gives you double, and when you give it freedom it does the same for you."

Fain walked over to Maeryn and gently wrapped his arms around her in a comforting hug.

"I can't hate you, Maeryn," he said. "Hating is too easy, and it comes back double; Tamala was right. You can't control your family's past."

Maeryn put her face onto his shoulder and wept freely. All of the guilt and anger over her family was coming out now.

"I know," she cried. "But I can't pretend that the past doesn't matter either. There is so much pain here because of my family. I have to find some way to fix this."

"You can't fix it," said Kaija weakly. "The hydra poison divides in the blood, and it has spread too far. We have to accept that my father is going to die."

"It's like cancer," said Max suddenly. "Dividing cancer cells."

Maeryn looked up, wiped her tears, and saw that the old sword of Edgard Zeig had begun to glow even brighter next to Jasper. She gasped as a thought struck her.

"I know why I'm here," said Maeryn. "I know why Gaia bought us together."

Chapter Twenty-two

Kindling

The Capital Road

"Kaija and I aren't linked in spite of our family's violent past, but because of it," said Maeryn. "Gaia's pulling us back together to fix what we've broken."

"Can Gaia do that?" asked Kaija.

"It depends on your religious views," said Fain. "Some branches teach that Gaia is an actual living being, while others believe that it is a cosmic energy field which harnesses the spirits of everyone who has ever lived."

Everyone looked at Fain, surprised that he had said something so insightful.

"What?" he asked. "*Oh wow, Fain knows a thing!* I'm Ms. Clara's best student, you dummies."

"Whatever Gaia is, it's real," said Max. "It preserved my mind, and brought me straight to Maeryn so that I could help her get here."

"Jasper is dying because of me," said Maeryn, "but I might be the only person who can save him. My dad told me that he was working on a cure for cancer. He said that it was nearly finished. Cancer cells divide, so his medicine would divide at the same rate as the cells and destroy them. It's exactly like the hydra poison. Max, do you think that you can find where the medicine is locked up?"

"I downloaded the MotherTech files earlier," said Max. "The medicine is at the main headquarters in your dad's office."

"Is he really going to just give it to us?" asked Kaija. "He literally tried to kill me earlier."

"I'll do whatever it takes to get the medicine," said Maeryn.

The tent flaps suddenly rustled in the wind and they heard a voice speak from behind them.

"How do you know that you can get back?" asked Ms. Clara.

Maeryn turned around to see that the old woman had entered the tent. Her eyes were red, but she watched Maeryn thoughtfully.

"I don't know," said Maeryn. "I can just feel it. Can't you, Kaija?"

The Bridge

Kaija nodded and looked toward the sword lying next to her father. It was glowing brighter with each second.

"That sword is ancient and mysterious," said Ms. Clara. "Even Edgard didn't understand its nature. It saved him in every battle but his last."

Maeryn stepped forward and picked up the sword, letting it fill her with strength and purpose.

"I have every reason not to trust you, Maeryn," said Ms. Clara. "But I *do* trust you. Please, save my son."

Maeryn visualized her father's office and swung the sword. Once again, it left a glowing slash mark that hung in the air ominously. There was a rip in the space in front of her, and she could see the interior of the MotherTech building through the slash.

"I'll need to leave the portal open this time," said Maeryn. "Just in case we need to leave quickly."

A rippling succession of pops suddenly erupted from outside the tent like gunfire.

"The Nomads!" Kaija exclaimed. "It's happening!"

Ms. Clara turned to Fain urgently.

"Tell the Monhegans to protect the tent at all costs," said Ms. Clara. "Do as you've been taught."

"Max," said Maeryn. "You stay and help."

"Are you sure?" he asked.

"Yes."

"Be safe, sister," said Max, and he flew off to follow Fain.

Maeryn stuck Edgard's sword into the ground a few feet in front of the slash mark. Kaija leaned over and kissed her sleeping father on the forehead.

"This is not goodbye," she whispered.

Kaija stood up, took a deep breath, and walked out of her universe.

* * *

Fain looked toward the Capital in horror. Dozens of Nomads were rapidly bursting into existence and firing arrows at the guards on top of the Capital's outer walls. The famous Edgardian archers returned fire and their metal arrows bent through the air toward the attackers, but the Nomads simply disappeared before being struck. A horn was blown and more Capital guards climbed onto its walls, holding up their arms and drawing in the power of Gaia. A great wall of fire suddenly erupted from the city, curving through the air and creating a perfect dome of flames over the Capital.

Max floated up to Fain and rapidly scanned the situation at the Capital gates.

"I'm going to stop as many as I can from coming near the campsite," said Max, and then charged ahead like a bullet. "Stay safe, fleshbag."

The Bridge

Fain's father frantically ran around the corner with a group of Monhegans following closely behind, all of them pulling out weapons and readying themselves for combat.

"The Western Blaze is attacking the Capital!" he yelled. "They're not going to leave us alone for long."

Fain watched the battle with a healthy mix of amazement and fear. As more Nomads and soldiers appeared, the battle spread out further on the plain and inched closer toward their campsite. Capital soldiers were climbing down the walls and joining the fight. Bursts of electricity, ice, and fire erupted into the air as the soldiers attacked. Despite the army's best efforts, the Nomads were simply too fast to be struck by a single attack.

"Dad!" Fain called. *"Look."*

Maddox turned to look toward the battle and his mouth dropped open. What had begun as a dozen Nomads was now growing into the hundreds. More and more were teleporting in with each second, and the air rippled with pops as they rapidly reappeared and disappeared through the onslaught of arrows.

"Protect our guardian!" yelled Maddox. "Don't let those monsters get near the tent!"

The Monhegans formed a circle around the campsite. Men and women that Fain had grown up around, ordinary people with jobs like baker or herbalist, were taking on advanced fighting stances. Just the other day, Ms. Clara's apprentice had chided Fain for not paying attention during math, and now here he was holding two axes that glowed with electricity.

What the hell kind of village am I living in? Fain wondered, watching as the nice old lady that lived next door twirled a trident over her head.

Fain backed up, standing closer to his father while watching the distant fighting. Nomads were scattered as far as the eye could see; there must have been thousands of them now. The entire Western Blaze looked to be converging here tonight. The new warriors were not just spacialists either; there were men and women of many ethnicities whom had sworn allegiance to Rugaru and gotten Nomadic tattoos. Fain spotted an internalist man holding a hammer that was bigger than himself. There was also a mentalist man who simply strolled around in silence and watched as the people around him dropped to the ground, crying in agony as they clawed at something invisible on their skin. Fain told himself to avoid that man at all costs; powerful mentalists could cause excruciating pain without laying a finger on you.

The Nomads turned their sights on the Monhegan campsite, and it became an all-out battle. The conjurist Monhegans began working together to create large bursts of wind that sent the arrows flying back toward the Nomads. Maddox suddenly reached up with blinding speed and caught a dagger out of the air inches from Fain's face. He squeezed his hand and the dagger snapped in half.

"Don't leave my side," Maddox commanded. "And watch out for—"

The enormous internalist suddenly leapt out of the battle, soaring through the air and swinging his giant hammer. Maddox summoned all of his internalist powers and concentrated them into his chest. The hammer struck him, ringing like a massive bell, and the weapon shattered into pieces. The force of the impact sent Maddox's body flying through the air and out of sight like a cannon ball.

Another Nomad appeared in front of Fain and reached forward. Fain dodged his touch by jumping backwards, but was simply grabbed by another attacker. The man laughed and whispered into his ear.

"Better learn to fly, boy," he said.

Colors flew past Fain's eyes, and he suddenly found himself teleported two hundred arms into the air over the battle field. The ground shot toward him in a rush of wind, and Fain knew that his body would be crushed if he couldn't slow down the fall. He screamed and twisted through the air, struggling to stay conscious, but at the last second Ms. Clara's words rang in his mind.

Do as you've been taught.

Fain held his hands out, pulled in as much energy as he could, and released it as a burst of wind. His body was suspended in air for a brief, disorienting moment before slamming into the ground. Fain stood up, very bruised and sore but apparently still in one piece. He stumbled as his eyes readjusted, and he realized that the Monhegan campsite was now on the other side of the Capital. A literal war was standing between him and safety.

Fain had always wanted to see what the high guardian's army was capable of, but witnessing a real battle was a horrible thing. There were agonized screams and explosions coming from all around him. The body of a Capital archer fell from the outer wall and hit the ground with a lifeless thud. Fain quickly looked away, suddenly finding that he could no longer control his breathing. Fighting a battle wasn't fun; it was chaotic and desperate.

He ran through the fighting bodies, using his short height as an advantage. A soldier to his left was struck in the face by a club and wetness splattered Fain's clothes. He tried his best not to think about what had just happened.

I don't want to be here, Fain thought. *This is desolation.*

A blinding dome of light suddenly appeared in the middle of the battle. There was a sound like lightning striking the earth, and when the light faded seven warriors stood in the center of a large crater. Fain recognized them immediately as knights of the High Seven.

They studied the scene around them without a trace of fear on their faces. Fain couldn't imagine how much fighting somebody would have to experience to be as calm as The High Seven looked. The Nomads immediately teleported away from the legendary relayers to other parts of the field, choosing their battles wisely.

Will Zeig, the conjurist knight, held his hand toward the sky and a massive tornado of fire began descending from the clouds. The other six knights dispersed to different corners of the battlefield. Fain stood in awe for a moment as he watched the fire grow larger, but then realized that if he didn't move the tornado would eventually pass right through where he was standing.

GAIA! he thought. *He doesn't care who that thing burns up!*

Fain took off running, desperately trying to find the Monhegan campsite amongst the chaos. Occasionally he would see an islander and run toward them, but the Nomads were grabbing people and sending them all over the place so rapidly that it was impossible to keep track of where someone might be.

He ran past Allie Zeig, the spiritualist knight of The High Seven, and noticed that she appeared to be reading a book as she strolled leisurely around the soldiers. A spear flew out of the darkness and headed straight toward her.

"Look out!" yelled Fain, but she didn't even glance up from her book. Right before the spear was about to strike her, an owl flew out of the sky and grabbed the weapon with its massive talons. It flew high into the air and dropped the blunt end onto the head of a Nomad, knocking him to the ground unconscious. Allie kept walking and reading, apparently unaware of what had just happened.

A metal orb shot past Fain, transformed into a little person, and hung in the air for a second. A Nomad appeared right before the spot where Max was waiting, and in the same instant the robot reached forward and sent a purple cloud into the man's face. The Nomad became limp and toppled over, asleep.

"Oh, hi Fain," said Max. "I just realized that the Nomads fix their eyes on the spot where they are about to teleport approximately 1.32 seconds before they reappear. I was able to create an algorithm that calculates their exact location within ninety-eight percent—"

A cry came out from the fighting crowd and Ms. Clara's walking stick suddenly spun through the air on its own. Fain ran forward, jumped, and caught the stick.

Fain's mind ordinarily moved too fast for him to keep up with his own thoughts, and he often regretted half the things he did. However, the moment that Ms. Clara's walking stick was in his hand, his mind became crystal clear. Time seemed to slow down around him and he could see things to the tiniest detail. Fain glanced around, taking in everything calmly.

The Bridge

"Max," he said. "I'm not sure what happened, but I'm like you now. I'm some kind of genius."

"I highly doubt that," said Max.

Fain held up his hand and opened it expectantly. An arrow flew out of the night and he caught it without trying before snapping it in half.

"Okay, that was impressive," admitted Max.

Fain dropped the pieces of the arrow to the ground and pointed at the outer walls. The Edgardian archers stood very still and were firing their bows in every direction.

"The Nomad's aren't attacking the archers anymore," Fain observed. "They're not trying to get into the Capital."

"Huh," said Max. "Sure. I noticed that too, of course."

A full moon was rising in the sky, and as soon as Fain saw it everything became clear. He remembered the strange room full of paintings at the Nomadic base in the mountains. A full moon had been painted outside one of the false windows. Fain thought of Johnathan York explaining how the painting was of the high guardian chamber, and then he visualized the hydra vine trapped in a tank while its poison was extracted.

"They're drawing all of the soldiers away from High Guardian Thomas," said Fain urgently. "Rugaru is going to teleport into the night chambers and poison him any minute now."

Fain gestured toward the dome of flames that encased the Capital.

"Can you get me through there?"

"I might be able to create a protective energy field," said Max. "I just need a second to think."

"We don't have any time!"

"I'm already done, dummy. I needed a *literal* second.'"

Max flew to the ground and became a silver disk, just big enough for someone to stand on.

"So here's my plan," said Max. "Climb aboard, jump head first into the chaos, save a king, and then rescue a princess or something. Don't worry, you have *hardly any* chance of exploding."

* * *

High Guardian Thomas calmly sat in his chamber with his eyes closed, gently stroking the green stone that he wore around his neck. Enormous amounts of Gaian energy flowed through him, and he stretched his mind out in every direction through the mental realm. The old man looked through the eyes of his army, seeing the ensuing battle from a thousand viewpoints at once. Thomas spotted one of his soldiers about to step in the path of an arrow and he whispered in the man's mind.

"Left!"

The solider moved to the left and the arrow sailed past him. Thomas smiled in satisfaction. He searched for his spacialist knight, finding him effortlessly. Elias Zeig was currently teleporting a large boulder over a group of Nomads.

"Elias," thought Thomas.

Elias perked his head up and smiled.

"Yes, high guardian," he spoke aloud.

"If this does not end soon, please come and teleport me to my Eurasian home."

"Yes sir," said Elias.

Was that the slightest bit of contempt that he sensed from his knight? Perhaps the days of trusting half-bloods was coming to a close.

Thomas's mind drifted away, receding from the mental realm, and Elias's image became like mist. He took his hand off the green stone and sighed. Usually the Nomads picked on small villages with weak guardians, and Thomas did his best to ignore them. They were getting bolder. Thomas stood up and took off his necklace. Relaying to this degree was leaving him feeling very drained in his old age.

Thomas looked up to see that a very large man had just materialized across the room, and he recognized him at once as the leader of the Western Blaze. Rugaru was holding a bow with the string pulled taught, and he fired an arrow straight toward Thomas in the near-instant of his arrival. The high guardian may have still been able to dodge, but his concentration was abruptly torn in half when the stained glass window behind him shattered and what looked like a boy on a surfboard came flying in.

* * *

Fain soared across the room, riding over the fragments of glass like a wave. The disc flew out from under his feet, liquefied, and wrapped around his hand until it looked like he were wearing a metal glove.

"For the princess!" Max cried out.

Fain hit the ground, pulled in an unbelievable amount of energy with Max's help, and sent out a gust of wind that shattered the remaining windows. Rugaru's arrow hit the wind and spun around only inches from Thomas's face, flying straight back toward the Nomad. The tip of the arrow brushed the back of Rugaru's hand and flew into the stone wall behind him. The stones sizzled and melted as the hydra poison in the tip of the arrow ate away at the wall.

Rugaru looked at the scratch on his hand in disbelief and then back up at Fain with a powerful, raw anger that made the boy take a step backwards.

"Twofold!" shouted Rugaru, sending spit flying through the air.

All of the remaining knights from the High Seven teleported into the room and darted toward Rugaru, who sent a final, threatening glare at Fain and then disappeared entirely.

The High Seven all turned their attention to Fain, who for once seemed to be speechless. Max had turned back into a wristband, not wanting to add more confusion to the situation.

"Well?" shouted Thomas. "Explain yourself, boy!"

"That…" muttered Fain. "I, uh… Fain to the Max!"

"You were supposed to say that to Rugaru!" whispered Max.

"Who said that!?" shouted Thomas, his eyes darting around the room in a fit of paranoia. "I sense another mind in the room! Get the boy; lock him up and interrogate him!"

The internalist knight, a man that was nearly twice Fain's height, suddenly leapt forward and grabbed him.

"What?" asked Fain. "But I saved the high guardian's life!"

"You got past my armies, the High Seven, breeched the Capital walls, and broke into my royal chambers!" said Thomas angrily, and then pointed at his knights. "Leave no corner of this boy's mind unsearched!"

"That's not fair, I—" Fain began, but was cut short by a menacing voice that spoke in his mind.

"Nomads, hear me," said the voice. *"This is Achak of the Western Blaze. High Guardian Thomas lives, and will likely*

flee very soon. Turn your strength on the city walls, and tear them down."

The High Seven stood silently, listening to the message. Fain guessed that the entire city must be hearing this voice, and he couldn't imagine the kind of power it would take to relay a thought into so many people's minds.

"Now, citizens of the Capital, listen well to my message. Only one death was planned tonight. We merely fight for the land that is ours, and we only act with aggression when it is acted upon us. Our brave leader Rugaru has been poisoned in an unforgivable strike against our people. We will meet your aggression; we will burn the Capital to the ground and kill every last citizen if your high guardian does not surrender his life."

Everyone in the room turned and stared at Fain, who suddenly wished that he could shrink to the size of Max and fly away.

"Allie," said Thomas. "What do you see ahead of us? Do the Nomads make it into the city?"

The spiritualist knight looked up from her book distractedly, and it seemed to take her a second to realize where she was.

"That depends," she said. "What day is it again?" She glanced at Fain and smiled. "Oh, hi Fain. Have we met yet? Is this now, right now, or is it already later?"

The Bridge

"Forget it!" screamed Thomas. "Elias, get us all out of here!"

The High Seven began linking arms, but the spacialist knight hesitated when reaching for the high guardian.

"*All* of us?" asked Elias.

"Yes!" yelled Thomas. "For my protection, in case we're followed!"

"The situation is already bleak outside the walls, sir. If we leave, the citizens will be completely unguarded."

Thomas snapped his fingers and Elias cried out, holding his face which had apparently been slapped by an invisible hand.

"Fine," said Thomas, glancing over at the conjurist knight. "Will, you stay behind. If the Western Blaze makes it past the walls and wants to know who poisoned their leader, *give them the boy.*"

* * *

Rugaru appeared on a beach in the guardianship of Zedland, halfway around the world from the Capital and the bloody battle that was surely ensuing. Crabs scurried away in the hot sand upon the large man's appearance. Rugaru held up his left hand and studied it for a moment. The gash on his skin where the arrow had brushed him only minutes ago was already turning black, and his fingers were twitching uncontrollably.

"A child…" he whispered to himself.

Rugaru thought back to the day that he had returned home to find his mother murdered by an Edgardian soldier. It had awoken something in him, and by the time the sun went down he had singlehandedly found and killed every single one of the soldiers that had raided his campsite. The next day, he tracked down their families. Barely eighteen cycles at the time, and already so much blood on his hands. It was the act of bravery that had elevated him to the leader of the Western Blaze, and he had been left without a single scratch. Tonight he had become the greatest spacialist of all time, utilizing the mythical technique of teleporting to a location that you have never been to by seeing it clearly in the mind's eye. To think that within the same minute he would be struck a blow that could easily end his life, by a child no less.

Rugaru took the dagger off of his belt and began relaying energy into the muscles on his right arm. He had never known his father, the coward having run off before he was born, but his mother often said something that had become Rugaru's creed.

"Kindling for the fire…" Rugaru whispered. "Every strike against you is kindling for the fire, and our people will burn brighter after this day."

The Bridge

He held the dagger firmly against his left wrist, and closed his eyes.

Chapter Twenty-three

True Strength

MotherTech Headquarters, Gaia

Stepping from a tear in space, Maeryn and Kaija walked into Dorian's office. They darted over to his desk and began rapidly looking through the drawers. The slash mark behind them filled the room with a pale blue light, and the Mother-Tech headquarters was eerily quiet compared to the muffled sounds of combat echoing from Gaia.

"The medicine is in a small vial," said Maeryn. "Max sent a picture of it to my contacts, and the last location on record was this room."

Kaija picked up a crushed soda can and tossed it aside.

"All I'm finding is books and old food," she said.

The Bridge

Maeryn pulled a battered sci-fi novel out of one of the drawers and threw it against the wall angrily.

"Why can't he be more organized!" she said, frustrated. "There must be some sort of secret compartment... *that's it!*"

Maeryn found a framed picture of her grandfather sitting on the desk, and she gently touched the glass with her fingertip.

"My father showed this to me years ago," she said. "It only responds to the DNA of someone in our family."

A wooden panel on the desk slid back, and a small compartment rose to the surface. Sitting in the compartment was a vile of gleaming, silvery liquid.

"That's it!" said Maeryn. She reached forward, but when her hand was inches from the container it sprang into the air and shot across the room.

Rosalie appeared in the doorway, looking fearfully in at Kaija. Dorian stood behind her; his eyes were sunken in and he looked like he hadn't slept since Maeryn had disappeared. He held the vial of medicine in his shimmering MotherTech glove.

"Maeryn," Dorian said. "You brought one of them here? After everything we told you? How... how could you?"

"We need your help," said Maeryn. "Kaija's father got poisoned because of me, and without that medicine he will die."

"Help?" asked Rosalie. "The Gaians are coming to us for *help*? Our own father disavowed his Gaian heritage because of their warlike nature. We can't fix their problems."

Kaija took a confident step forward.

"We're not the violent ones," said Kaija. "You almost killed me. I never did anything to you, and you tried to stop my heart."

"I was doing whatever it took to save my niece's mind," said Rosalie fiercely.

"That's insane," said Maeryn. "Kaija wouldn't hurt me."

"You think that you can bring over your friend from this other world, and that's the end of it? Once the divide is breeched, more and more people will become aware of it. There are people on Gaia who could set off every quantum bomb on Earth by simply thinking it. We will never be safe around them, and I'm not so sure that they're safe around us either."

"It never ends with one, Maeryn," Dorian agreed. "Not even here on Earth. A compassionate act opens the floodgates, and then immigrants with less noble intentions will follow. It's simple history."

"Rosalie, you told me yourself that so much of history gets left untold," said Maeryn. "Do you want to know what I learned on Gaia about our own history? Edgard Zeig was going to run away from the guardianship and start a family, but Duncan killed him anyway. Ever since he died the world has been in chaos, and a terrorist group has been taking over. Kaija is his granddaughter."

There was a calculating silence from Rosalie.

"Is this true?" asked Dorian, and Kaija nodded.

"Yes," she said. "My father is the rightful high guardian of the continent, but he's been poisoned." Kaija began fighting back tears. "Please, help us. We've tried everything else."

"We can set things right," said Maeryn. "We can make up for the suffering that Duncan caused."

Rosalie shook her head.

"The Gaians have too many reasons to hate us," she said. "This won't change anything. If they find out we're here, they will destroy this world and every last safe place to kill us." She pointed to Kaija. "Leave us, and don't come back."

Kaija and Maeryn looked at each other, instantly getting a sense of what the other was feeling.

"No," said Kaija.

Rosalie lifted her hand and the MotherTech glove began glowing and sparking. A white-hot ball of energy appeared in her palm.

"LEAVE US!" she shouted.

Maeryn walked up to Kaija and took her by the hand.

"No," said Maeryn.

"I'm trying to keep us safe!" shouted Rosalie. "I'll do anything to protect my family."

A voice spoke from the back of the room.

"I understand."

There were suddenly gentle footsteps coming from behind them, and Ms. Clara stepped through the glowing slash mark. She held Jasper in her frail arms, and his breaths were a slow death rattle.

Clara dropped to her knees and began openly crying.

"Please," she cried. "This is my son Jasper, and he became my whole world when he was born. I gave up a guardianship for him, and I would destroy an army to keep him safe. But there's nothing I can do anymore, so I'm begging you. Help us. I've lost too much already; I can't lose him. *Please*."

Rosalie stared coldly at the old woman, and Dorian gave his sister a searching look.

"Rosalie…" he pleaded.

"I'm sorry, brother," she said, and then raised her voice. "Sedate them!"

A MotherTech drone shot into the room like a rocket and fired darts toward the Gaians. Maeryn screamed, closed her eyes, and held out her hand. A great fountain of energy began flowing through her body. There was a collective gasp in the room, and Maeryn opened her eyes to see that the darts were frozen in mid-air. Gaia was flowing through her fingertips, and she felt as if she were holding the darts with her mind.

"That's impossible," said Rosalie.

The Bridge

"No," said Maeryn. "Gaia came with us when I made the opening. Don't you feel it?"

Dorian took a cautious step toward the blue light, reaching up and letting it touch his fingertips.

"Yes," he said softly. "I… I do."

Maeryn gently relayed the power of Gaia, turning the darts in mid-air and pointing them at Rosalie.

"You have to help us," said Maeryn. "Or… or I don't know what I'll do."

Rosalie held out her hand and sent shockwaves through the air with her MotherTech gloves. Each of the darts exploded and sprayed fluid in every direction. Several more drones flew into the room and pointed their weapons at the Gaians, now aiming to kill rather than sedate. Rosalie held her palm toward Clara and energy began rapidly growing in the MotherTech glove.

"I can have an army of Guardian Angels here in minutes," screamed Rosalie. *"LEAVE!"*

The drones began exploding one by one, bursting into hot flames and then dissolving into no more than dust. Ms. Clara had taken a step forward toward Rosalie with a ferocity in her expression that Kaija had never seen before.

"You think that I won't fight you with my dying son in my arms?" Ms. Clara asked.

The entire building began shaking and the room suddenly felt like a hurricane had materialized from thin air. Rosalie had to brace herself to remain on her feet against the screaming wind. The MotherTech suit began spreading across her body, and the ball of energy in Rosalie's hand grew larger still.

"Look what you've brought into our world!" shouted Rosalie. "One Gaian can start an earthquake and bring this building down. Imagine what an army could do." The energy in her hand was now filling the room with a piercing heat.

"Why are you like this?" asked Maeryn. "I always looked up to you, but now I know you're just too angry to see clearly."

Rosalie looked at her niece and for a fleeting second Maeryn thought that she saw a trace of hesitation, but then her eyes darted to a camera in the corner of the room. It was pointed straight at Rosalie, and a little green light on its fixture blinked on and off.

"I... I don't have a choice," Rosalie said, almost inaudibly. "I've never had a choice."

As crazy as it felt to admit, Maeryn could have sworn that Rosalie was talking to someone else. Someone that nobody but her could see.

Kaija's voice suddenly spoke in Maeryn's mind.

"I can feel her emotions, Maeryn. She's not angry."

Kaija stepped between her grandmother and Rosalie, stopping only inches away from the glowing ball of energy in the woman's hand.

"You're afraid," said Kaija. "And you're looking for an enemy, because then you could take out your fear on us."

She turned to look back at Ms. Clara.

"We can't give her the enemy she's looking for, grandmother."

The intensity in Ms. Clara's face slowly drained away, and she nodded in understanding. The building abruptly stopped trembling, and the wind ceased blowing. Kaija turned back to look at Rosalie, but the woman did not lower her MotherTech glove.

"We're not going to fight you," said Kaija. "But we're not leaving, either. Kill me if you have to; you've already tried once. I don't hate you for that, I just want your help."

Rosalie's arm trembled, but the ball of energy remained pointed at Kaija.

"Please, Rosalie," pleaded Maeryn. "Help us. I thought you were strong."

Dorian suddenly spoke up, walking slowly toward the confrontation.

"No, she's not," said Dorian. "Your aunt's afraid like I am; I can feel it too. But I'm done letting fear guide me." He looked at Kaija and gave a weak smile. "True strength is asking for help from those that you have every reason to hate. Rosalie, this young woman is strong in ways that you will never be."

Dorian turned around and gently took Jasper's body from Ms. Clara. He held the dying man in his arms and looked down at his face. Jasper's eyes opened weakly and met Dorian's.

"I'm Dorian Kacey," said Dorian. "It's a pleasure to meet you; I believe our fathers knew each other."

Dorian looked up at Ms. Clara and smiled.

"I worked desperately on this medicine to save my father," he said, "but he was an old man, and I was fooling myself in thinking that he could live much longer. Maybe I was making it for you all along. I can't make any promises; the medicine has proven too strong in all of the tests, but I will try my best. Come with me."

He turned around and walked past his sister without a second glance. Rosalie's cold eyes never left the Gaians, and the ball of energy remained sizzling in her hand as they walked past. One by one, each of them left the room, and one by one, Rosalie let them go.

* * *

Rosalie lowered her hand and the glowing ball of energy dispersed. In the silence of the office, she looked from the slash mark in the air to the photograph of her father on the desk. Maeryn was right, she could feel Gaia's presence. It was unlike anything she had ever experienced, but something was wrong about it. The sensations coming from the other side of the opening were horrible and desolate.

"The suffering of an entire world," she said. "Is that what you wanted? Is this what you predicted?"

Silence was the only response. The guilt-free image of Duncan the Crucifier smiled at her mockingly from the photograph. Rosalie took off her MotherTech glove and threw it across the room in anger. The security camera in the corner swiveled and watched her actions.

"You're on your own," Rosalie said.

A deep voice spoke quietly from the speakers in the room.

"Desolation draws closer on the branches, Rosalie, *especially* after what you just let happen. The devourer of worlds does not care about or even comprehend your compassion. You must—"

"I'm invisible," Rosalie interrupted, and the voice was immediately silenced.

The light on the camera turned from green to red.

* * *

The Capital's walls were falling. Once Achak had carried the news of their leader's injury, every single Nomad had turned to attacking the structure itself. Thousands of warriors fired lightning, heaved boulders, and struck the stones of the wall with their bare fists as the entire Capital trembled. The dome of fire was now flickering out as the conjurist guards on the wall were struck down one by one. Edgardian soldiers dwindled as the Nomads teleported them to every corner of the globe. Some of the soldiers simply ran, knowing that the high guardian and his knights had chosen to save themselves.

Maddox Monhegan found his partner sprawled out on the abandoned battlefield, clutching at her leg and crying out as blood soaked through her pants.

"Maddox!" she screamed. "I lost Clara's walking stick, and I can't find Fain! Our son's gone!"

Maddox picked up his injured partner and trembled as he stared at the chaos erupting at the Capital.

"It's over, Delia," he cried. "Edgardia has fallen. We need to gather the Monhegans and leave the continent. Fain has to be alive somewhere; *he has to be.*"

Delia looked toward the sky, and a strange look spread over her face. The stars were blinking out one by one, and the moon had completely disappeared. The temperature dropped rapidly as black storm clouds materialized in the sky.

There was a sound like the world splitting in two and thousands of lightning bolts streaked across the clouds, arching in the same direction. The spider webs of electricity converged upon a single point in the sky over Edgardia and cast the silhouette of a man into the churning heavens.

The Bridge

A figure floated in midair, holding his sword erect as the electricity of one hundred thunderheads surged through the weapon. The man seemed to glow like a star and his hair whipped wildly in the wind as he cast his eyes down at the chaotic battle. Nearly every single Nomad and Edgardian soldier dropped their weapons and ceased fighting as they saw the great figure floating through the sky.

"STOP!" he called. The sound shook the ground and silenced the insects for stretches in every direction. His voice pierced through the veil of the mental realm and echoed in the minds of a thousand fighters like an explosion. Men and women began kneeling to the ground and crying aloud.

"Son of Gaia!"

"Edgard has returned!"

Delia and Maddox exchanged a look of understanding.

"No," she said. "It's not Edgard. It's—"

"Jasper," finished Maddox. "Our guardian."

Jasper pointed his father's sword at the battlefield and patterns of light flew from its tip, spiraling in fractals toward the ground. Hundreds of Nomads blinked away at once as they fled the scene, while those incapable of spacialist relaying simply ran screaming. The grass beneath their feet began growing like hydra vines and snaked around the bodies of the fleeing warriors. The points of light struck thousands of Nomads simultaneously, and they all fell to the ground, unconscious.

Jasper floated to the ground in the center of a ring of cheering Monhegans. Kaija, Maeryn, Ms. Clara, and Dorian stood amongst the rapturous crowd with tears in their eyes. Soldiers from the Edgardian army began running for the campsite, calling out for their savior.

"Son of Gaia!"

"Edgard!"

Jasper took a few trembling steps forward, mostly ignoring the shouting behind him. Kaija wanted to run to her father, but she simply stood in awe of him. His voice spoke quietly in her head.

"I missed you, Kaija."

Jasper glanced at the hundreds of approaching soldiers and then back at the Monhegans. The entire group had suddenly become quiet, everyone wondering what in the world was about to happen next. It was as if they could feel history itself about to branch one way or the other.

"I suppose this is it," said Ms. Clara, breaking the reverent silence. "This is when everything changes. Those soldiers believe you are the son of Gaia, Jasper, and from this moment on the entire world will—"

Jasper's eyes widened and he held up a hand to silence her.

"Is *that* what they think?" he asked. He scratched his cheek in thought for a second before decisively proclaiming *"No thanks!"*

The Bridge

Jasper swung his sword into the ground and a dome of light shot up around the campsite. The air around them began to ripple and glow as the surrounding battlefield turned to mist. The calls of the soldiers suddenly became faint as more familiar sounds came into the foreground.

Wind.

Waves crashing against the rocky shores.

The crowd recognized their new location at once. The entire campsite and all the villagers had been teleported back to Monhegan Island in a single stroke of relaying.

Jasper dropped his sword, wiping the sweat dripping from his hair, and looked around at all of the surprised faces.

"Well, that was something," he said with a weak smile. "I could sure go for a nap and a big slice of—"

Jasper took a step forward and then abruptly collapsed onto the soft grass, snoring loudly.

Chapter Twenty-four

The Frost Flower

The Capital Prison

Fain leaned against the dirty wall of the prison. Max had snuck away nearly two hours ago to get help, and the boredom would have nearly driven Fain crazy if it weren't for the amazing things that he had seen out of his cell window. A man in the sky had stopped the largest battle since the Gaian Global Wars, and Fain heard whispering in the hallways about how Edgard Zeig had returned.

But Fain knew the truth. Maeryn and Kaija had done it; they had saved Jasper and returned the sword to its rightful owner.

A guard walked up to the cell and sneered in at Fain.

"I brought your breakfast," he laughed, rolling a plain potato under the door and into the dirt.

"Is that all you have on the menu?" asked Fain. "I'm a little potatoed-out at the moment. Since I saved the world and everything, surely I deserve at least a carrot or something."

The man slammed his fist against the bars of the cell and gave Fain an angry look.

"Don't you backtalk me, boy," yelled the guard. "You have no idea how much trouble you're in. I could snap you in half without even…"

He stopped in midsentence and stood there without moving a muscle. His mouth hung open and drool dripped down his chin.

"Um," said Fain. "Mr. Guard, are you okay?"

The guard was absolutely frozen in place. Fain walked to the door of the cell and was about to poke him when High Guardian Thomas came around the corner, followed by Ms. Clara.

"Don't worry about the guard, boy," said Thomas. "He won't even remember you were here after I let you go."

Fain smiled at his teacher.

"I did it, Ms. Clara," he said. "I stopped and thought about my actions for once, and I saved the high guardian's life!"

Ms. Clara shot an angry look at her old friend.

"Yes," she said severely. "And I'm sure he's rather thankful for it."

Thomas simply stared back at her.

"Well, they did lock me up in a pretty nice cell," said Fain. "Dinner could have been better, though."

Ms. Clara took a step toward the high guardian and poked him in the chest with her walking stick.

"You know, Thomas," she said. "I didn't want to believe the stories about you fleeing the castle on the night Edgard died, but I'm having an awfully hard time not thinking the worst about you right now."

"Cut me some slack, Clarice," said Thomas. "I thought you were dead for the last forty cycles. Tonight a Nomad breeched the Capital's defenses, I was saved by a teenager flying on some metal *thing*, and now people are saying that Edgard himself stopped the battle. Could that have been your little boy, I wonder? What do you expect me to do, act like my world hasn't been rocked in the last hour?"

Ms. Clara whacked the high guardian on the back of the head with her stick.

"I expect you to thank him!" she commanded.

"Yes, Ms. Clara," he muttered.

Thomas turned to Fain and gave him a fake smile.

"Thank you for saving my life, Fain. You are free to go."

Thomas took out a key and unlocked the cell. Ms. Clara took Fain by the arm and began walking with him down the hallway. She suddenly stopped and glanced back at the high guardian.

The Bridge

"I can feel you prying at the edges of my mind, Thomas," she said. "Yes, that was my son that you saw tonight. My son, and the son of Edgard. True high guardian."

Thomas's eyes became suddenly very wide.

"That's right," said Ms. Clara. "So I suggest you get your slimy fingers off that gem and leave my mind alone. You leave *us* alone, and we will leave *you* alone."

Thomas's hand quickly sprang back from the stone he wore around his neck as if reprimanded by his own mother. He nodded grimly and watched as his old companion departed. Just before Ms. Clara turned the corner, the high guardian called to her.

"Members of my army reported that many of their lives were saved by a group of civilians," he said. "Men and women came out of nowhere and fought with skills that surpass many of my best trained soldiers. Would you know anything about who these people were?"

Ms. Clara smiled.

"I would imagine that, wherever they're from, they have a very good teacher," she said, and then walked out of sight.

As soon as Ms. Clara departed, the frozen guard sprang back to consciousness.

"...without even breaking a sweat," said the guard, and then looked around in confusion. He kicked at the potato on the floor with his foot, and then jumped when he saw Thomas standing right behind him.

"High guardian!" he exclaimed. "I was just talking to… well, honestly I'm not quite sure any more. I suppose I was talking to that potato. My head seems to have gotten fuzzy."

Thomas patted him on the back and walked off.

"Carry on, young man," said the high guardian. "We both need some sleep."

* * *

Monhegan Island

"Maeryn, look!" cried Dorian. "I'm doing it!"

He held out his hand, and a tiny pebble was hovering in the air in front of him. Fain looked at it and gave a big smile to the man.

"Amazing, sir!" he said.

"I'm a regular Dumbledore," agreed Dorian.

"Dad," said Maeryn. "They don't understand our cultural references here."

"Still not going to stop making them," said Dorian, flying the stone in zig-zags around his head.

"A high guardian in the making if I've ever seen one," said Fain. "A true inspiration to relayers everywhere— ouch!"

Kaija had poked Fain in the ribs with her elbow, and they both started laughing. The whole group had slept for half the day in the cabins of Monhegan, and then eaten an exotic feast with the entire village as they traded stories from their two worlds. Now the sun was sinking in the sky, and an entire day had passed since the battle outside Edgardia's walls. Max sat on Ms. Clara's shoulder and was engaged in a heated philosophical discussion about one of the books from her library. Kaija and Fain were trying to teach Maeryn and her father the basics of relaying.

"Maybe you're not an externalist," said Kaija, flicking the pebble out of the air while Dorian frowned. "I've heard that Duncan was an amazing internalist."

"Yea, dad," said Maeryn. "Try relaying some energy into your body, and I'll hit you with a big stick to see if you can block the impact."

She grabbed a stick from the ground and began chasing her dad around the hillside. Jasper came walking up from the village, yawning and rubbing his eyes behind his glasses.

"It's the wizard himself," said Dorian. "How many naps is that today?"

Kaija ran up and hugged her father.

"I've lost count," said Jasper. "I did enough relaying yesterday to last a lifetime. The sword woke me up. It started glowing again, just as bright as the first time I saw it."

"Strange…" said Dorian. "I was just thinking that we needed to go back to, well… *Earth*. Maybe the sword read my mind; could it be that we've found some sort of *MAGIC SWORD*?"

"Go?" asked Maeryn. "This is the first time I've gotten to experience Gaia without being locked in jail or on the run from a carnivorous plant."

"I know," said Dorian. "But I've got four thousand employees wondering where I am, and I'm worried that your aunt might smash my bass guitar collection if we stay away too long. Besides, I'm looking forward to my retirement."

Dorian looked around and breathed in the fresh air of Gaia.

"Maybe we'll do some traveling. I've always wanted to visit all forty-nine states. Heck, *I'm rich*; we could see the world."

"Worlds," Maeryn corrected him. "We could see the worlds."

* * *

Jasper retrieved his father's sword and met them on the hillside, offering the weapon to Maeryn.

"No," she said. "It's not mine."

"I don't know if it will respond to me like it did yesterday," said Jasper. "Everything that happened in Edgardia is a blur now."

"There's only one way to find out," said Max.

The Bridge

Jasper closed his eyes and visualized the world where his life had been saved. The sword glowed bright, Jasper pointed it ahead of him, and a great big hole split open in the fabric of the world near the edge of the cliff. Dorian, Maeryn, and Max gathered their things and stood before the gateway to Earth. All of the Monhegans that they had met gathered around to say their goodbyes.

Dorian held out his hand to shake Jasper's, but Jasper grabbed Dorian with his massive arms and pulled him into a hug.

"Don't break me, strong man!" cried Dorian, and Jasper let go.

"Thank you for all that you've done for my family," said Jasper.

"Oh…well, I'm not so sure that I deserve your thanks. If anything, I hope that you can forgive me and my father."

Ms. Clara walked up to Dorian and gripped his hand firmly.

"We can't forget what is in the past," said Ms. Clara. "But things have changed. I can't believe that I'm saying this, but I'm glad that Duncan got to have a family. Caring for someone changes your perspective, and I'm sure that he became something totally different from the man I knew all those cycles ago."

"Dorian?" asked Max. "Is it okay if Fain comes over to our universe to play sometimes?"

"Wow," said Dorian. "That is a really interesting question."

"Would it even be possible?" Maeryn asked to the group. "I mean… we did what we were brought here to do, we fixed what was broken; didn't we? Will Gaia keep us linked together?"

"Yep, we're heroes," said Max. "Although we did start all the problems in the first place. But isn't that the American dream?"

"No," said Ms. Clara. "You were given an opportunity to set things right, and both of you could have ignored it."

"But do you think that Gaia's done with us?" asked Maeryn, suddenly feeling very melancholy. "I mean, we have Gaia in our blood; this is our real home. I can't imagine never talking to Kaija again."

Kaija's voice spoke in Maeryn's mind.

"I don't think we have a choice about that one, city girl."

Maeryn smiled and approached the gateway to Earth with Max and her father. Max turned to see all of the emotional looks on the Gaians' faces.

"I guess that, in the end, friendship was the real bridge," said Max.

Ms. Clara raised an eyebrow.

"What the heck is that thing talking about?" she asked.

The Bridge

"Somebody has to sum up our whole adventure in a shallow way," said Max. "And nobody's seen more bad movies than me."

Nearly a hundred blank expressions looked back at the robot.

"Okay," said Max. "How about *poisoning a stranger's father can be the start to a wonderful adventure?*"

"Let's leave before you embarrass yourself anymore," said Maeryn, taking the little robot by the hand.

* * *

Monhegan Island

Kaija sat at the edge of the cliff where she had first met Maeryn, and there was a glazed over look in her eyes. Snow drifted from the sky and was lit by the light of a half moon. Fain jumped from the trees and relayed a small snowball at Kaija. It splashed her in the face, but she simply sat motionless.

"Kaija?" he asked, gently shaking her shoulders. "Are you in this universe?"

Alertness came into Kaija's eyes, and she smiled upon seeing Fain.

"Hey, Fain," she said, but then frowned. "Why is my face wet?"

"I honestly have no idea," said Fain. "What have you been up to?"

"Maeryn and I were just watching a movie."

"Any good?"

"Eh," Kaija said, concealing a smile.

"Really? I promise not to be jealous."

"Oh my gosh it was amazing!" Kaija exclaimed. "People were flying in machines through the stars and having battles with sticks of light."

"I wish I could have been there."

"It's okay. Tomorrow I'm going to show Maeryn the electric lobsters on the south side of the island if you want to come. Oh, by the way, Max says hi."

Fain tried to smile, but he couldn't fake it any more. His conflicting feelings had been getting worse over the past few months, and he had to come clean to Kaija.

"Kaija," he said. "Is this how it's going to be forever?"

"What do you mean?" asked Kaija. "Is this about Maeryn? You're still my best friend."

"I know that," he said, turning slightly red in the cheeks. "I'm not jealous, I think Maeryn's amazing and I'm glad that we can still talk to her. It's just…"

He sighed, gently reaching over and taking Kaija by the hand.

"Things are so good now," said Fain. "Your dad's alive, Ms. Clara's been a lot nicer to us, and we have two new amazing friends from another universe who are teaching us all these interesting things, and…"

Fain teared up, and Kaija scooted closer to him.

"I used to take things like this for granted," he said, "and the old me would have thought that this could last forever, but on the mainland everything was horrible. Those Nomads killed that nice man's horse without hesitating. I saw people dying and falling from the Edgardian walls. One of the soldiers next to me got hit by a club and his blood got on my clothes. Any of those people could have been me, Kaija. Or my parents… or… or you. My brother never got to be this happy."

Fain was now openly crying.

"Do you think that these things will stay away from the island forever?"

"My father will protect us," said Kaija. "This is the safest place on Gaia."

"Your father is my hero, but a single thorn almost killed him, just like the hydra poison probably killed Rugaru. Heroes aren't supposed to die. Do you think we can really be the only ones that know about this secret world for our whole lives, and that nobody will ever find out? That there will never be any consequences?"

Kaija took all of this in, but she had no response. With all of the excitement in discovering a new world, the consequences of their actions had simply not been a consideration.

"I just know that I'm happy now, Fain," she said. "Constantly worrying about what happens next; that's no way to live. I don't know if things will stay like this forever, but maybe that makes moments like this more important, not less."

Fain wiped his eyes and smiled.

"I should go," he said. "I made some conjurist vultures angry earlier, and they've been circling my cabin for the last hour."

He took a few steps toward the village, but hesitated. There was something that he desperately wanted to say, but he lacked the courage to do it out loud. Fain simply thought the words as hard as he could, hoping that Kaija would hear his message in the mental realm.

"I meant it, Kaija."

Kaija turned around and looked at him.

"Fain?" she asked. "Was that you?"

He nodded shyly.

"You meant what?" she asked.

"What I said in your dream," he said. "That was really me, and I think it every day. You're the most perfect thing in any world."

Fain turned to go, but Kaija grabbed him by the arm and pulled him in close. She wrapped her arms around him, and they kissed under the Gaian stars to the sound of the thunderous ocean.

* * *

Hours later, Kaija walked along the rocks in the now abandoned Gull Cove. There was still a black mark on a large boulder where lightning had struck the hydra vine. She nervously held the sword of Edgard Zeig in her hands after having snuck it out of her father's cabin. Jasper never used it, not enjoying the overwhelming responsibility he felt every time he touched the blade. She had so much to tell Maeryn, but she wanted to do it in person.

Kaija held the old sword and opened herself up to the mental realm.

"Take me to Maeryn," she thought.

Nothing happened.

Kaija concentrated on the energy in the air around her, relaying a massive amount of it into the blade.

"I want to see Earth," she thought, but again there was no response. The blade did not glow; it just sat in her hands like a useless antique.

Kaija dropped the sword on the rocks and sighed.

"Every night," she told herself, disappointed.

Kaija picked up the sword and began to gather her things to head back to the village. A voice spoke up from behind her, making Kaija jumped in surprise.

"Don't melt, frost flower."

Kaija jumped around and held out the blade defensively. A blonde woman with purple streaks in her hair sat on the rock in Gull Cove, quietly strumming a ukulele.

"Any requests?" asked the woman. "I can play a mean Paul Simon."

"Who are you?" asked Kaija.

"I'm sorry," said the woman. "I keep forgetting that we haven't met yet. That's what happens when you dislodge yourself from linear time, I suppose. I'm Allie Zeig, spiritualist knight of Thomas's High Seven."

"How did you get here?" asked Kaija.

"Frog," said Allie simply.

Kaija waited for further explanation, but apparently there was none.

"Oh… okay," said Kaija. "What are you doing here?"

"Just here to see the frost flower. *What's a frost flower*, you are about to ask? A frost flower is when thin layers of ice curl from long plants in the autumn or early winter, forming pedals made of pure frost. A very rare occurrence in nature."

Kaija looked around, seeing no flowers made out of ice. Allie slapped herself on the forehead.

The Bridge

"I don't mean literally, you normie!" she laughed. "Kaija, *you* are the frost flower; a rare occurrence in nature, perhaps the rarest occurrence! You are a mindbridge! It is not unheard of for two people's minds to overlap in the mental realm, it happens once or twice every generation between those who share similar circumstances. Becoming fully aware of a mindbridge and being able to control it is even rarer, although not unheard of. But for the overlap to happen across worlds? You and that other girl from Earth are a freaking frost dandelion!" Allie grabbed Kaija's face and tilted it, looking into her ear. "Is the Earthling in there right now? Amazing! Why do I always forget to bring my camera; you would think I could have foreseen that."

Kaija pulled herself away from the woman, her head absolutely swimming with confusion.

"How do you know this about me?" asked Kaija. "And how did you find me?"

"Oh, about fifteen cycles ago I felt tremors in the mental realm. Some digging brought me to this island and I've been popping in and out, keeping an eye on you ever since."

"*Fifteen* cycles? That was before I was born. Can you see the future?"

Allie put down her ukulele and stood up, her blue eyes darting around oddly.

"Nah, dude," said Allie. She suddenly reached up into the air and grabbed a fly with her bare hands. Allie observed it for a moment, and then casually popped the insect into her mouth.

"Um…" said Kaija. "*What?*"

"Oh, sorry," said Allie. "Frog was hungry." She swallowed loudly. "Anyway, nobody can see the future clearly. What I can see are the shadows that the tree of time casts upon the ground. I believe that you and Maeryn have something to do with where the branches are heading. Edgard Zeig's spiritualist knight, Páigus Zeig, wrote an apocalyptic folk song about forty cycles ago, and I think it may have been about you. You might want to hear it; I'll skip the ten minute free-jazz section at the beginning."

Allie picked her ukulele back up and began singing.

"Born in worlds of isolation, they build the bridge toward Desolation."

She abruptly stopped, held up the ukulele, and it vanished in a cloud of sparkles.

"The rest of the song is mostly about how much Páigus enjoys coffee. That was Desolation with a capital D by the way, you know… the *third* world. Or do you know? Have you been licked on the forehead yet or talked to the toaster ghost?"

Kaija could manage little more than an *uh* in response.

"Oh, never mind," said Allie. "I'll talk to you in the Helenic Guardianship after Jasper's finger grows back. Bye! Places to see—"

"Wait!" pleaded Kaija. "I'm a mindbridge? Did Gaia pick me for a reason? What am I supposed to do?"

"Oh, stop it with your tired chosen one tropes. Gaia's a force of nature, do you think I hang out with hurricanes in my spare time? Speak their language? Why is a plant stalk picked to have thin layers of ice curling around it? What does it mean?"

"I don't know!"

"Exactly."

"You can't say something like that and just leave!" said Kaija.

"Leave? Is that what you think?" asked Allie with a laugh. "I was never here, Kaija. Didn't I tell you that yet? I'm projecting my consciousness through the mind of a particularly powerful mentalist frog." She snapped her fingers. "Aha! There it is: *that's* when I say it. Farewell, little frost flower."

And with that, the wind blew and scattered Allie's image like dust. She had been replaced with a tiny frog that was sitting on the rock and croaking loudly.

Kaija briefly considered waking Fain and telling him what she had just seen, but she decided to keep this moment to herself. Maybe it was better that she had not talked to Maeryn, Kaija thought with a blush. Perhaps this was a night for secrets.

Epilogue

Home

Interstate 95, Earth

Kai awoke on the hyperbus just before it crossed the state line from New Vermont to Maine. The driverless vehicle shot down the road at nearly two hundred miles per hour, veering around the autocabs with sophisticated precision. As the bus crossed onto the bridge over the Piscataqua River, the old man smiled. He missed his dog, but he knew that his friends in Garfield Park would take care of her until he returned. Every year Kai managed to scrap together enough money to take this pilgrimage.

He closed his eyes contently and found himself thinking about that young girl he had saved in the park. She had been on his mind a lot recently. It was simply too big of a coincidence that Maeryn Kacey would run into him on one of the strangest nights of his life. He had looked for Maeryn the next day, but the entire Kacey family had disappeared and had not been seen in months.

The bus stopped in Portland and Kai was transferred to another bus for the remainder of his trip. Two hours later he arrived at his destination, and the artificially intelligent tour guide called out to Kai.

"We have arrived in Boothbay Harbor, Maine," said the robotic voice. "Enjoy your vacation, Kai. Have you made any interesting plans?"

"Family reunion," said Kai. "But first: ice cream."

The old man pulled out a few crinkled dollars and bought an orange-chocolate ice cream cone on the harbor. He strolled around aimlessly, watching the street musicians, painters, and magicians with mild disinterest. Kai stopped through Orne's Candy Store, bought some chocolate, and made his way to a ticket-booth that sat by several passenger ships.

"Can I help you?" asked the ticket seller skeptically. "We don't have any spare change."

Kai laughed and pushed his roll of money under the window.

"I'm not here to beg," he said. "I'm a millionaire; can't you tell?"

"Oh," said the seller, embarrassed. "Sorry, sir. Where to?"

"Monhegan Island."

* * *

Kai's alarm woke him up just past midnight in his room at The Treetop Inn. He made his way out of the hotel and looked toward the night sky. Even all the way out here, the sky had a slightly orange glow that obscured every single star. The old man hiked his way through the pitch-black woods, shivering in the bitter cold as he traversed the familiar landscape.

Eventually he emerged onto the cliffs of Lobster Cove. Kai stood for a moment, listening to the waves crashing against rocks below.

"Home…" he whispered.

Kai took in a breath of fresh air, sat on the edge of the cliff, and simply waited in meditation for a long time. His mind became dark, and he found peace in that familiar silence. However, something was different about his usual meditations. There was a tiny light in the black abyss of his consciousness, floating as if it was searching for its home. Kai recognized it at once and reached for the light, bringing it into his heart where it flickered and became a raging fire.

He opened his eyes urgently and stood up, taking in heavy breaths. Cold rain had begun to fall from the sky, but Kai barely noticed. A sensation was filling his body that he had not felt in a very long time.

"It couldn't be…" he thought. *"Not here."*

Kai raised his eyes to the sky, and the rain began to bend and twist around him as it fell. Somewhere in the distance a bolt of lightning shot from the clouds, arcing over the water and toward the cliffs of Lobster Cove.

In the same instant, Kai reached out calmly as the blinding light approached. Time seemed to slow down as his reflexes were intensified a thousand-fold. He opened his wrinkled hand, and caught the lightning.

"Gaia."

To be continued…

Connect with the Author

and a free preview of The Mindbridge Trilogy Book II

Want to see what happens next and learn about Kai's origins? Join my mailing list to read the first chapter of *A Path of Branches* for free! Here's what else my mailing list gets:

*Chances to read the next books in the series early.

*Monthly book and music recommendations from me.

*Automatic entry into monthly giveaway drawings, including *The Mindbridge Trilogy* merchandise, gift cards, and free books/audiobooks.

Join below. One of us! One of us!

https://astounding-trailblazer-618.ck.page/41fe578511

Already joined my mailing list? This link will still work for you. Unsubscribe any time. Heck, for all I care, get your free stuff and run. Stick it to the man!

Oh wait, I'm the man! Forget I said that.

-*Joe Luegers, writer/musician*

Author's Plea

To those who made it this far: I am already more grateful to YOU than I can possibly express. Yes, *you*, _____insert name here_____. If you are a young reader, let your friends know about this book. Help me get rich and famous! Also, clean your room, young lady/man.

Adults: if you didn't like *The Bridge*, thanks for at least finishing it before tossing it on the book burnin' pile. If you *did* like the book, please allow me to get on my metaphysical knees and make one final plea on behalf of myself and all self-published writers. After finding time to fulfill my responsibilities as parent, husband, teacher, musician, and writer, I also need to make an attempt at being a one-man marketing team. I don't care so much about sales figures (heck, I'm already an elementary school teacher, I don't really need any more gold to swim in), but I do want people who might be interested in reading this book to actually know it exists.

Here are some *free* things you can do to help not just me, but *any* independent writer:

*Leave an honest review on Goodreads or an online retailer. If you do anything, do this: PLEASE! I really want to hear what you think, good or bad. It will literally make my day.

*Like my facebook page at https://www.facebook.com/Luegerswriter/ and invite your friends list to like it too.

*Sign up for my newsletter to keep in touch and get previews of upcoming books. https://www.luegerswriter.com/newsletter

*Recommend the audiobook to someone about to go on a long drive. New subscribers on Audible can get it for free.

*Name a baby after one of my characters, and raise them to promote my work at every given opportunity. (Okay, maybe not so free.)

Now, please allow me to go from my metaphysical knees to the metaphysical floor itself, crying out for help as you, the reader, stand above me while taking pity in my shameful self-interested groveling.

If you are feeling absurdly generous, consider contributing to my Patreon page:

https://www.patreon.com/luegerswriter

Anything that I make through Patreon will go directly back into my writing, helping me purchase ISBNs, better recording equipment for audiobooks, advance reader copies, online advertisements to help me escape obscurity and finally achieve mediocrity, and basically help increase my budget from ZERO (or, as it stands now, *less than zero*). Patrons will receive regular perks, including early access to audiobook chapters, behind the scenes videos, and shout-outs in the acknowledgements section of future works.

Rock and roll!

-Joe Luegers

Acknowledgements

Special thanks to my beta-readers who gave me the confidence to move forward: **Travis Humbert**, **Brilee Knight**, **Caleb Spurling**, **Jasmine Withrow**, **Elliot Withrow**, and **Isaac Scheller**. Having six people read my book was already enough to fulfill my greatest ambitions, and I can eventually die happy because of you.

The first time I sent a book to **Emily Bernhardt** for editing, I told her that I'd already been over it ten times and it was fine if she didn't find very many things to fix. A few weeks later she had bookmarked *literally* hundreds of amateurish, obvious mistakes that I had made. So, thank you Emily for having the colossal task of making me look slightly less stupid.

Emily's also a wonderful musician. Listen to her music here: https://emilybernhardt.bandcamp.com/

If there were an award for *"Most Hardworking, Multi-Talented Human Who Has Every Right <u>Not</u> To Be As Humble As They Are"* then give it up, losers, because the award goes to **Ashley Ellen Frary**. When she sends me cover art, the excitement robs me of a preposterous amount of sleep.

Check out the amazing *Mindbridge Trilogy* merchandise that Ashley created here:

https://www.redbubble.com/shop/ap/73662194

Maybe the academy spoke too soon, because if you tried to thank **Travis Humbert** for saving a burning bus full of nuns and puppies, he would just shrug and say "eh, whatever works." Travis, please lower your thanks-deflecting shield and accept my appreciation for your audio-book mastering.

And, most of all, thank you to my wife **Alax Luegers**. Firstly, for being such a skillful narrator in the audiobook edition, but mostly for just being *her.* If I am ever off doing a cool thing, it is only because Alax is currently trying to keep alive the two little people that we created. The best of what I am, I got from you. I can neither confirm nor deny to the general public the existence of my wife as a character in this book itself. I love you, Alax. Thank you for helping me fight the patriarchy.

-Joe Luegers

About the Author

Joe Luegers is a guitarist, pianist, organist, composer, teacher, and writer. He lives in Evansville, Indiana with his wife Alax and their two kids, July and Rory. Joe published the adult horror novel *The Gears That Watch the Clockmaker* in 2018 and has since turned his focus towards writing young adult fiction. He performs frequently as a soloist, alongside his amazing wife on vocals and ukulele, as well as in an eclectic range of ensembles including the opera rock band The Tapestry.

Check his social media and website for information and release dates for the next two books in *The Mindbridge Trilogy*: Book II, *A Path of Branches* and Book III, *Songs of Desolation.*

Get in touch: joe@luegerswriter.com
Facebook: https://www.facebook.com/Luegerswriter
Instagram: https://www.instagram.com/joeluegers/
Patreon: https://www.patreon.com/luegerswriter
Website: https://www.luegerswriter.com/

CPSIA information can be obtained
at www.ICGtesting.com
Printed in the USA
BVHW071143220521
607791BV00001B/97